To Be Continued

by

Charmaine Gordon

Vanilla Heart Publishing

To Be Continued

by Charmaine Gordon

Copyright 2009 Charmaine Gordon

Published by: Vanilla Heart Publishing

www.VanillaHeartBookAndAuthors.com

10121 Evergreen Way, 25-156

Everett, WA 98204 USA

This book is a work of fiction. Names, characters, places, and incidents are either the product of the author's imagination or are used fictitiously, and any resemblance to places, events, or persons living or dead is purely coincidental.

ISBN-13: 978-0615902203 ISBN-10: 0615902200

10 9 8 7 6 5 4 3 2 Second Edition

First Printing, October 2013

Printed in the United States of America

Dedication

I wake up each day and think, "This is a plus."

Acknowledgements

From a chance meeting with Chelle Cordero leading to Kimberlee Williams of Vanilla Heart Publishing, I give a bunch of thanks. I couldn't ask for a warmer welcome into the family of VHP authors.

And to my friend, Kathleen Kubik who stepped in and rescued me when she retyped To Be Continued, a blessing on your blond head.

The Writers Salon women, meeting for several years every other week to offer constructive suggestions while dining, are terrific pals. I thrive as a writer with their help. Thanks to Ellen Belitsky, Jenny Kalsner, Kathy Kubik, Ann Letzter, Donna Litz, Barbara Rosenthal, Sheila Servetar, Arlene Shapiro, and Bobbi Werzansky.

Special appreciation goes to Lynn Brustein-Kampel P.C. for her gracious time and attention to my questions.

To my husband Don who says, "What's for dinner?" and understands when I reply, "I'm writing." You are the best, my dear.

See what I mean? This is all a plus.

Chapter 1

Sun sneaked through blinds. *Eyes shut tight. Not quite ready to open.*

Elizabeth Malone wanted to revel in memories of the great sex she and Frank, her husband of forty years, had last night. *At his insistence, for God's sake.* She practically had to seduce him before they did it anymore; was on the verge of suggesting those little blue pills the girls talked about, when out of nowhere he became amorous. And it was great. *No...wonderful. No...Fan—fargin'—tastic!*

"Mmmm."

Fingers crept along the sheets searching for her mate. They groped to where Frank could be found most early mornings except on golf days or scheduled surgery. She touched the edge of his pillow but no Frank.

Turning her head, she called his name. At the same time she saw an envelope lying on top of the pillow. *Never like Frank to leave a note but how sweet is this?* A smile tugged at the corners of her mouth and she sat up. The sheet slipped down and there she was. Naked. *Liz, you're such a slut. Where oh where is your nightie, you naughty girl.* A heap of green satin lay on the floor next to the bed, evidence of last night's pleasure.

With care, one long polished nail sliced through the envelope. The nail snagged on an edge and broke. "Shit." Nothing was going to spoil the moment because this was the first letter from Frank in all the years of togetherness and she planned to keep it. She withdrew the letter.

Stumbling off the bed, letter clutched in her hand, she groped for reading glasses, found them, dropped them, on hands and knees patting the carpet, found them again. Naked on the floor, she read:

Dear Lizzie, It's not you. It's me. I have been uncomfortable in my own skin for a long time and have decided I must make a change in my life. I sold my half of the practice to George. You, dear Lizzie, are well taken care of. Call Bruce Bradley. He has all the papers, investments, everything you will need to live in comfort. The house is yours. Last but not least, I signed my portion of divorce papers so whenever you want to, sign yours. Bruce will take care of it."

She leapt up—made it to the toilet and retched. Foul taste in her mouth, Elizabeth returned to the bedroom and stared down at the despicable letter. "He called me Lizzie. Twice. He knows I hate that name. Liz was okay but the despised Lizzie, never." Her skin crawled with pain and fury. "Oh God. What am I going to do?" No answer in the silent room. "Divorce," She shouted to the empty house. "People like us, we don't divorce, you stupid..." Tears streaming, she pounded her chest with the letter, crumpled it into a ball and flung it across the room.

She staggered to his closet, slid open the mirrored doors, heard empty hangers clicking against each other before they came in sight. Gone. Wiped out. Nothing left but dust and a few empty shoe boxes, lids tipped over. Elizabeth's knees buckled and she sank to the floor, head in hands. After a few moments, her head snapped up. *When did he do this? Maybe he slipped a little something in my drink last night to make sure I slept while he packed and flew the coop.* "That son of a bitch. That God damn son of a bitch."

She tore sheets from the bed not caring if they ripped to shreds and stuffed them in the laundry chute where they'd land in the basement; imagined Frank stuffed in the chute, hurtling into the mouth of certain doom.

Standing, careful not to fall, she trailed a hand along the wall 'til she reached the bathroom and flicked the switch. Blue and yellow tile gleamed under the bright light--double sinks were illuminated. His cabinet stood open, empty except for a rusty razor blade on the top shelf. *Too rusty to slash my wrists.* Wild eyed, hair standing on end. Her reflection stared back for a second. *Who is this stranger?* A small clenched fist pulled back, trembled; the urge to smash her image was strong. She wanted, needed, to demolish something. If she cracked the mirror, maybe she'd sever an artery and bleed to death. The trembling fist pounded her head, one, two, three. It hurt and she cried. Beth sobbed with the woman in the mirror.

In the shower, under the pulsating stream of hot water, Beth emptied an almost full shampoo bottle on short brown hair. "I want my forty years back," she whispered through tears choking her throat. Too much conditioner followed the abundance of shampoo as she braced trembling arms against the shower walls and sudsy water sluiced down her body. The hot water gave out and so did she. Wrapped in a striped blue and yellow bath towel, she dripped her way over to the crumpled letter, stomped on it and walked barefoot to the small balcony outside the bedroom.

Shivering in the chill of a late March morning, Elizabeth Malone surveyed the property as far as she could see. The beautiful pool slept under a green cover soon to be removed and she'd swim every day in the heated water. Water so warm you could make soup in it, Frank would say. Would—past tense.

"Why?" she cried out. "Why?" and ran inside. Shaking from the cold, she called George Lehrman, Frank's partner. Maybe he was still asleep; she didn't care. Sure enough, a sleepy voice answered the phone. Marilyn, his wife. Marilyn who never liked her.

"Marilyn, it's Liz Malone. Let me speak to George, please."

"He's sleeping, Liz. Do you realize it's not even nine o'clock? We were out late last night."

"Marilyn," Liz's voice rose a notch, "If you don't put George on, I'll be at your door in ten minutes." She heard two muffled voices and George picked up.

"What seems to be the problem?"

By now the knuckles of the hand gripping the phone were white. "George, I need to know when Frank arranged to retire, what excuse did he give you and do you know where he is."

He cleared his throat and sighed. "I'll tell you what little I know." She heard him ask for a cup of coffee. "A few months ago Frank said he wanted to retire, sell his half of the practice to me and leave town. I thought it was settled so this call comes as a surprise to me." *He's lying.*

"George, we've known each other a lot of years and you're loyal to your partner, but if you're lying to me and I think you are, I'm coming to the office tomorrow and screaming in front of patients so you better tell the truth." Liz, naked and shivering in a wet towel, didn't know or care where she got the nerve to say this but she did. Now she waited for him to change his story,

Rapid breathing and whispered consultation from the other side. "I'm sorry to tell you but Frank was determined to move on and I bought him out. I swear that's all I know." He paused. "That's the whole story. I paid him and that was the end of thirty years of a close working relationship. If there's anything we can do for you, just call. Goodbye, Liz."

And that was it. *Fini* as far as George and Marilyn Lehrman were concerned. Who else could she turn to? Sharon, of course, her one and only best confidante at the club. She dialed her number. The maid said they were away for two weeks. To Antigua on holiday, she said. Any messages? No.

Wonderful how she took off with the devoted husband at a moment's notice without telling me. Maybe she ran away with Frank. Oh God, I'm off the wall like Humpty Dumpty. Liz could hardly catch her breath as she sank to the floor still wrapped in a wet towel and cried and cried.

She caught her breath and tried to think. *If Mom were alive, I'd call her.* More tears. Where did they come from? *Mom, I need you. You were the one who told me to marry*

Frank. Thoughts tumbled over; Liz held her throbbing head, tried to think coherently to no avail. Past and present mixed in a kaleidoscope. *Frank loves me 'cause I'm a winner/ No-nonsense Coach says "Go to college on the scholarship—train for the Olympics." Mom/Frank/Coach pulling me until I almost fell apart. I have no one to turn to except for daughter Susie who idolizes her father. How did everything that seemed so right go so wrong?*

Liz shivered and cried out, "I gave up swimming, a chance for Olympic gold, my college scholarship for you, Frank. Doesn't that count for something? The first time we met, when I won the State championship, you said you loved a winner." She pulled at the towel wrapped around her. "When did I stop being a winner and become a loser?" The empty house had no answer. Hurling the towel toward the bed where it landed with a soggy splat, Beth looked at her nakedness. She lifted small breasts and let go, no bounce; gazed at all her parts in pretty fair shape from swimming and diving for more years than she wanted to remember. She cried out, "Not young enough for you, Frank?" Her voice ricocheted around the room and boomeranged back--not young enough--not anything enough--not enough.

Chapter 2

From the bedroom came the insistent ring of the phone, jolting her back to the present. One, two, three rings. The answer machine picked up. Frank's authoritative voice delivered the message. "Leave the time and date of your call. We'll get back to you as soon as we can." Like an automaton, stiffly she walked back to the room she intended to vacate as soon as possible and listened.

"Hi Liz. It's Sally Morton. If you and Frank are free this afternoon, Jim and I would just love to play twilight golf with you and have a late dinner at the club."

Frowning, Beth wondered what was the real reason Sally, who had never called this number in the twenty years they'd known each other, wanted to be chummy.

Sally took an audible breath and plowed on. "I called Frank's office for an appointment Saturday and was told he retired. Jim and I are interested in what your next step might be. If you plan to sell your gorgeous home, my Jim is a real estate broker. He'd be pleased to lend a hand to make any transition easy for you. Oh, the time is nine forty five, Sunday morning. Please call."

Shaking not with cold but with rage, Beth jabbed her forefinger at the delete button. Another nail broke. *The club gossip wants to wheedle information so she can spread the word about the Malone's private life and Jimmy boy can make a fat commission by selling my gorgeous home. Fargin' bitch.*

Storming her way to the closet, Liz searched for appropriate clothes. Restless hands fluttered like butterflies over a rack of bright spring outfits, finally lighting on a black shirt and matching black pants. *Black in mourning for the death of my marriage.*

Towels plummeted down the chute with a vicious shove, another image of Frank as she pushed. She hurried to the bathroom, lathered up with lotion, rummaged deep in the lingerie drawer for a black bra and panties and dressed. The woman in the mirror was sad, heartbroken. Frank, the only man she'd ever been with, was gone. Forty years of okay-ness. That's what marriage was all about, right? A lot of sex dwindling down to occasional sex, one child although she'd wanted more and he hadn't, disagreements and he always got his way so why argue. Marriage. Unsuccessfully, she tried to breathe through a nose red and swollen from all the damn crying. *Loser.*

Time to call daughter Susie. *She'll be torn apart.* Always Daddy's little girl, he was the favorite parent, the one she ran to. Now Susie was thirty, divorced, living with someone named Javier and calling herself Suzette. *Suzette? It's hard to call her Suzette.*

The phone rang and rang. Susie answered laughing and said, "Hi."

"It's Mom. I have something terrible to tell you."

"Oh hi, Mom. If it's about Dad, he told me he was going to leave. I think it's a mid-life crisis. Don't take it too seriously. I mean, I've heard about things like this and the husband always crawls home."

Stunned, for a moment Liz couldn't speak. "He told you before he sneaked out in the night?"

"Well, yeah. Dad and I have always been close. Don't worry, Mom. He'll come back."

"I'm his wife and he tells you first? Why didn't you call me?" *Don't cry, don't cry, don't cry.* "First your father betrays me and now you."

"Mother, calm down. I'm sorry your feelings are hurt." She called out to Javier to wait. "Mom, Dad leaving like this was a

14

rotten thing to do. Javier and I have an appointment. We'll stop by later."

Liz's voice rose. "Hurt? You have no idea. . ." Her daughter had hung up.

I thought I had a life. Liz glanced around the room with swollen eyes. *Now I have nothing.*

She sat down on the edge of the bed, forgetting for a moment this was a place she didn't want to revisit ever again. Moving to the dressing table, still holding the phone, she reeled from the knowledge that Frank had told Susie. All Liz could do was shake her head. How did she let this happen? Could she have prevented the erosion of her place in the family?

When Susie was born, Liz was the happiest she'd ever been. The little house was immaculate, she cooked and baked each day, their garden was a showplace, and the baby was delicious. Frank brought friends home to show off his talented wife's accomplishments. He was always in the nursery picking up the freshly changed Susie, handing her over for Beth to do the feeding, diapering, bathing. He knew how to play with the baby and forgot how to play with his wife. As time went on, Beth slipped into the role of the housekeeper and Daddy's coming home meant fun time for Susie.

Maybe when Frank asked her to sit in the backseat of the car so he could talk to Susie, she should have said no. He said, "I work long hours and don't have enough time with our daughter." From then on, that was her place; the backseat. No wonder Susie thought of her mother as a second class person. The feisty winner Frank fell in love with had flat-lined, like the water in a swimming pool when the race ended and the swimmers went home.

Retrieving the crumpled note, she smoothed it carefully. Maybe it didn't say what she thought it said. Glasses perched precariously at the end of her turned-up nose, she read aloud, "It's not you, it's me." *A joke from a sit-com starring*

Elizabeth Malone. He wrote 'call Bruce', his best friend and lawyer. She dialed the number.

"Bruce Bradley here."

"It's Liz. Liz Malone." *Don't cry, don't cry, don't cry.* She cried.

His voice changed from jovial to oily smooth. "Ah Lizzie. I'd come right over but I have a tee time shortly. What can I do for you?"

Tee time. "Where is he, why did he leave, and who did he go with? Tell me or I'll show up at your office or at court and scream."

"Calm down, Lizzie. I'll do my best to answer all your questions. Oh, there's my ride. Call you back." He hung up.

Dumbfounded, she stared at the dead phone, then banged it down. "Lizzie? Why didn't I say shut up, you fool. You'd never hang up on Frank. Never, never, never." *If I throw things, I'll have to pick them up so what's the point?* Instead, she pounded the floor until both hands hurt and she tried to hold on to her senses.

Chapter 3

Somehow the morning sun had risen high and it was afternoon. Bewildered, Liz struggled to focus. All she could do in the house was wring her hands together and wander from room to room. Images from the past jerked through her mind like a silent movie. The young couple—Frank and Liz holding hands, a moving truck, doors opened in the background. Workmen building a major addition ten years later, a youthful Beth swollen with pregnancy; prosperous Frank swaggering around. Susie's curly blonde hair nestled in Daddy's neck as she pretended to sleep. The small house transformed into a sprawling mansion on acres of land cleverly purchased by the eminent Doctor at a low price. *Purchased with money from my inheritance when my dad died because he was just out of med school and had no money of his own.*

When her internal clock felt lunch closing in, automatically she glanced toward the picture window thinking Frank should be back from spring golf by now . *Stop. No more lazy Sundays by the pool.* Happy homemaker hands Frank used to call them. Always busy, never still; she did everything but churn butter and make shoes. He'd brag about her. My wife. *Yeah. He left out the part where he was going to leave the handy wife behind after forty years. My breasts aren't perky enough for you, Frank?*

Tentatively, Liz stepped outside. There must have been a rain shower she hadn't heard; puddles lay all over the pool area. She wanted to lie down on top of the green pool cover in spite of the dirty cold water settled there. The diving board beckoned. A sense of satisfaction rose when she recalled a long ago shouting match with Frank. He didn't want the Olympic size pool but she held her ground and he caved. Mental note--

Call the pool guy and tell him to open the pool ASAP. She needed it.

Full night had settled in and she was too tired and cold to go in and too frightened to stay out. Backyard sensor lights clicked on flooding the entire area with white light. A sigh of relief escaped from Liz as she pushed the sliders open. Locking the doors, she punched the security code and felt safer. A shower, warm clothes and uh, oh yes, must eat. *See, I can take care of myself.*

The fridge still had the uneaten food from last night's dinner. No way was she going to eat a meal planned to please Frank. She scraped the expensive meal into the garbage container. The insistent beep of the answer machine demanded attention. *Damn, it was a nuisance.*

First message: "Hey Liz, it's Lisa Marcus regarding tennis round robin tomorrow. Hope you can come. Heard Frank retired so maybe you'll be busy with him."

Word's out so soon. Next thing they'll know is he also retired from me. I don't know if I can ever go back there.

The phone rang. It was Susie. "Mom, we're at the front door. Open up or we'll break a window. Javier cooked one of his specialties."

She ran to the front, threw open the door and fell into Susie's arms surprising both her daughter and herself. They hadn't hugged in a long time. "Come in. I'm a mess."

The three of them entered the house, Javier holding a container filled with tempting aromas.

"Don't worry about Dad," Susie said. "He's always been so selfish. Me, me, me. Everything about him. That's all he ever talked about. He'll get tired of being alone and come running home. Javier wanted you to have something fresh and hot." A quick pat from Susie, a shy smile from Javier and they were gone.

Grateful they'd come, Liz wished they had time to stay. Now she was alone again but she had food. Nice of them to come by and thoughtful. Maybe she could begin to build a mother/daughter relationship now. Never too late. She cried as she carried the food upstairs and wondered where to settle down. Too late for her marriage. She'd never take him back but why did he leave? Must be another woman. And where did he go?

Tears fell as she went for a robe. *The stairs seem steeper, higher than before. They must have multiplied since I came downstairs hours ago. I'm not a young chick anymore. Stop whining. Susie brought food.* Charity meal balanced in one hand, Beth searched for a place to eat; somewhere in the house where Frank's ghost wouldn't haunt her. Mentally she ran through a list of rooms; laundry—he never did laundry but who wanted to eat where the air smelled of bleach, detergents, dirty gym socks, smelly underwear. Powder room? Uh, no. Combination sewing room and athletic gear. Not bad. How about Susie's bedroom/guest room? *Turn it into a grown-up room for me?*

She took the stairs two at a time to prove she was still able and limped to the Susie/guest room. A small table sufficed for the solitary plate and little bottle of Chardonnay, no glass. Toilet tissue served as a napkin, fork and knife forgotten in the kitchen. Yet when Liz unwrapped the foil from the still warm plate and inhaled aromas from chicken and vegetables in a spicy sauce, her taste buds perked up. *They included a fork and knife. How thoughtful. Just when I gave up hope, a daughter came through.*

After dinner, Liz peeled off her clothes and dressed in flannel pajamas; she wondered where to sleep, the master bedroom no longer an option. Visions of Saturday night's delightful dinner, Frank surprising her with chilled champagne, two dozen red roses, *throw out the roses*, dark chocolate. . . Was it only twenty four hours ago? He was touchy-feely, charming, funny. Talked more last night than he had in. . .how long? Years. The son-of-a-bitch.

Wandering, she found herself back in Susie/guest room, sitting cross legged in the middle of the bed. *Good mattress.*

Firm. Not broken in, broken down, like my mattress. Like me. Damn. "I want my forty years back. Is anybody listening?"

The alarm clock set for 7:30, Elizabeth Malone crawled between pink sheets in her daughter's childhood bedroom and cried herself to sleep. . . .and to dream.

Late. Frank was late. Liz wrung her hands and wondered what to do? Stuffed baked potatoes were ready, his favorite salad chilled in glass bowls. But the filet mignon? To start the grill or wait 'til he walks in? And his cocktail. He likes it shaken and poured just so. She fussed with the short hair he didn't like, ran to the powder room, applied a drop more lipstick--the garage door went up. Frank was home.

Doctor Frank Malone made his entrance, one hand behind his back, one in front bearing a gold box with a red ribbon wrapped around it; a bottle of champagne tucked under his arm completed the picture. "Honey, I'm home," he crooned in his sweet Irish tenor. "Oh, what's all this? It's not our anniversary, is it?" Liz felt a flush rise in her cheeks. Maybe she was supposed to give Frank a gift, too.

Setting the package on the table, two dozen red roses in the sink, and a bottle of champagne on the counter, Frank swept his wife of forty years into his arms and pressed her body very close. He whispered in her ear, "This is a fine how do you do," and taking her by complete surprise, ground his erection between her legs. And all she thought of at that moment was, "Is this what he's calling it? A fine how do you do? And where's it been hiding all these months when I've tried wearing little lacy outfits."

What she said was, "Well, hello Frank." And when she mentioned dinner, he poured champagne. When she said salad, he slipped a dark chocolate between her lips, and when she said more champagne, he lit candles and walked her upstairs. Foreplay.

Until then, she was positive Frank thought fore play was a golf term and candles were lit only when there was a power outage. The geriatric gymnastics that followed just about killed the two of them. His appetite was voracious, like honeymoons you dream about. Satiated, she slept to wake up.

Liz's eyes flew open. She raced to the bathroom and threw up. Threw up thoughts of Frank's letter, the sex, vomited all the disgust she felt for him and for herself. After teeth-brushing and a mouthwash rinse, Liz crept back to her daughter's childhood bed for a test drive of the single life ahead.

Chapter 4

Two calls to make before Liz did anything else. She had to leave a message at Susie's "Susie, thanks to you and Javier, I had a delicious meal last night. I appreciate your thoughtfulness. I'd like to see both of you again very soon. Please call."

"Lisa, sorry to call at the last minute. I can't play this morning. Uh, yeah, sick. Thanks. "

No tennis. Not today, maybe not ever. For sure not today.

Early Monday morning, she punched in the pool guy's number. Weather forecast was for another string of sunny days. Temp in the high forties going into the fifties. *With the warm water pool, I can swim every day. Might save my sanity.*

A deep husky voice answered. "Maverick."

"Oh, are you the pool service person?"

"Yes, Ma'am."

"This is Mrs. Malone. We, uh, I have a contract with you to open the pool early spring and I'm calling to open the pool."

She heard a shuffling of papers and footsteps as he picked up the phone again. "Okay, Mrs. Malone, usually Doctor Malone calls to set up a time but Monday's your day. Since today is Monday, I guess you want me to come over."

"Okay." She hung up. *My first business call since I left work so many years ago. Imagine that. Frank always made the calls. A man's voice gets the job done, he'd say. I'll handle it.* "Now what do I do?" she asked herself, and the door chimes rang. "Answer the door."

Liz hurried downstairs, walked past room after room of the large house 'til she reached the front door. It was Maria, the cleaning woman who'd been with Liz since they built the first section of the house. Maria exchanged greetings at the door and bustled off to work. *What next? Breakfast to keep up energy. Pool guy opens pool, pool heats up, eat to have strength to swim. It's a start. Coach's voice emerged from the past and shouted.* "Sink or swim, Liz O'Brien. Make the right choice or get off the team."

Forcing down tea and toast with orange marmalade, promising she'd work on eating, Liz began a to-do list and stared blankly at the page. She looked around the kitchen, trailed a hand along tile counter tops she and Frank picked out so long ago. Clutching the blank list, Liz walked from room to room with tears streaming down. Everywhere, everything in the house had some small memory of Frank. Wherever he'd run off to had no memories of her, especially the smooth body lying next to him. Knowing Frank, *guess I didn't know him that well*, never a loner-- he didn't leave alone.

Dropping to her knees in the entrance hall, she looked up at the skylight. It would have been better if he died, she thought, as the clear sky and warm sun looked back. *Oh God forgive me.* Raw pain wracked her body. Time heals, someone once said. Sure. She scrambled to her feet and rushed to the powder room to throw up. Somehow Liz made it back to the kitchen to make some coffee. Maria's voice interrupted her.

"Excuse me, where are Doctor's shirts? I am ready to wash now."

And Liz stared at the pleasant face asking the same ordinary question she'd asked for many years and sobbed as her heart broke in a million tiny pieces; Maria enfolded her in the warm expanse of a generous bosom.

"Doctor is sick?"

When Liz could speak, she said, "He left me."

Maria nodded and stroked her back. "Sorry to hear this. You are a good person and Doctor is sick to leave you."

A muscular man knocked at the slider doors, tall and rugged in a denim jacket and boots. He waved.

Maria said, "Pool guy."

"Thanks, Maria. I'll take care of him. It's business about my pool. Time to take the cover off."

She opened the sliders and he stepped in, his energy filling the room, bouncing off the walls. By contrast, Liz felt faded and inconsequential.

"Hey, Miz Malone. I can come back later. Don't want to interrupt you."

"I was about to make coffee."

No time to look in the mirror and she didn't care what pool guy thought. What would the so-called friends at the club say when the word about the Malone's got out. Liz measured cups of water in the gleaming pot. One cup, *Liz Malone couldn't keep her husband happy.* Two cups, *he found another woman.* Three cup of water, *I'm surprised he stayed this long.* Four cups. Tears eked out, spilled down thin cheeks just missing the trembling water cup. She made eight cups of coffee.

"Thanks but I don't need any right now. Maybe later. Better get to opening your fine pool and setting the heater. You'll want to be swimming soon as possible, I guess."

Why did I make so much coffee? Sharon's away. She's the one who'll offer a shoulder to cry on and advice. Where've I been all these years? Play golf and come home; play tennis and rush home. Sorry can't stay for lunch; have to do something for Frank... They'd laugh. Clean the dirt out of his golf clubs. What?

So she sat by the glass slider doors in back watching the pool guy. *What's his unusual name? Martino, Mercutio. No. Maverick. Yes.* Watching Maverick, the pool guy work. Maybe

25

now he'd like a cup of coffee. Never one to be idle yet here she sat idle, lost in thought with too much time on her hands.

Knocking at the slider door interrupted the reverie she'd fallen into. "All finished. Added a big dose of Shock to clear the water. Be back tomorrow to vacuum, add chemicals, and get the heater going. By the end of the week you can swim." She nodded and began to close the door. "Miz Malone, Doctor pays the first bill today, if you don't mind."

Liz stared into the kindest blue eyes she'd ever seen. "Monthly bill?"

"Opening the pool is a separate fee. It's paid at the time I do the work. I keep careful account of my books and this pool is so special . . ." He waited. When no envelope appeared, he said, " Doctor Malone's always here to settle up at eleven." The silence became awkward. "Said he always took Mondays off after morning procedures. Stopped home to change and pay me."

Frank took Mondays off? Since when and why? "I'll get the check book.

Where is the bill?" He reached into a knapsack, pulled out an envelope with Malone on the outside. *Organized young man. Where's the business checkbook and where are my glasses?* "I'll be right back."

Hurrying down the hall to Frank's study, Liz hoped the checkbook was in the top middle drawer of Frank's desk. It was. And reading glasses they sometimes shared were next to it. More confident now, she marched back to the kitchen and sat at the kitchen table, prepared to write her first business check in the long ledger style checkbook. Her name was on the account right under his name although Frank always told her he'd take charge of the business end of writing checks for household expense. Certainly Liz was capable. She had been the office manager of a mid-size company and moved into an executive secretary position over ten years. *Why didn't I stand up for myself back then? He rode over every thought until I lost the steam to fight.*

The bill was open on the table. She glanced up to see Maverick, tee shirt stretched across his tan muscular upper body, arms folded across his chest. He grinned a lazy grin.

"Thought I'd save you some time by opening the bill. Hope you don't mind."

Flustered, no longer accustomed to transactions other than buying groceries, clothes, and other homey items, Liz said, "Uh no. I don't mind this time but I'll have to. . . get. . . used. . .to it." *Don't cry, don't cry, don't cry.* Tears splashed on the checkbook. She turned her head away, sniffled, searched for a napkin. A callused hand pressed one into hers. She heard the scrape of a chair against the tile floor as it was pulled close.

"Miz Malone, did something happen to the Doctor?"

When Liz turned to him, they were almost nose to nose. *He smells like coconut oil; blue eyes filled with concern for a stranger.* In that isolated moment, he was her only confidant. "The Doctor's gone," she said.

"Gone? Like away on a trip?"

"No. Gone like he flew the coop." When Liz realized he didn't get it, a string of words poured out. " Gone like bye-bye, hasta la vista, ciao, fare thee well, auf weidersehn, have a nice day." A helpless gesture of her hands and she giggled and couldn't stop. She laughed all the way through writing a surprisingly large check for the one thing she fought for years ago and Frank finally had to give in. *Major upkeep.* The check was entered in the register; Liz tore it out and handed it to Maverick.

Quiet, respectful, he received the check, wrote a receipt and the transaction was complete. An awkward moment passed before he said, "Sorry for your trouble." He slid the glass door open and half turned. "I'll take good care of your beautiful pool."

The door closed the rest of the way and Liz caught her breath. *Did that really happen? Did I spill my guts to the pool guy?*

Passing the length of mirrored walls in the foyer, she caught a glimpse of a skinny woman dressed in some kind of sad-sack black shirt and ill-fitting black pants, short hair sticking out every which way. Liz stopped. "Oh my God. It's me." *I walked around in front of Maverick looking like this. What happened to the pride I've always had in my appearance?*

The phone rang, the answer machine picked up and when she heard Frank's voice saying no one was home to take the call, please leave your name and number, she removed her shoe and threw it at the phone, ending the message.

"Bingo," she yelled, picking the phone off the floor to listen for dial tone. Still working. How to change the message was a mystery. Noise out in the back indicated maybe Maverick was still there. He'd know how to change a message. She ran to the slider in time to see his boot, some wheels and hoses disappear around the side of the house.

"Maverick," she called running after him.

He was almost at the van in the driveway but stopped, swung his blond head around, gave her a worried blue-eyed look. "Something wrong, Miz Malone?"

Suddenly standing there in front of this stranger seemed like a stupid idea. Her cheeks burned and she ran both hands through the idiot hair-do. When she finally spoke, her voice was thin and breathy. "I'm basically a techno-dummy and machines have always been my mortal enemy." She fidgeted. *Don't suck your thumb, nitwit.* "I know it's an imposition and you have a busy schedule but no one's here to help me and I must change the message on my answer machine. Now." *Or I will lose my mind and kill myself if I hear his voice in my home again.* She searched her weary mind for incentives to offer Maverick. "I'll pay you for your expertise." *Please, please.*

He packed his equipment in the van, locked the doors, and said, "Okay. It's easy to change the message. I'll show you." He walked along the garden path, commented on the forsythia bushes in full bloom as daffodils and tulips she nurtured over the years competed in a beauty contest and they entered the house.

A few buttons pressed, Frank's voice deleted forever. Maverick made no comment, asked no questions until he said, "Okay, time for you to record your message."

She pointed to her chest, "Me?"

"Yup. Your house."

"What'll I say?" Liz felt panic rise high in her throat about to choke off sound and breath. His warm, rough hand closed over her hand and gently squeezed.

"Any white wine in the house?" She nodded and pointed to the bar in the recreation room nearby. A small refrigerator was built-in. He opened it and poured a half glass of wine in a crystal glass hanging from a wooden rack. "Sip this, Miz Malone. It'll relax you. I'll get my lunch from the truck and keep you company, if that's okay." He was out the door before she had a chance to say thanks.

Wine finished, Liz felt much improved as Maverick predicted. He checked his watch, noted the time and said, "Let's record the message."

Two deep breaths and she said, "I need some advice and since no one else is around, you're elected. Please?"

Curious, he said, "If I can help, sure."

"My name is Elizabeth but he called me," she shuddered "Lizzie. I hear his voice calling that name and I hate it. I have a strong urge to change it to Beth. Is that stupid or what?"

When a lop-sided grin spread across his face, Liz felt like a fool, sorry she trusted her thoughts to a stranger. And then Maverick said, "My name was John. One day I thought to myself that I had enough of John." He spat out the name. "I was different from the other kids. Yeah I was a good jock and a really good student but I didn't like hanging out, drinking, doing nothing with my time. And one day, I became Maverick. Been feeling good ever since. So Miz Malone, if Beth is what you want, be Beth."

He understands and approves. Marvelous. She regrouped, breathed deeply and said, "I'm ready. Hi. You've reached Beth Malone. *Sounds just right.* Please leave a brief message and your phone number. I'll get back to you as soon as I can. Thanks for calling."

He played it back and smiled. "Sounds good. Please don't pay me. It's my pleasure."

She escorted him to the door. "Thanks for all your help. I'll be paying the bills from now on." They walked out the back way and she gestured to the space over the pool and just for a moment, felt like a kid as she spread her arms to the sky. "Have you ever done a heated enclosure?"

His eyes lit up and he rubbed capable hands together as if in anticipation. "Yes, Ma'am."

"Let's talk about it in a couple of weeks when, hopefully, I feel more human."

Maverick gave her his business card. She watched the white van with the whimsical logo painted on the side, drive off. A large calf, head looking over the shoulder, no brand to be seen. A maverick. Separate from the herd.

Frank separated me from the herd when he fargin' left me without warning. Well, fuffa him. Took Mondays off, huh?

The tears came hard there in the driveway and Beth ran to the front door but it was locked and she had to run all the way around her big house, too big for one person, and hoped the back door was open and she cried all the way through the rooms, one, two, three, four, five, and stopped counting—too many rooms and that was only the downstairs, and then up the stairway, up, up, up, and fell on the master bedroom bed where she had the best sex in years but that made her feel dirty so she moved into Susie's innocent room and lay down wishing she'd sleep to wake up and find the whole thing was only a nightmare..

Chimes rang out demanding attention. Maria was gone. *No one but little old me.* Beth dragged herself out of bed,

30

caught sight of her rumpled self-swollen red eyes, hair on end. *What a sight*. She dragged her fingers through hopeless short hair and called out, "I'm coming."

Through the peephole, she could see Bruce Bradley. Too late to pretend she wasn't there and what a mistake to think she had to answer every ring. Indoctrinated by Frank never to miss a call or respond to the door was a habit she'd have to break. Bruce waved hello, gave her his winning smile and waited impatiently for her to open up. With trepidation, she opened the door.

"Lizzie, so sorry I had to end our conversation so abruptly. My ride was blowing his horn and I was stuck." He stepped back and appraised her, then opening his arms wide, he enfolded his best friend's deserted wife with gentleness. One hand held a huge bouquet of flowers readily available at any greengrocer in town. As if he owned the house, Bruce led her to the homey kitchen. Beth caught his glance at the wine bottle and one glass on the table and it was just two in the afternoon. He'd have a lot to report back to Frank about how awful his wife looked and 'by the way, Frank, she's drinking alone early in the afternoon.'

Taking both her hands in his, he said in his most sincere, insincere way, "If there's anything I can help you with, please call day or night. Alicia and I will be in touch."

"Call me Beth from now on, Bruce. And uh, Bruce, all I want at this moment is to know what assets Frank left in my name, money market, stocks, bonds. And I need a copy of the will. The note he left said I'm well taken care of. Is that true?" She tried to assess what lie behind his façade and couldn't. The legal papers would tell the truth.

"Believe me when I say Frank left you well provided for." He moved with assurance, mission accomplished. "I'm off." At the door, Bruce pressed too close then waved from the bottom step. "Goodbye, uh Beth." This was becoming her theme song. She tried to recall her thoughts before the door chimes rang. *Oh yes. What do I do next?* Dumping the flowers in the trash, she took action.

31

What a fool I am. Call the bank. See how much money I have. Did he really provide for my future? If so, the next best thing after financial security from a faithless husband, was what? I just don't know. But I do know I can't go to the bank looking like a rag.

The bank manager set up a meeting that afternoon with the President of the bank, Raymond Ross. She wondered if she had to legally change her name to Beth or just use it. *The least of my concerns. A man who couldn't fulfill his wedding vows wrote something in a letter. Not to be trusted.*

When she walked out an hour later after being given the red carpet treatment, Beth was relieved. Frank had more money than she ever dreamed of and she was well provided for. Where did all that money come from, she wondered? Vaguely Beth recalled an uncle in California leaving something in his will to Frank a few years earlier but he'd said it didn't amount to much. Hmmm. He'd lied before and she never called him on it. Why not about the money?

That burden off her shoulders with no one to share the information, she wondered how she'd ever face the club members, townspeople, the social strata they lived in for so many years. The gossips would have a field day with this bit of news. Humiliation at being deserted, Beth hurried to the black Mercedes and sped home. She didn't want to bump into anyone. Money could not be discussed with her daughter. Susie knew how to badger and dig in like a detective and she'd want what she would consider her share of the spoils. Absolutely not. She was a teacher and Javier worked at something. Together they'd carve out a life. *Hopefully with better results than mine.*

Chapter 5

No round robin tennis again and oddly, Beth missed it. She wasn't ready to face the club yet. Playing with different partners every forty minutes and recording your scores with an awards dinner at the end of the season was fun, even though Frank always put it down as foolish and too easy. Not like the one-on-one gladiator sport of golf or singles tennis, he always said. Patterns of a lifetime breaking up all over the place because . . . *I'm allowing what Frank did to me to upset every aspect of my life and therefore I must make some kind of a plan. He did. Well thought out over months, I bet.* A nagging thought hit her like a brick. What if he came back? Then what? Susie would be ecstatic and say, "See Mom, I told you." He'd say, "Midlife crisis. Just a glitch, sweetie. Sorry." *Plans? I can barely think straight let alone plan for the next five minutes. The pool will save my life. Breathe in, breathe out.*

Chilly air hit the warm pool and mist rose almost as high as the diving board where Beth poised to take her first dive. Shivering when she climbed the steps, she relaxed and breathed. Coach's hoarse voice called, "Chin down, Liz O'Brien Time for chin up after the plunge." She sailed arms wide, then knees tucked and last, knifed clean through the fog below. Frank forgotten for a while as she went through the routine established when she was a winner.

Beth began to make sense of every day. A small room upstairs became her office where a computer and all component parts were attached. Before her lay plans for dinner tomorrow. Two months passed as Beth and Maverick searched for perfect plans to build an enclosure for the pool and tonight they would finalize costs and a time frame for construction. As a reward for all the extra hours he'd put into the project and because she felt like cooking and good company, Maverick was coming for dinner.

Always a terrific cook, she searched her memory for something wondrous to prepare. It had to be beautiful to look at, delicious to eat, and for an experiment, cut down on calories and fat. Phooey. Whatever happened to butter, whipped cream, yummy cream sauces? Gone, she sighed, in the age of awareness of counting this and that and taking a lot of joy out of cooking. Quiet, oh so quiet in the house built forty years before. Before the wreck. Quiet as she tried to control herself and succeeded. *Focus on the present.*

Tomato and mozzarella salad with black olives and Italian dressing, chocolate mousse with a swirl of whipped cream. *Protein? A big guy, Maverick needs grilled steak.* Beth added steak to the menu. *Carbs? Stuffed baked potatoes.* Braid vines from the morning glories to lay across the table and purple irises in a crystal vase as centerpiece. Cookies? Didn't know if she had time. Fun. This was stimulating. She hadn't planned a dinner except to please Frank for a long time.

Time for bed. The mirror reflected a fit tanned woman, the dull look in her brown eyes taking on some life. Brown hair bleached by too much chlorine and sun but growing longer. Didn't look too terrible. She allowed half a chuckle as the shower beat down on tired limbs. She'd call her daughter. They were growing a little closer although she wished Susie's farewells didn't always include the positive remark that her dad would get tired and soon come home. Beth wondered if Frank was in touch with Susie. Today she'd ask.

Chapter 6

Wishing her heart weren't beating so fast, *I gave birth to this kid*, she waited for Susie's phone to ring and hopefully be picked up by her and not the person she lived with, Javier.

"Hello?"

"Hi, it's your mother."

"Oh. Hi Mom. I'm rushing to go to work. The kids this semester are a handful and I can't be late but I can talk for a minute. How are you getting along?"

"We haven't talked for a while, Susie, and . . ."

"Suzette. Did you forget?"

"Oh. Well, yes. It's hard for a mother to suddenly start calling her daughter another name, but who am I to talk?" Beth laughed. "I decided I didn't like Liz anymore so I'm calling myself Beth now. What are you doing after teaching hours today? Any time for a visit?"

"Beth? Okay but I'll still call you Mom. I have some time after school before Parent/Conferences night. If you make some of my fave chocolate chip cookies and a sandwich to go with it, I can stop by about four. Bye."

Beth hung up, happy Susie was coming and there'd be a chance to chat. She didn't know if her mental conversation would take place but she'd try. *Even if your father begged to return and he won't, trust me on this. Should've, would've, could've. So many opportunities to be close to a little girl and I let them slip away. So what if you never wanted to cook with me or swim or decorate. I should've—there's that word again—paid more attention to what you liked to do. You're a born teacher. I never noticed you had a gift for organizing friends in games. And the way you are with babies and small children.* This was an opportune time to mend fences with Frank out of the picture, Beth thought.

At four sharp, her daughter arrived looking a bit tired yet very professional. A perfunctory hug at the door and Susie kicked off her shoes and headed for the comfortable kitchen. She sniffed the air.

"Thanks for taking the time to bake my faves, Mom. I really appreciate the effort." Chomping on a cookie, she said, "Javier thinks you're very brave, Mom."

Javier thinks I'm brave. How nice. I thought I was a cowering bag of. . .

"He said mothers should be revered and taken care of, especially in time of need and that I better clean up my act." Susie bit into another cookie, swallowed and started in on the toasted ham and Swiss cheese Beth prepared for her.

Beth thought for a moment and said, "That's lovely of Javier. This has been the worst time of my life and I'm virtually alone in dealing with my loss." She sat next to Susie and tried to explain her feelings. "Our relationship isn't a good one as we both know and I grieve not only for the loss of my husband walking out but for the loss of you."

Susie looked up and continued eating.

"Somewhere along the way, I failed you and I take full blame. You didn't like the activities I liked and no matter how I tried, they weren't your thing. So I didn't dig to see what my daughter was made of and we drifted apart. You found your niche and I lost contact. But Susie, I've always loved you and felt left out when you and your father had secret jokes and special times together." Beth stopped to catch a breath and noticed Susie finished her sandwich and glass of milk and sat watching her. "I just hope we can find a way back to a simpler time, a Mother/Daughter time when we can help each other and recapture the love we once had." It was more than Beth had said in a long time. *I really need a shrink.*

"Mom," Susie stood up ready to leave, "Unfortunately, I have to get back to school. You're right and Javier is right. And Mom, please don't take all the blame for what's happened in the past. I'm old enough to admit I've been acting like a brat." She kissed the top of Beth's head. "We'll talk some more but maybe instead of talk, we'll act on it." She placed her dishes in the sink and walked out, calling over her shoulder, "Dad's a jerk, Mom. He'll come back."

"Wait." Beth ran after her. Her daughter was already in the car. "Is he in touch with you?"

Susie said with a grin, "Of course, Mom. I just know one day he'll show up." She waved and backed out of the driveway.

Shocked to learn he was still in touch with their daughter, disgusted she had to ask yet glad she did, Beth dragged her bones back in the house. At least this time she spoke her mind.

Beth prepared for tonight's dinner with her only friend so far. The pool guy, Maverick.

Old skills rose to the surface as Beth pulled dinner together. By the time the table was decorated, steaks ready for the grill, she had just enough time for a shower and another black outfit. *It's a friendly business dinner.* Beth applied a little more mascara. *Then why all the fuss?* She adjusted the new black Wonderbra. *Why not?*

Maverick arrived at the front door briefcase in one hand, a bottle of wine in the other. To Beth's eyes, the man cleaned up just fine. "Right on time, as always. Welcome to the front door." Something citrus, men's cologne, filled the room as he passed by and Beth's senses went into overdrive. *Business dinner, remember.* "It's a lovely evening. We're dining on the patio." They passed room after room and she noticed his head turning side to side, taking it all in. Through the sliders and out to the patio where citronella candles kept the bugs away and flowers attracted a few Hummingbirds.

Maverick touched Beth's shoulder and said, "So beautiful." He placed a bottle of Merlot on the table just as a butterfly poised on the edge of Beth's water glass, then fluttered away.

She smiled at her handsome guest and said, "Butterflies bring good luck." The evening began.

He licked the platter clean, almost. Beth was amused and delighted at Maverick's response to dinner. Afterward, they went over every aspect of the project and Beth signed her name to the contract. Two more weeks and she'd be swimming all year. At the door he leaned over to kiss her mouth. Beth felt the pull but turned her head at the last moment and the kiss landed on her flushed cheek. When the bolt clicked, his heat remained on her skin as she leaned against the door breathing deeply. *What if. . .*

Chapter 7

"I've got to stop doing this," Beth Malone said, punching the garage door opener and watching its ascent. She sat in the Mercedes until the garage door closed. With a practiced motion, she balanced two bags on a hip, unlocked the interior door, and set the bags on the kitchen counter in the silent house. *Almost ten pm and I'm sneaking home with groceries, for God sakes. What a wimp. Start buying groceries in my own town.* Beth made a note to herself and posted it on the fridge. *Got to face the world. So what if they whisper behind my back. I know the son-of-a-bitch left me. By now, everyone knows. Certainly the women in the round robin tennis today knew from the odd looks and cold shoulders. Who gives a flying fuffa.* "I do," she whispered and felt a trickle of tears begin.

Eleven weeks of not playing and Beth couldn't hit the damn ball. Then something awful happened followed by something interesting. Abruptly Beth tore open a fancy dark chocolate bar she'd planned to keep for an emergency treat. Sinking her teeth in, she bit off a large piece and chewed. *Breathe in and out and sit for a minute.* The next bite melted in her mouth as the scene at the club replayed.

Two hours of keeping a stiff upper lip while used-to-be-friends were pleasant but distant, Beth was in line to report her poor scores when she saw Sharon hurry past. Sharon, her closest friend in the social circle. Sharon who hadn't called in all the weeks since Frank flew the coop.

"Sharon, over here." Beth left the line and ran over. "What's going on? I must have called half a dozen times since

Frank walked out and the maid keeps saying you're not home." Avoiding Beth's eyes, Sharon seemed to search for an escape. "Sharon, look at me. Just because I'm alone doesn't mean I'm not the same person, the same good old girl I've always been." Close to tears, thinking don't cry, don't cry, don't cry, she waited for an answer.

Sharon said, "I really feel bad about this but we're a couples crowd. We all discussed your problem and the truth is, you don't fit in anymore as a single woman. Be realistic. Where would you sit at a dinner or bridge or in doubles when we play with our husbands?" And Beth stood there dumbfounded to hear the way old friends coldly picked the sad situation apart and banished her from everything that was fun and familiar for most of her adult life. Sharon gave Beth a stiff-armed hug and said, "If there's anything you need, please call." She turned her back and racquet on shoulder, sashayed away, short white tennis skirt swaying in the mild May breeze. Sharon moved with confidence away from a momentary encounter with an old friend, back to the smug life where single women were excluded.

Lisa, the tall heavy set woman in charge of round robin play, appeared and taking Beth by the arm led her to the table where she kept Round Robin scores, whispering all the while. "I overheard what that woman said to you. I experienced almost the same thing when my ex left me."

In shock, Beth heard as if from a distance but felt the warmth from this woman's voice. Lisa, a newcomer to the club since last year always pleasant and helpful, Beth found it hard to believe Lisa had suffered. When Lisa suggested getting together for lunch, Beth agreed. She thanked Lisa and said she'd call soon. *Someone to talk to? Be careful. Hard to know who to trust. Sharon Moore, the closest to me of all the women, turned out to be an ugly bitch. Damn her.*

Cold food went into the refrigerator, the other bag stood neglected in Beth's haste to change clothes. The pool always broke the sadness pattern. It was a start for Beth. A series of hurdles. As she stripped, the mental list took shape: 1.shop in town, 2. explore some kind of work. *I put Frank through medical school while I worked in an office, receptionist, typing, bullshit work, yes sir, no sir, finally office manager, then executive secretary to the president and I learned how to invest money. For God sakes. Did I really do that?* Suited up in the new black lycra one piece, thinking time set aside, Beth glanced in the mirrored closet door. Everything was tucked in and ready to dive.

Fast. Beth Malone's feet flew fast down the carpeted stairs, through quiet rooms no longer holding the faintest echo of family life. At her touch, the patio alarm turned green, the lock to the sliders opened and Beth stepped out into the brisk night air. She had to stop, catch her breath, watch little puffs blow away. Late May nights were chilly but steam rose from the heated pool calling the swimmer. Whenever grief threatened to overwhelm Beth, she ran to the pool. Diving, diving, diving 'til old Coach's voice yelled in her ear, "Enough."

Afterward, in the pink frilly bedroom where she slept, Beth wished she smoked. She never liked smoking. And wished she craved booze and, and, marijuana. A half glass of Chardonnay sent her spinning sometimes and the one attempt at marijuana set off a migraine. There was a life out there—a better life ahead and she had to make it happen. She had to find a way to be continued.

Chapter 8

Feeling overwhelmed night after night with crying spells, grief and confusion, Beth wondered who to talk to. And then Frank's personal nurse for twenty years, Doris, called. Doris had been more than an employee. A comfortable woman who went through life's tribulations with her head up, she always spoke to the doctor's wife in a confidential manner.

"Elizabeth, I'm so sorry I haven't called sooner. Frank was a rotten shit leaving you like that. Is there anything I can do for you, my dear?"

Don't cry, she said to herself. "Thanks. As a matter of fact, there just might be. I wondered whom to turn to and here you are." *Deep breath.* "I'm having a difficult time getting through each day and wondered if you knew a therapist I could speak with."

"Wait a minute." Beth heard Doris rustling through papers. "I'm retiring soon and moving to Florida to be with my daughter. Okay, I found it. Here's the name of a well-known therapist. She's busy all the time. Use my name and best to you. You deserve it."

"Thanks so much, Doris and tell your daughter I think she's fortunate in having such a terrific mother."

"Thanks and goodbye, Elizabeth."

Another tie broken and another goodbye, Beth. Definitely my theme song.

Therapist Jenna Stanley welcomed Beth into a cozy setting. No sharp edged dark furniture here. Antique ash wood, watercolor fabric in shades of blue covered the sofa and chairs. The attractive doctor wore a beige silk shirt and matching pants on her slim frame. She walked with a loose limbed athletic stride and listened with kind eyes, totally concentrating on Beth.

"Tell me why you're here, Beth."

Why am I here? "Where do I begin?" Beth cried, arms outstretched to the ceiling. "One minute I'm married forty years and the next minute, there's a note saying he's gone." Jenna passed a box of tissues toward her. "No," Beth pushed them away. "I've cried enough. I just want to know. . ." and then to her surprise, she cried hard.

When the well finally ran dry, Jenna said, "What happened just before you found the note."

"Okay," Beth sniffled, "Get ready for a soap opera script." Beth paced the floor as she spoke. "Frank came home for Saturday dinner as always. We hadn't had sex in months no matter what advice I followed in all the magazines. I even borrowed a few blue pills from my former best friend to slip into his drink . Instead he comes home, initiates amazing sex like there's no tomorrow, I fall asleep and wake up the next morning to find a note. Gone! There is no tomorrow. And I'm a laughing stock, old friends want nothing to do with me and I'm barely getting along. It's like a charade I'm playing. A disguise." She dropped into her chair and held her head.

After a short silence, Jenna said, "What kind of a marriage did you have, Beth?"

Peering up through a mess of hair, Beth said, "I thought it was fine, like everyone else we know, knew. He was the boss, made the decisions, I was the homemaker although I did put him through med school, paid the bills, bought the house with the inheritance from my father. After Susie was born, I was just Frank's wife, Susie's mom." She sipped water from a glass on the table, relieved to talk about life as Frank's wife. "When Frank and I met, I was the State swim champion. My dream was to win gold medals at the Olympics and I had potential. Coach said I did. Then maybe movies like Esther Williams. Colleges were offering scholarships. All I had to do was choose one. I. . ." tears fell again, "I chose to marry Frank and give up my future for his. Not too smart." The ache in her heart threatened to crack open. "Forty years ago I made the wrong choice and I'm paying for it now. At fifty eight, what can I possibly do to continue my life?"

After a silence, Jenna said, "You were about seventeen when you had to make momentous choices?"

Beth nodded. "About. Finishing my junior year in high school. I didn't have to decide 'til the next semester."

"And who helped you decide what to do?"

Beth laughed. "Who helped? Coach was furious. He practically tried to shake sense into me; said I was throwing my chance away for that smooth talking Irish who wanted a winner and then he planned to change me. I argued, said Frank wasn't like that. He said, 'Wake up Missy O'Brien, I've known guys exactly like him'. Mom was thrilled. I'd be close to home, working like all the other girls she knew and engaged to a future doctor. And Frank talked about our future in glowing terms while he petted my body and made me feel like a woman."

"So you were torn?"

"Oh yes. Torn to shreds. The only thing I did right back then was to swim and dive. I lost myself in the routine and competition, pushing myself to the limit, won every title." Tear fell again as memories flooded back. Beth lifted her head and cried out. "But it was all for nothing. Frank and Mom were merciless. He even promised to build me a swimming pool when we could afford it. So I turned my back on my future and show up forty years later, bawling my eyes out over a bad choice."

"You were young. Without the proper guidance, even adults make bad choices. Let's take a look at what you accomplished, Beth. You got a job, must have worked your way up to a good position to pay bills and eventually bought a house. Yes?" Again Beth nodded. "Remarkable. No wonder he believed you were a winner. You took over and pulled him through what was certainly tough times and then, when he became the breadwinner, what happened?"

"What happened? Why, I gave up my career as executive secretary to the president of the company and became a homemaker. Had Susie, cooked, decorated, planted a garden, nagged Frank 'til a pool was built."

"How did you feel about giving up a career you'd worked so hard for over a long time?"

"You're digging deep, Jenna." Jenna waited. "Sad, relieved, sorry to turn my back on people who'd come to rely on me, trust in me." Frowning, Beth said, "Kind of the way I felt about Coach when I walked away from the promise of the Olympics and scholarships and all the effort he'd put in training me."

Jenna stood. "Our time is just about up, Beth. Can you come back next week and we can work on your situation?"

Beth nodded and rose to leave. "There are support groups I can recommend in addition to our sessions," Jenna said. Beth shook her head no. "See you next week."

Driving home, Beth thought she'd feel relieved to get feeling out in the open. She pulled to the side of the road and threw up again and again. At home she lay down, a cold cloth pressed to her forehead as thoughts of the past whirled around. No good. She tried to sleep. Precious sleep eluded her. What have I done, she wondered. Talking to Jenna was like opening Pandora's box. *In forty minutes, I exposed thoughts hidden for more than forty years.* Shivering, Beth wrapped the pink flowered down quilt around her and dozed. Her last thought was that she couldn't survive 'til next week's appointment. Call Jenna tomorrow. Must talk about Susie.

Hair wet from a sudden rain shower, Beth huddled at Jenna Stanley's door waiting for it to open. A door closed, footsteps approached and Jenna stood there, a welcoming smile on her serene face.

"Raining," said Beth, stating the obvious. "Got caught."

"Come in. I'll get a towel for your hair. Your clothes look mostly dry."

"Ran."

Jenna handed Beth a white towel and sat down opposite her.

"Thanks and thanks for making time for me today. I was kind of off the wall when I left with my thoughts colliding and didn't know if I'd survive until next week." She dried her hair with the towel.

"This is my last appointment of the day and very often I choose to leave it open in case of emergency. You sounded as if you needed to talk."

Beth nodded. "I don't know if this happens to other people but I feel like a can of worms has been turned loose because I opened up to you and now. . .I have to tell you about my daughter. She's an only child because Frank said he was satisfied with one. I wanted, craved at least one more. Why didn't I fight? Why did I wind up lying under Frank's steamroller every time?"

"Why do you think you did, Beth?"

Rain pelted against the windows as precious therapy moments ticked by.

"Because it was easier."

"Yes. Very often it's easier to give in rather than argue."

"I kept doing that, giving in, and I was diminished not only in Frank's eyes but in mine"

"True. Very perceptive, Beth."

"So when Frank said I should sit in the back seat of the car so he could talk with Susie in the front seat, I should have said no. I think, above all, that was the beginning of her seeing me in a secondary position."

Jenna said, "Quite possibly."

"Is there any way to change her perception of me? She's thirty and has always been her daddy's girl."

"What do you think?"

"A question answered with a question again." She let out a big breath. "This is hard work. Be myself and let her see me as I am. I can't do more than that."

When Beth left, the rain had stopped and she felt more positive about her future. Time to swim.

Coach yelled for everyone to line up, toes curled, and he blew the whistle. No turning back.

"There's something new that's come up in my life," Beth said toward the end of the third therapy session. "I feel like an idiot talking about it. I'm almost 59 but. . ." Jenna motioned for her to continue. "I'm having a pool enclosure built so I can swim all year. And the young guy who's doing the work came over for dinner and uh, bent down to kiss me when he was leaving."

A nod from Jenna. "And how do you feel about that?"

"Well, uh, I or rather we were going over final plans and I needed to sign the contract and uh, I thought it would be nice to have dinner with him and. . .he's about early forties." Heat flooded Beth's cheeks. "Oh my God. I practically invited that kiss and uh maybe more, didn't I?"

A resounding applause came from the therapist. "A breakthrough. You're learning more about yourself. On that happy note," she stood up and ushered Beth to the door, "see you next week. Call if you need to talk."

Tying up loose ends on her to-do list was the way Beth thought of the call to Bruce Bradley, their lawyer. She made an appointment to go over all of the papers Frank referred to in the famous Dear Lizzie letter he'd left. Bruce was away on a conference followed by a trip with Alicia and wouldn't be available for a month. Regarding a divorce, she'd have to eat nails before her mind could wrap itself around such a concept. *"Keep your options open," Jenna said. I will.*

Chapter 9

Deep in concentration following along with the yoga video the next morning, voices from somewhere pierced Beth's solitude. *From the street? Not in this village. Not ever.*

An excited shrill female voice combined with a deep male voice came closer. Louder.

Oh my God.

Beth jumped up, almost fell as she tried to untangle legs and arms from the lotus position.

There in the entrance to her domain were daughter Susie-- and lover, swarthy Javier. What the fuffa! Beth attempted composure with difficulty.

"Hi kids. I was just finishing my yoga. I do this every day. I wish I'd known you were coming so I'd be more prepared." There was an awkward silence. Beth mopped her brow.

"Maybe next time, you'll call before dropping in."

With satisfaction, she watched Javier back away but daughter dear, whom she hadn't spoken to since an intimate conversation weeks ago, remained in the doorway, hands on ample hips. *Ample hips? Skinny Susie dressed in a shirt stretched tight over an expanded belly.*

"You're pregnant?"

"And married, Mom."

Pain shot through her system but she hid the feeling. "Congratulations." Beth crossed the quicksand territory when it came to mother/daughter relationship. She didn't want to sink.

"Why didn't you tell me, honey? I would love to have been a part of your ceremony."

No reaction from the rounded face, although hazel green eyes so like Frank's blinked a few times. Curly strands of blonde hair escaped from beneath the baseball cap Susie wore.

Pretty. She looks pretty and happy.

"Javier wanted to but I figured you've been so upset about daddy, you didn't want to be bothered with me."

Beth pulled Susie close and rubbed her back trying to soothe hurt feelings the way she'd done when her child was little. "No, no honey. We talked about all that. You're all I have left and you still come first the way it's always been since you were born. Honey, please don't shut me out. The only difference is I'm learning to make a new life. Alone. Privacy is very important to me. I forgot you had a key."

Mother and daughter gazed at each other. "Okay Mom. Maybe it was the hormones that made me so forgetful. I'm sorry. We'll sort it out as we go along. Susie turned and headed toward the stairs. "When we discovered the pregnancy, we made it legal." Over her shoulder, she said with an impish grin, "We were going to ask you to sell the house and move in with us. You could live downstairs."

Beth said, "Downstairs? You mean the basement?"

A laugh from Javier at the bottom of the stairs. "No, Mother Malone. Our house is split-level. You would live on bottom level."

Susie said, "Uh huh. The bottom. But now we can sell our place and with the gorgeous pool and what you've done with the house, I guess we can move in with you." She laughed the silver bell laugh Beth loved when her baby was small. She came close to Beth and hugged her.

"Only kidding, Mom. We like our privacy, too. Besides, when Dad comes back there won't be room for anyone else."

50

Mother Malone. . .move in with me. . only a joke. . .Frank returning! I can't take a joke. Head in a spin with the audacity, the selfishness in her world gone mad, Beth used every resource she'd learned in the past few months. With the aid of several deep breaths, she said, "I have an appointment and don't have time for a chat, not even a cup of tea. I'll call soon, we'll get together. I want to hear about the baby, your plans for the future." Escorting them to the door—*"here's your hat—what's your hurry"* ran through her mind, she said, "Let's celebrate all the good news soon and please, next time call first."

Chapter 10

Late. Again. Always punctual before Frank walked out, Beth never arrived anywhere on time these days. *Another new habit to break.* She was eager to meet with Lisa Marcus, hear her story, get a feeling about trusting someone.

Beth dropped 2 quarters in the parking meter and hurried in to the Kozy Kitchen, a checker cloth old fashioned restaurant in the heart of town. Raw damp weather with a hint of rain in the forecast chilled her bones and she hungered for a bowl of hot soup. Curious about Lisa who always presented herself as nothing but upbeat, Beth spied her in a quiet corner of the bustling lunch crowd. Seeing Lisa alone at the small table for two, Beth sensed the same isolation in her that she'd felt since Frank left.

Lisa glanced up and smiled. "Hi. Thanks for coming."

"Sorry I'm late. Thank you for asking. You're the first friendly person I've spoken to since. . ." Beth draped her jacket on the back of the chair and sat. "Before we say another word, I must tell you this." She took a deep breath. "My daughter just stopped at my home with her new husband to say they got married and she's pregnant." Lifting her hands palms up, Beth shook her head. "What is wrong with this picture?"

After a quick search of the lunch menu, she sighed. "Excellent. Chicken vegetable soup with dumplings." She dropped the menu on the table. "Have you eaten here before?" Lisa said no. "Carole's soups are famous and I need something hearty to stick to my ribs. Weather's crazy for end of May. Warm one day, chilly the next." She took a good look at Lisa; the full face, dark eyes and curly long dark brown hair worn loose today.

Overweight by about thirty five pounds, in her late forties, maybe. "What are you having?"

"You tell me something as momentous as that and now you talk about food?"

"I had to get it off my chest right away and you're here. Let's order. We'll talk about Susie another time."

Lisa's face reddened. "What I crave is a chocolate hot fudge sundae, extra whipped cream. What I'll have is the matzo ball soup, same as you."

Their eyes met and they laughed. The noise level rose and fell around them but they connected.

Orders placed, Beth tilted her head as if to say, "So?" Hot coffee arrived and Lisa began. "I moved here a year ago. I lived in Chicago in one of the Northern suburbs with a nice home, two sons—twins, attractive husband, taller than me." Tears welled up, she sniffled, and stirred sugar and cream in the cup. Beth sipped coffee and listened.

"We went to high school together; then on to college where his major was pre-law and I had a head for investment banking and business related subjects. But I got pregnant.

Oops. He had a fit. I wasn't thrilled. We weren't married, a lot more school ahead, he pushed me for an abortion and here's where our families got involved. Soup's on."

Bowls of steaming soup were placed on the table by Carole herself. She and Beth were longtime acquaintances. Oyster crackers and hot bread in a wicker basket came next.

"Beth, dear lady, haven't seen you in a while. You're looking a bit peaked. Who's your friend and where's the good doctor?" Before Beth had time to reply, the apple-cheeked woman wiped her hands on a red checked apron and greeted another patron.

In a low voice, Beth said to Lisa, "I'm looking peaked because the good doctor ran off after forty years of what I thought was a fine marriage and my new friend is about to finish another tale of marital horror. Otherwise, Carole, everything is perfect."

Again the shared laughter and they agreed it was better than the buckets of tears shed over unworthy husbands.

Beth said, "Better eat the soup before it gets cold."

"You sound like my Jewish mother."

"Irish." A spoonful had Beth rhapsodizing. "Mmmm. Carole is a great soup cook.

Not too sincere but what a cook. My forte is beautiful tasty food—no soup."

Lisa started to eat and finished before Beth was half through. "Delicious. I'd love another bowl and a chocolate sundae."

"Really? Didn't anyone ever tell you to savor the taste, not gulp every spoonful as if enemies were at the border?" Lisa appeared stricken by her comment. Reaching over, Beth touched her hand. "Sorry. It's none of my business. That was so rude of me."

Lisa said, "Beth, I never behaved like this until Kenneth walked out. I gained thirty pounds in a month, continued to blimp up and finally realized I had to start over, fresh, where no one knew my name and past history. I researched the area, knew a position in my field was available and no waiting list at the country club so here I am."

"And your sons? Where are they?" Beth spooned the last vegetables from the bowl.

Finished and full. She wanted the recipe and knew Carole wouldn't part with it.

A wistful smile softened Lisa's face. "They're freshmen in college. Summer session. Up in Boston. They'll come to me for Thanksgiving. Maybe a weekend visit before."

Somehow the restaurant had emptied out and the sound was muted. Beth said,

"Better keep our voices down. You never know who's listening. Small town gossips."

The waitress asked if they wanted dessert. Lisa said, "No, just the check please."

The bill was split; they shrugged into jackets and walked out together. Outside, they continued the conversation as if they were old friends catching up. Beth—slender and fit, medium height and Lisa—tall and heavyset. They caught sight of their reflection in the glass and once again laughed.

"Like the old cartoon Mutt and Jeff?" Beth said.

"Not for long," Lisa said. "Can't change my height but with a little help, I sure can change my habits." A solemn nod from Beth.

Beth gestured to a stand of willow trees next to the pond in the village square. "See the tallest willow? That was our donation to the beautification program. I planted it about twenty five years ago. Brings back memories."

Lisa's voice dropped to a whisper and Beth leaned close. "I was like a willow a long time ago."

"You were?"

"Now I'm like a Sequoia, still tall but thick." Silence as the wind picked up and a light drizzle began.

Beth said, "That's how you see yourself, a tall thick tree?"

"Uh huh."

Horns beeped at the stop light, people jostled by unfurling umbrellas as they hurried along.

Beth frowned, wondered if she should talk to Lisa about her business idea. She said, "Before you go, I have two things to say. In response to the Sequoia image, get over yourself and do something about. You may not realize this but you started already, in the restaurant. By the way, this insight comes directly from my therapist."

"I did?"

"Yes. When the waitress asked if we wanted dessert, you said no, bring the check."

By now the rain fell steadily and they didn't have umbrellas. Lisa's face, dripping with rain, glowed with pleasure. "I already started."

"Number two is a question."

"Shoot."

"You mentioned investment banking was a major interest years ago." Lisa nodded. "Are you in that field now or any related work because I'm seriously thinking of starting a small business and need someone to bounce off. Since Frank left no one wants to talk to me. Everyone in our social circle dropped me as if I were contagious. We've been friends with this crowd for many years and suddenly. . .another loss. You saw an example of it at the club." A helpless shrug. "Oh shit."

Their eyes met, standing outside in the misty rain, as people hurried by and Lisa said, "I want to talk to you. Bounce off me."

"Oh? Do you have time now? You can follow me home. I have dry clothes you can. ." and they both grinned with the thought of Lisa's large frame fitting in Beth's skinny clothes.

"Oh, just follow my car."

"All right. I'll call my office and advise them."

Chapter 11

Lisa's silver Lexus followed Beth's car through the winding streets north of the center of town and finally around the circular driveway. A mad dash in the pouring rain and they were in the impressive entrance of what Frank called 'the Malone palace.'

Beth hung jackets to drip dry, showed Lisa the way to the powder room where there were towels to dry off. She lit a fire in the stone fireplace and ran upstairs to change into dry clothes. Grabbing a one size fits all robe for Lisa, she knocked on the bathroom door and handed it in. Beth put a kettle on for tea.

She found Lisa curled up near the fire, dressed in the robe, hair wrapped in a towel.

"Calling your beautiful bathroom a powder room is a misnomer. Very elegant."

You're too much, Beth. Meeting you today is the first good thing that's happened to me since. ."

"Me too, kid."

"Beth, this is the way I work and you better have a tough hide. Always remember, it's not personal, we're talking business. First you explain what your needs are and I'll play Devil's Advocate. Expect me to be merciless, okay?"

Lisa hung her skirt and blouse near the fire burning well enough to spread heat.

Beth ran upstairs, came back with a notebook and settled on a couch opposite Lisa. She consulted notes, found the page and got right to business. "I've thought about my options and requirements.

1.   A service of some kind-I want my work to benefit others.

2.   I love to cook and decorate.

3.   Most of all—at age 58 soon to be 59—I want more meaning to my life."

She glanced up at Lisa for a reaction and to see if she was paying attention or just being polite. What she saw was a different persona from the 'club' Lisa and the 'lunch' Lisa. Head erect, eyes bright with the reflection of dancing flames, she sat forward, chin on folded hands. Again they connected with a 'go on' sign from her new friend.

"A couple of years ago, a used-to-be-friend went to a recycling-single-men party. Her husband died and she thought it might be a way to meet someone new. Every guest was sanctioned by another. For example: You dated Jim, a nice guy not right for you but you want to recycle him to a friend. The chemistry might click. Everyone knows someone they can recommend. Since then, I've never heard of another singles party that sounded so safe." *Cut to the chase.*

"So here's what I've been thinking about for a business for me. Bringing mature unattached people together in an attractive setting—my castle—delicious food, catered by guess-who-me, all for a fee. Sounds so right." She inhaled deeply and exhaled. "The discussion is open."

A barrage followed. "Strangers in your home? Are you crazy? Strangers, unknowns are a potential danger so, throw a notepad to me." She reached for the notepad and wrote: small groups-from a cursory glance--your home can accommodate twenty guests comfortably. Small wait staff-possibly hired through a security company. She looked up. "Each guest must be approved as in investigated so start small with references from say. . ." she thought for a moment, "our club."

Amazed by the concise assessment without mincing words, Beth said, "You're the perfect Devil's Advocate, Lisa. I'm so naïve. How can I be so trusting and just plain dumb?" She searched the ceiling for an answer. "Mindset is stuck in another era. Thanks for the wake-up."

"Beth, you must've led a sheltered life for a long time. Don't beat yourself up."

Then Lisa grew quiet, lost in thought for a few minutes. Beth waited and wondered what was going through her mind.

Lisa leaned forward again. "We barely know each other and personally, I'd like to see a lasting friendship develop. So please don't take offense at anything I say, okay?" Beth nodded.

"Your business idea is interesting and different. In order for it to be successful, you must carefully plan every step. That means taking your time. I believe you're pushing yourself in your haste to prove something. I'm willing to give you all my expertise every step of the way but don't hurt yourself by rushing, careening through to get it all done.

When did you have in mind for the first party?"

Beth almost choked. "First party? Uh, maybe September or maybe after Thanksgiving when people make plans to travel or celebrate holidays and maybe so and so will meet at my party and have someone to be with." She inhaled, exhaled and felt better.

"What do you do in your daily life? This is fact finding, not an interrogation, Beth."

"Oh sure. Well, I swim and dive every day and hope to get back to my tennis form although I don't have partners anymore. And I'm about to begin as a volunteer at St. Paul's soup kitchen once a week. Exercise, gardening; not a whole lot of activity."

More relaxed now, Lisa said, "You're doing well for a woman who had the rug pulled out from under her a short time ago. Very well.

"Once upon a time I was a winner. I'm trying to find my way back to the feeling."

"A winner, huh? Sounds like something I want to hear. About the tennis, I've watched you the past year and think you're one of the smartest players at the club. How about the two of us teaming up? I was Number one tennis doubles State champion before I moved here."

Astonished, Beth said, "Who me?"

"No one here but us chickens, girl. Think about it. Now let's get back to business."

She was on a roll. "Your home and cooking—perfect combination. I can help with sources for advertising and getting the word out. At this point, drawing from the affluent Westchester towns, a night of possibilities might be worth $100 or more."

"Stop." Beth grabbed the note pad, gaining confidence as she drew. "That's it. The perfect name—A Night of Possibilities—recycling unattached gentlemen and gentle women. Beaming, she held up a rough sketch of the new logo. "Needs work, first draft."

Lisa said, "I need a brownie."

"Like a hole in the head."

Quiet for a minute, Lisa said, "Here's another thought for free marketing."

Beth's eyes lit up.

"You and I go to the club."

"The club? They've been so cold and. . .mean.

"Not all of them right?"

"Uh, no, but. . ."

"Listen to me. You've been a club member for how many years?"

"Twenty five."

"The club is a perfect source so use the bitches."

Beth couldn't suppress a laugh.

"Make it a charitable thing you're planning to do, a philanthropic venture. It's not as if you need the money or do you?" Beth smiled, giving her a thumbs up about the money. "Good. Make this a necessary service with all profit going to ..."

"Got it."

"So we have a salad. Yes, a salad with a squeeze of lemon for dressing. Spread out papers, flyers, whatever. I finish and leave. I'm positive those nosy club members will be dying to find out what we're working on. Have a sign-up sheet ready.

Let them come to you. Be enthusiastic and friendly. You'll come away with leads.

Oh—one more thing before we have some tea and a fat free goodie like lemon meringue pie. Consider CCTV—closed circuit television to monitor guests. It's an investment but an important one. Also it may very well be tax deductible."

As Lisa spoke, she rose to a towering six feet tall, removed the robe, felt her clothes and slipped into the skirt and blouse. Beth had an impulse to say, "Stay, please stay." She restrained herself. "What an afternoon. Thanks for simply everything... A cup of tea, no pie before you leave. Are you really free for a quick lunch tomorrow? And is it too soon to gather names and spread the word?"

"I don't think so. Tell them it's in the planning stages."

Lisa unwrapped the head towel and a wild mane of dark hair fell to her shoulders.

"Scary, isn't it?" She grinned at Beth. "For you, I'm free. Otherwise I charge. I'm #1 consultant on investments at the National Bank of Westchester. I made a lateral move from a major bank in Chicago. Let's drink a toast to A Night of Possibilities."

At the club the next day after Lisa finished lunch and business ideas were tossed around, she squeezed Beth's shoulder and left. Beth continued to flesh out ideas and pick at the salad. Soon, as Lisa predicted, acquaintances sauntered past, peered over her shoulder and asked questions. With enthusiasm and authority Beth didn't know she had, she explained the concept of the parties, making it sound more philanthropic than a business.

Free advertising—word of mouth. If it's successful, I'll donate the proceeds to a charity.

Everyone knew a divorced, separated or widow/widower; someone seeking companionship.

She spread out a sign-up sheet for contact names, phone numbers and addresses. In a short time, thirty five approved prospects were listed. Maybe a mailing of flyers with an introductory letter instead of advertising in publications at first. Also post a flyer at the club and other posh establishments in nearby town. Beth Malone was in business.

Beth dialed Lisa. "Hey Ms. How are you?"

"Beth, good to hear from you. I wondered what happened after I left you at the club. Wait a sec. Just poured a glass of Chardonnay to have with some dee-licous fat free cheese and crackers to match. Need something to munch on while we chat."

"You sound thinner already."

"Uh huh. Only forty pounds to go."

"Are you sitting down because it turned out exactly as you predicted. The women came by to see what we were up to. I was enthusiastic and they gave me the names of every unattached person from here to the Mississippi. I have enough for at least the first party if everyone reserves." A whoop of laughter from Lisa.

"Ya done good, partner. I bet you finished the poster and typed the letter."

Beth heard a crunch of crackers on the line. "That's what I wanted to ask you about. First, are you available, say Saturday early evening? If so we could go over my work because I need your final approval. And then maybe dinner and a movie or something?"

"Am I available? You bet your ass I am. I haven't had a date since I moved here. Of course when you look like a Sequoia and don't want to go out with a giant Redwood. . .I'm flattered you want my final approval, Beth. I'd love to take a look and be merciless. Also there are more aspects to consider so let's do it. Everything. And thanks for having faith in me."

Booting up the computer, Beth selected fonts, drawing tools and began to sketch, happy she'd become proficient with the drawing program. An Evening of Possibilities, she wrote discarding night as too seductive. An upscale motif without being trite. Second draft, Beth did an impressionistic background of soft colors and tried bold script on an angle across the top. *So far so good.*

Now the text: I offer, she deleted I and typed in the royal we.

We offer a comfortable setting in a private home, where sanctioned unattached gentlemen and gentle women may enjoy delightful cuisine and stimulating conversation. Why remain alone when The Singles Salon beckons. We are not a bar nor a noisy singles' dance. We are an intimate gathering of soon-to-be friends in Westchester County.

Phone 915.358.3939 for reservations

The next Salon is

She reread, proofed, and selected another font until she was satisfied.

Make it work. Maybe no one will call. Oh fuffa. It will work.

Tired of sitting, she rose, stretched about to turn off the computer and stopped. *Copies, one for herself, save one in a file, email one to Lisa.* The copy in color was rewarding.

She printed and pinned one to the cork board.

On impulse, she ran to the exercise room, turned on Fleetwood Mac's "Don't stop thinkin' about tomorrow, yesterday's gone" and danced until laughing she fell to a mat in the corner.

Towel wrapped around her neck, she gulped down a bottle of water and swaggered back to the office. *Beth Malone, entrepreneur.* On second thought, the boss needed a bite to eat and a good night's sleep. With reluctance, she closed up shop.

The next morning, she placed a call to Lisa to confirm their date for Saturday.

"Lisa Marcus, please." Beth waited on hold as elevator music butchered Cole Porter's 'Dancing in the Dark.'.

"Lisa Marcus here," answered the voice of her new best and only friend.

"Hi Lisa, it's Beth calling about plans for tomorrow. I hope we're still on."

"Does a bear poop in the woods? You bet we are. I was hoping you'd call. It's been a hectic week and I feel like just hanging out at my place with you, having a bite to eat and schmoozing. Does that sound about right or were you counting on something fancier?"

"I never saw a bear poop in the woods but I'm sure when they poop, the woods is their bathroom."

"It's a Midwest expression." They both chuckled.

"Your idea of a laid back Saturday night sounds perfect. My week has been filled to overflowing. Much to discuss. Where do you live and what time?"

"You know the new condos—they call it Eastern Horizons for Discerning Adults—north of town about twenty minutes from you? Until I bought this place I didn't know I was."

"Was what, discerning?"

"No. An adult. Anyway, I'm in the newest section, corner condo #101. I'll leave word at the gate. He'll mark a map. Bring a flashlight. How about six o'clock?"

Beth said, "I haven't been up that way but I'll find it. Can't wait. Bye."

A few months ago I couldn't find my ass with both hands. Just now I said I'd find my way to a place I've never heard of before. Instead of moping alone—I'll be with a real pal.

New beginnings and full steam ahead. Two words for you Frank, and they ain't Happy Birthday.

Chapter 12

Saturday evening at six, Beth set out to find Lisa at Eastern Horizons. And find it she did with the help of Map quest plus the new Global Positioning System recently installed in the Mercedes. Now she was both pilot and navigator negotiating the rocky course through life, responsible only for herself.

The gatekeeper mumbled something unintelligible when Beth announced her name, passed a map through the window and opened the gate. With what appeared to be a police baton used to crack skulls, he gestured right and left and closed the gate behind Beth. The GPS directed her to Lisa's doorstep.

Dressed in a long white cotton shirt knotted at the waist, jeans and sneaker, Beth carried a wrapped bowl as a contribution to the evening. No time to research a new recipe, she fell back on low fat—low calorie shrimp filled tomatoes. It was only when Lisa greeted her that Beth realized it might not be appropriate. "I made a shrimp appetizer and I don't think it's kosher."

With a straight face Lisa said, "It isn't and neither am I." She pulled Beth in and shut the door. "Welcome, friend."

Surprised to find Lisa living in ultra-modern surroundings, Beth wandered around the open spaces, floor to ceiling glass walls, over-sized couches, chrome legged tables, everything white, black and beige with peach accents.

Beth said, "I pictured you in a cozy cottage with hooked rugs and calico throws."

"Why?"

"I have no idea. Midwest image, little house on the prairie. I'm so sophisticated, you know." She hugged Lisa. "Just kidding."

"Beth, I'm from Chicago, a major city, very cosmopolitan."

Spreading her arms wide to indicate the whole panorama of the interior she could see, Beth said, "This is gorgeous, elegant. Makes my home look worn out." Lisa stood there, tall and proud. "And you're melting the weight off. Do I see cheekbones emerging already?"

"All I needed was tough love from someone who cared. You taught me to say no to myself."

Lots of laughs followed as they put a meal together and settled down for dinner. With a Chardonnay toast, Beth said, "As senior member of this friendship, I caution you not to say no to everything that appeals to your palate."

"I'll drink to that although I don't know what you're referring to." She drank sparkling Perrier with lemon. "This will have to do for now."

"Have you dated since moving here?"

"No. No one asked." Wistful, Lisa said, "There is a guy who banks with us." She pushed the last cherry tomato around the salad bowl before popping it in her mouth. "I'd like to jump his bones." Again Lisa surprised her, this time with a blunt declaration of lust.

"What's stopping you?"

"Not 'til I lose at least another ten pounds." She leaned across the table. "There's something personal I want to ask and if it's too personal, answer anyway."

Intrigued, Beth said, "Ask away."

Clearing her throat, Lisa said, "You're older than me and I've seen you up close on the tennis courts and in the locker room and I wonder how come you look so," she searched for a word, "youthful. Have you had plastic surgery?"

An explosion of laughter came from Beth. "Actually, my body stays in good shape from daily swimming but the wrinkles are in my face. There's a saying that when you have sex, never get on top and look down or you'll look really saggy. So the answer is no, I haven't had plastic surgery but husband Frank did. He had an eye lift thing and now that he's on the loose, he probably will tighten up everything that sags."

By now, the women were having a fit of giggles.

Mopping her eyes, Beth said, "Okay. Let's clear the table and curl up on the couch."

Settled in the low comfortable couch, Beth pulled a peach silk pillow close to her chest and wrapped both arms around it.

"What I really want to hear is more about your life, Lisa."

"My life." Crossing to the glass walls, Lisa activated a switch to shut the draperies. Ivory silk brocade pleats swayed in a graceful dance and settled in to seal off the outside world.

The dimmer switch softened lights and the atmosphere became up close and personal.

A few strides with endless legs and Lisa curled up on the opposite end of the couch from Beth. "You sure you want to hear the whole sad tale?"

"Absolutely."

She lowered her head, closed her velvety dark brown eyes like a child playing 'you can't see me' and in a soft monotone she began.

"So there I was pregnant in college and Kenneth wanted me to have an abortion. Right away—first thing he said. I cried, said we should get married, finish school and manage. Shit happens but I knew I was up for it and loved him so much and wanted his baby. I'm very close to my folks and his parents so I told them. He was hysterical. They insisted we marry, they'd all help financially, and it was going to be fine. The two sets of parents were understanding and supportive. Kenneth was a total schmuck. We married, had the twins, graduated, I juggled the boys, a career, and for the next seventeen years, he cheated on me, but the guy was a decent father. When the boys left for college, he'd been living with some lawyer from his firm for years but kept up a front as if he still lived at home and I let it happen. Anyway, we're divorced, I gained weight like a fool and finally cut my ties, sold the house, big profit and moved here to make a new start. Kids are in Boston. We alternate holidays. I won't see them until Thanksgiving although they might come in sooner. It's their choice and their father gets. . ." her voice cracked. End of the story.

Beth waited in silence while Lisa gathered her dignity. "It's a little soon to be thinking about Thanksgiving but it occurs to me, you and your sons would make the perfect addition to my table. I'll ask my pregnant daughter and new husband and I will definitely need the support of a good friend if they come since daughter Susie is difficult and I barely know Javier. So what do you say? Please come to my rescue."

Dark eyes peered over at Beth. "This isn't a mercy invitation, is it?"

"Oh honey, it'll be a mercy to me if you'll celebrate with us."

"Tell me about once upon a time you were winner. I'll throw in a few cookies."

Beth laughed. "I'll dust off my trophies and tell the whole sad tale next time, maybe."

She got to her feet and stretched. "Time to go home. By the way, what's with the gate guy?"

"He's a Marlon Brando wannabe pretending to be tough. Really he's a, what's the word?"

Together they said, "Numbskull." Enough cause for Beth to grin all the way home.

Chapter 13

July was a month of anticipation. Watching the enclosure take shape, business plans going full swing, still struggling with the see-sawing Mother/Daughter relationship. *Discuss this with Jenna next session.*

Early Sunday dinner started off pleasant enough. Susie's favorite ham topped with pineapple slices and brown sugar sauce, baked potatoes and salad served soon after the young couple arrived was received well. Not the meal Beth wanted to prepare but pleasing her daughter came first. They dined politely on the patio under an umbrella.

Beth said, "What do you do Javier, if you don't mind me asking."

"Not at all. I design automobiles."

Susie said, "He began as a mechanic growing up in Miami; studied engineering and design all paid for by The Borg Corporation. We met when Artie and I were on our honeymoon.

He's becoming well known in his field."

Javier flushed under his dark complexion but said nothing.

They met when she was on her honeymoon. After the beautiful church wedding. Oh my God. I failed my daughter by not teaching her proper values.

Then her daughter asked for a tour of the nearly finished enclosure and an explanation of why it was necessary and how much it cost and at some point, Javier touched his wife's arm, soothing her rising temper. Beth, flustered and upset that another opportunity might pass for mending fences, changed the subject. Javier proved to be an ally and a gentleman conversant in a wide variety of subjects. Aside from art and engineering, he had cooking expertise from working for a well known restaurateur in Miami.

A few digs were thrown at her mother before they left when once again Susie said, "When Dad returns, please let him come home. It's only fair, Mother. Look at all he left for you to live on."

Pasting a smile on her face and praying the headache waited a few minutes, Beth said, "Please understand this. Your father will never again enter this house. He walked away—left divorce papers at Bruce Bradley's for me to sign. I'm making a life for myself with the help of a therapist. If you want to come with me so you and I can sort ourselves out, maybe we can fix our relationship before the baby comes." A long deep breath and she looked at Javier and then her stunned daughter. "You have a good man here. Welcome to the family, Javier. I look forward to getting to know you."

This time it was Beth who said, "Goodbye."

Early the next morning as Beth prepared breakfast for one, she heard a knock on the sliders. Susie waved. Beth ran to open the sliders and there they were, face to face, mother and daughter. Susie, dressed for work, tears in her big blue eyes walked into Beth's arms and sobbed.

Susie looked up at her mother. "Sorry I was such a bitch yesterday. Can I blame it on hormones?"

Beth smiled and shook her head no. "Your husband said for you to clean up your act. You don't want your baby to treat you like that."

"Mom, you've been sleeping in my pink bedroom since daddy left."

Beth held her at arm's length. "Yes. I couldn't go back to the master bedroom. For now, I'm in your room where you were an infant, where I rocked you and fed you and where you grew up."

"When my baby is born, sometimes may I bring her to your house and let her sleep in that room? Please Mom?"

Mother and daughter gazed at each other until they grinned with the lifetime of knowing so much and yet so little. Beth said, "Sure. I'll buy the portable crib I was looking at the other day."

They walked around the house to Susie's car, arms linked. Susie said, "Were you really looking at baby furniture?"

A pat on the baby mound and a kiss on her daughter's cheek as Beth shut the car door. "Sure."

Breakfast never tasted so good to Beth as it did this morning.

Chapter 14

At last the enclosure was finished and Beth thrilled to the sight of the new structure, her concept. A unique pool enclosure, tall enough for an expert diver. It glowed in the mid-June night, beckoning like a lover. *Mmmm.* Beth ran to the enclosure, pressed a series of numbers, turned the handle, slid the door open and shut. Locked in.

A tropical paradise greeted her. The idea was to reproduce a picture from a travel brochure with foliage compatible with chlorinated water. A lot of research went into the project and she found the computer not to be as scary as some of the women thought it was. Warm moist air wrapped around her while she hung up the towel and sweatshirt on a rack, kicked off sandals, adjusted a swim cap and prepared to swim. She pressed a button on the side of the pool; the water went flat. Silence.

She lowered chin to chest, took deep breaths and climbed the ladder. How long Beth was in the water diving and doing laps, she didn't know. She never stopped until her body said 'no more'. Mind-set still in the rhythm of the water workout, she hoisted up out of the pool in one big splash. First thing off was the hated swim cap and she hurled it toward the area of the towel rack. Knocking at the door frightened her. Who the hell was out there? She grabbed a towel, wrapped it around her dripping self and yelled, "Who's there?"

"Just Maverick. Open up, please."

Annoyed to have her privacy disturbed, she double-checked through the door, making sure he was alone. Opening the door enough for him to enter, she locked it again and said, "What in the world are you doing here?"

He shuffled around in his boots looking ashamed for disturbing her and then picked a towel off the rack and patted water from Beth's arms. "Sorry. Didn't mean to frighten you. I uh, was passing by, saw the lights on in the pool house; wanted to tell you about, uh, to make sure you were okay." He dried Beth's arms, and looked into her eyes.

"What are you doing?"

They were close; so close she dripped on his cowboy boots. Beth noticed once again the age lines around his eyes, creases next to the nice mouth. No way was he a young kid. He was, what? maybe late thirties—early forties and she was definitely fifty eight. What was the question then? She'd heard this somewhere. Ladies locker room at the club. How many times does forty go into fifty eight? Oh, for God sake.

He kissed her. Stopped with the pats, pulled her wet self closer, and kissed the hell out of her. The climate controlled air upped a notch, bare toes left the puddled surface and steam came from Beth's lycra swim suit that suddenly felt a size too small.

"Whoa," Beth said.

He didn't whoa. Instead he nibbled his way down Beth's neck to her shoulder, slipped off the left strap and licked her skin. Beth shivered. A gentle pull meshed their bodies together as he continued with merciless kisses, a tongue Beth dreamed of when she was young and every night since. "That day. . .I intruded on your private time and watched a beautiful lady dive and swim, graceful with so much power. I've wanted you ever since."

Overcome with desire, knees weak, Beth said, "Maverick, I . . ."

And didn't get to finish because he said, "I want to make love to you right now, if that's okay."

She glanced all around the steamy area, wondered for a moment where to do it and nodded. "Okay."

Maverick carried Beth to the padded lounges on the side stopping long enough to lower the dimmer switch. Now the only lights came from the pool. Setting her down, he leaned over for one more delicious kiss.

Transfixed, Beth smiled and watched his muscles ripple while he kicked off boots, unsnapped a Western shirt and struggled with tight blue jeans. She tensed with the sight of the soon-to-be lover, *was this really happening?* stood up. Stood up, literally, in the smallest underwear she'd ever seen. Black and she couldn't tell anyone about it. No one. *Oh my.* He pulled a packet from his jeans. Condom. *Condom? How cute is this? Oh, my God. Beth Malone, you slut. It's about time.*

Slap, slap. The sound the two lounge chair cushions hitting terracotta tiles resounded in the humid air. "Looks comfortable. What do you think?" Maverick said.

She didn't have a thought in her head other than the vision of the man with the crooked grin, high cheekbones, protrusion in the scrap of fabric covering his nakedness. "Hey," is all she managed and laughed when he swooped her up and with the sweetest care, laid her down. "I smell from chlorine."

Burying his face in her hair, he sniffed like a puppy. "Mmmm. My favorite scent and I didn't know it." He sniffed some more.

"I could shower. There's nice soap and sham . . ."

"Later," he said, lifting her arms above her head and rolling until she was on top. "Surprise."

So hot but a corner of her mind flashed, *hide your face when you look down so it won't sag*, she shook her straight wet hair and it hung like a curtain across his cheeks. He closed his blue, blue eyes, big grin on his face.

"Lots of clothes on, Miz. Malone."

What a time to blush but there it came. *At least it's not a hot flash.* The right strap of the bathing suit came off in all the ruckus. "Call me Beth." *Clever repartee. Almost naked and that's the best line so far.*

Chapter 15

Coffee. The aroma of strong coffee wafted somewhere close mingling with chlorinated air. *Chlorinated air? Real coffee—not the decaffeinated crap I've pretended to like for years--and chlorinated air? Where the hell am I?*

Beth managed to force one eye open. Steam curled from the coffee mug on the floor right next to her. Naked, an over-sized beach towel tucked under her chin, she stretched out on the cushion Maverick threw on the floor before last night really got interesting.

"Would you mind if I took some pictures?" Maverick's deep voice echoed across the water.

In one swift motion, Beth covered her head with the towel. *Pictures of rumpled-Beth-skin? Not on your life or mine, lover.* "To remember me by? Can't I autograph something instead? A check for good work maybe?" She heard the whir of a camera. "I mean, the good work you accomplished building the beautiful enclosure."

Boot steps retreated. She peeked from under the towel. He was photographing the pool structure, plants and all. His question was rhetorical and she was talking to herself. She sipped coffee, wondered if he planned to join her, felt insecurities rise and beat them back. Decision reached when she glanced at the big clock on the wall. Seven a.m. Wrapped in the towel, Beth made a dash for the door.

"If you're hungry, I'm scrambling eggs. See you in the kitchen."

By the time Maverick sauntered in, Beth had scrambled more than eggs. The fastest transformation in her history left the energetic woman radiant, flushed with afterglow and full of creative ideas. What next for the future was on her mind and it did include the not-as-young-as-she-thought-he-was man who entered her more than once last night and was about to enter her home as if he belonged here.

He brushed a kiss across the back of her neck at the same time as she laid crisp bacon on two plates. *Laid. The thought, the action, the kiss. Oh fuffa*! Heat rose in her cheeks and spread all the way down to dark places. Who cared about breakfast with him so close? Strong hands reached around her, lifted, *oh shit*—the plates and carried them to the table. Apparently he cared about breakfast.

Beth, a smile pasted on, slid back a chair harder than she meant to, the scrape against the floor caused her to shudder. *Don't be a jerk. Have fun. Take charge.*

"Hey," he said, and took a large bite of toast. His eyes crinkled in the corners as he shoveled in eggs and bacon along with more toast. "You make a mean breakfast, Beth. What're the green sprinkles in the eggs?"

"Secret ingredient." Blue, those blue eyes again. She couldn't look at them without picturing him above her. *Don't be a fool, Beth. You got laid—it was amazing. Move on.* She nibbled on cooling eggs and bacon.

Mopping crumbs from his mouth, Maverick finished the last drink from the coffee mug." I decided, with your okay, of course, to make a photographic display of the enclosure. People have been asking me about my work; like what else I do beside build and maintain pools. When I mentioned the enclosure and described the design, there was interest in seeing pictures. Actually, last night I stopped by to tell you about this and. . ." He paused, the slow crooked smart-ass grin took on special meaning." One man wanted to see it but I said that wasn't possible and he doesn't know what town you're in, so. . ." He spread muscular arms wide and grinned. "What do you think? It would be a terrific boost for my business."

How could she say no? He said business. *Keep it business, Beth.* With a straight face, she said, "It was my baby from the beginning. I helped you design it, Maverick. What's in it for me?" *What's in it for me. Did I really say that?*

June winds kicked up blowing leaves torn from the trees against the glass sliders. Beth's attention focused on the design of the pool enclosure. When she first asked the pool guy if he built such a thing, it was like a seed way back in her mind. Almost an idle thought to make her feel better, to help heal what felt broken. They talked, drew diagrams, researched and the project grew. Sure, enclosures were available, packaged like huge erector sets. Too easy. The Malone pool, Beth's pool was special; a dream come true and it was saving her life.

Rain splattered leaves on the glass, then washed them away. One stubborn leaf clung to the center, slipped and slid with the hard rainfall. Beth crossed to the slider, pressed her hand to the glass and traced the leafs descent. The eight a.m. sky turned dark, sensor lights clicked on in the pool house. Ominous signs of a summer storm.

Blonde eyebrows lifted as her words registered and once again the slow grin lit his weathered face. "Partners? You design, I'll construct."

"Did you make love to me because you wanted the pictures?" No answer. "Don't lie, Maverick."

She felt his heat, arms around her waist, cheek pressed close. Their reflections blurred in the fogged glass.

He said, " Guilty as charged, Beth. Kind of. The business idea was cooking for a while and late yesterday, this really big bucks customer asked what I planned to do over the winter. He made me a great offer after I described your enclosure and I was so excited, I just wanted to share it with you. See what you thought so I drove by and there you were, in the pool and I've been crazy about you since the first day when you were busted up sad and. . ." He turned Beth around. "It's the truth."

She looked way up, assessed his attractive face. So earnest and she still liked the man holding her, no lie detector available. "What a night, Maverick." With a careless shrug,

Beth moved toward the digital camera lying on top of his bag. "You clear the table, I'll check out the pictures. See if there's anything worth enlarging."

Enlarging. One of those words again. Damn.

"Partners then?"

"No." She glanced over her shoulder. *No big deal, cowboy. It was just sex.* "You install enclosures, you're reliable and I'll recommend you. What we did together. . .what we created together was because of my pool's special size." *Oh dear God.* She attempted to turn her full attention to the camera and clicked away until the best ones remained. "Okay. These are, in my opinion, the best. Good job. When the pages are printed, stop by. I'd love to see them." She smiled, displayed all the pearly whites he'd licked the night before, and noted to her delight, Maverick was mystified by her behavior.

So was she. Beth Malone was coming-of-age.

Thinking he was rebuffed and gone, Beth sighed and turned to lock the sliders before heading somewhere in the vast empty house to start over. Startled, she saw Maverick , nose pressed against the rain drops on the glass, like a kid at a bakery shop window—forbidden cookies—out-of-reach. Like the grown-up she almost was, Beth did what any red blooded woman would do. She invited the starving man in.

Beth said, "Don't think every time you show up . . ."

Wet and chilled, Maverick dropped his knapsack in a corner, yanked off damp boots and lifted Beth high in his arms. "Where to?" He headed toward the stairs. "How 'bout the exercise room, with the mirrors, hmm?"

She was about to suggest the same.

Chapter 16

Despite her disastrous end of a marriage, Beth was fortunate to have the financial means to sustain herself and decided to give back to the community in some way. An article in the local news covered the prominent St. Paul's Church located in a town not far north of where she lived. They had a highly regarded soup kitchen and always needed volunteers. The idea of feeding the hungry appealed to her. The following Thursday night, Beth planned to show up.

Big sign--**St. Paul's Welcomes You**. *This must be the place.* A sharp right turn; Beth pulled in, dodged a bunch of shabby folks hurrying toward well-lit doors. *Seems too early for soup kitchen recipients to line-up but what do I know. Never too early when you're hungry.*

Parking the Mercedes at the far end of the church lot, Beth took a moment to check her appearance. She fished for the big amber compact in her purse, fumbled for the clasp, brushed powder off the glass and caught her reflection in the poor light. Not pretty. The severe hairdo didn't help. She snapped the compact shut. Heard the click. *Does anyone still have a compact?*

Get rid of it and put a smile on your face. Purse tucked out of sight, Beth opened and locked the car door.

Rain slammed down with sudden force. She skidded, almost fell; a strong arm steadied her. He pulled the hood of her slicker over her head, mumbled, "Careful," waved, tie flying as he raced past and disappeared in the distance.

"Thanks," Beth said and carefully walked toward the church.

Inside was a welcome atmosphere just like the sign advertised. Drenched from the storm, she searched the faces of people gathered; children clinging to parents, grandparents, some alone.

She forgot about Beth Malone's life, how she looked. There was a job to do. A purpose. Beth approached the petite woman dressed in black, clipboard in hand, in control.

"Hi, I'm Beth . . ."

"First names only here," said the woman in a voice rich with an Irish brogue. " 'tis more friendly. Sister Mary Margaret."

When the little nun spoke, Beth pictured an Irish pub serving corned beef and cabbage, shamrocks adorning the bar, pints and quarts lined up.

She glanced up from the note pad, blue eyes swept over Beth and she grinned, her face a marvel of wrinkles. "To the cloakroom with you, Beth. Dry off quickly. You'll be . . ."a gnarled finger traced the list, "ladlin' potato soup. It's a favorite."

Beth said, "But I. . ."

"A virgin, eh?

Bewildered, Beth wondered if that was a qualification for ladling soup. "No. Uh, sorry.

Married forty years."

The nun patted Beth on the shoulder. "Just a figure of speech, m' dear. There's a first time for everyone who comes here. One of the volunteers will show you what to do. There are four of you tonight and, as you can see, a lot of hungry folks. Now off you get." She pointed the way toward a corridor and Beth marched on.

Never met a nun like her. Beth shouldered through the restless crowd, found the cloakroom, hoped for a bathroom.

At the mirror, the cutest spitfire of a woman with white curly hair waggled a mascara wand toward the back. Her high pitched voice rang out.

"You're almost late. Locker rooms next to the john."

She continued to apply mascara to stubby lashes. "Gotta get me some phony lashes one day." Finishing, she looked up to find Beth at her side. "Don't just stand there gawking, girl. Move it. Hungry mouths to feed. Names Lucy. What's yours?"

"Beth."

Lucy's voice followed her. "Grab an apron from the counter. You got three minutes."

Wet slicker hung on a hook in what Beth hoped was a secure locker. *Next time, if there is a next time, bring a lock.* She hurried, tying the green and white apron with the church logo embroidered in gold thread across the front. Property of St. Paul's.

Lucy, face made up as if she were going on a date, *a bit heavy-handed with the mascara*, grumped approval.

The next two hours blurred; a sea of grateful humanity shuffled along, trays in hand.

Beth mentally cursed the high-heeled shoes she wore while muscles reserved for swimming ladled steaming potato soup into endless bowls. And she was hungry, famished. *Hope the food doesn't run out.*

Every so often, Beth glanced at the other volunteers. To her left, Lucy doled out dessert; cupcakes and puddings—one to a customer, no exception. A wooden spoon held in one veined fist looked as if she wouldn't hesitate to rap a greedy person over the knuckles.

At the station to Beth's right, stood a young girl, dark wavy hair in a pony tail, apron bulging in front. *Oh my, very plump or very pregnant?* Popular with the crowd, she sliced beef like a pro, spooned gravy and heaped veggies with a flourish. Every so often, she'd press one hand in the small of her back and grimace.

The man at the end, the fourth volunteer, piqued Beth's curiosity. *Must be the man who saved me from falling in the parking lot; covered my head with my hood. Gallant gesture.*

85

In charge of bread, rolls, and crackers, and some sort of greeter. He speaks to each person, makes notes in what appears to be an electronic notebook after they walk away. All accomplished without anyone noticing except for me, the detective. A warm smile crinkled the corners of his mouth and eyes. *A grown-up man in his fifties, at least. How come wrinkles and gray hair are distinguished on a man and on a woman, she just looks old? This line-up is all wrong: bread comes first, soup next, meat and vegetables are third and then dessert. Beth the organizer. You couldn't keep your husband but this soup kitchen, you can put in proper order.*

"Soup, please." A child's voice interrupted Beth's reverie. Embarrassed to be caught off guard, she looked up, way up. Perched on tall skinny shoulders, sat a serious little boy about three. "Me and Daddy like two soups. Please." He held up two semi-clean fingers. The father nodded with pride.

Beth smiled at the close pair and placed the order on their tray. "Careful. It's hot. You have nice manners."

"Daddy teached me." The father moved along carrying his precious cargo.

The last few stragglers came through the line and it was over. Quiet before sighs of relief were heard. Beth sunk into the closest chair, unzipped and kicked off the foolish shoes.

Applause echoed through the large room with high ceilings. Sister Mary Margaret entered, clapping small hands together. "Great job, everyone." She sailed up to each volunteer, hand extended.

"Lucy, you are a wonder, you are. We need more like you." To Beth, she said, "Beth, new volunteer, your feet may not forgive you but you did yourself proud." She grasped Beth's hands, added an extra squeeze and like an expert politician, said, "May we count on you next week?"

Caught off guard, Beth stammered an affirmative. "Uh, sure. Yes, okay." *Smooth and do I really want to make such a commitment?"*

Moving along, Sister hugged the young girl who winced in apparent pain. "Are you all right, m' dear? Being on your feet right now seems a bit of a burden."

"But I love working here, Sister." Blotting tears with a leftover napkin, she repeated, "I love it here."

"We'll find another job for you, Karen. In the office. After the baby comes, you can hire on as the cook. We'll take good care of you. I tasted and tasted the pot roast tonight." Karen brightened with the news.

Beth felt as if she were watching an old movie—"The Bells of St. Mary's." Something with Barry Fitzgerald as the funny priest and Bing Crosby warbling a tune.

"Chow down, folks. You've earned it." And the little nun moved on to the man at the end. His apron lay across a chair and he looked like a quick get-away was his preference but her firm grip stopped him.

Beth squeezed aching feet into her shoes, filled a bowl with soup and walked to the communal table nearby. "Mmmm." Potato soup, the best she'd ever eaten, bar none. Some kind of drama was taking place not ten feet away between the man and Sister Mary Margaret, hands planted on both hips, but she was too tired to care.

"Good job, Beth."

A poke from Lucy who sat nearby got her attention. "Thanks, Lucy. It was a challenge."

"Karen cooked everything. She's amazing. Went to culinary school, got knocked up—decided to keep the baby—don't know about the father." Lucy munched on a chocolate donut.

"Did I get it right, Karen?"

"Close enough, "said Karen from an old chair, feet propped on an ottoman. "Billy's still my boyfriend, my fiancé¢ and we'll be married as soon as he graduates."

To Beth, Karen's words sounded like wishful thinking. She hoped Karen's dreams would come true. Daughter Susie's declarations of love for Artie a few years ago ended in disaster and here she was with Javier—a baby on the way. *I'm in church. Take a moment and pray for a happy outcome.*

Mopping the last bit of gravy from her plate after eating the beef, Beth said, "Karen, the pot roast is delicious. I'm a good cook but this tops my recipe."

She waved away the compliment as if were no big deal. "I know it's delicious." Karen struggled to a stand from the over-stuffed chair she had collapsed into. "I've won prizes with my secret recipes." She smiled at Beth. "Thanks." Groaning, she placed a hand at the small of her back. "Back's hurting worse than usual today. Any idea what that means?"

"What month are you in?"

"Five months." She leaned in close to Beth and whispered, "I have a lot of pressure."

Beth whispered back, "Any spotting?"

The young woman wilted. "No, but a lot of a. . .mess, like discharge." She grabbed Beth's hand. "Sorry to talk like this to a stranger. I don't want anyone here to know there might be trouble. I could lose my job."

She seems big for five months and what she's describing could be serious. "When is the next doctor appointment?"

"Whenever. I go to a free clinic." Slowly, Karen walked toward the cloakroom.

Too painful for Beth to watch, she ran to the girl, touched her lightly on the arm and said, "I don't want to frighten you but I've had experience with difficult pregnancies and you must be seen right away. Tonight. Promise me you'll go right now."

Karen held her gaze and finally nodded. "Billy will take me."

Back at the mirror in the cloakroom, Lucy touched up her lipstick.

Beth said, "You look nice after working so long. Are you going to a party?"

"Uh huh." A final pat to the white fluff of hair. "My new fella's picking me up."

Beth shook remaining rain drops from her slicker.. "What's the name of the other volunteer?"

Lucy packed her make-up kit and walked along with Beth. "Larry. Larry Cooper." Her blue eyes twinkled with mischief. "Divorced, I think, if you're single and interested. And here's a plus. . ."

Beth smiled a question. "He's a real catch. . .a Doctor."

Oh Lord. Beth, stay clear of this man.

Sister Mary Margaret was nowhere to be found so Beth left a note on her desk regarding Karen's condition and telling of Karen's fear about losing her job. Conscience cleared, it was time to go home.

Exiting the church, Beth paused, wished her car wasn't parked so far away, when a hoarse voice called her name. It was dark, still raining with gusty winds, the lot desolate. *What the hell.* Hands fumbled for pepper spray buried somewhere deep in her bag.

A shabby man moved out of the shadows in her direction. She'd read about attacks. They happened suddenly. A weapon—find a weapon—keys, pepper spray. Heart pounding, mouth open—ready to scream. *Where was the damn pepper spray?*

"Don't be scared, Miss. Doc Coop had to go. He said to make sure you got to your car safe."

Doc Coop "Oh, Oh, Oh." Beth said and forced herself to calm down. "Very kind. It does look nasty." *Why didn't he warn me? I'll wake up tomorrow with a wide white streak in my hair.*

He grunted and grabbed a fistful of her sleeve. "Spread sand all over. Don't want Sister M & M to fall.

Cute. He calls Sister Mary Margaret M & M.

Half skidding--half walking, he propelled Beth to the Mercedes. When she tried to offer money for his service, he shook his great mane of shaggy hair. Rain drops flew in every direction. "Doc Coop takes care of Harold," he said and lumbered back to the shadows.

A soggy business card was tucked behind a windshield wiper. Wet fingers pulled it free and as the windshield wipers swiped back and forth Beth tried to read the ink-blurred words but couldn't.

On the other side, in raised gold letters: Lawrence Cooper, MD

Practice Limited to Psychiatry

5 Parkland Avenue

New York, NY 11130

212.815.2100

email lcoop@brainfood.net

website www.LawrenceCooper.com

Oh no. A shrink. Now what? Get home safe is what. Slow cautious driving helped Beth feel peaceful all the way home.

Exhausted, she left a trail of wet gloves and sodden boots on the way to the stairs. Even the slicker slid off and landed on the tile floor. *To swim or not to swim is the question. Early enough—only 8:30 at night. Coach's voice shouted from the past, "One more lap."*

Abused feet crept up the stairs; the railing became a rope tow as hand over hand, Beth pulled herself along. *Hot shower and sleep sounds right—exercise tomorrow.*

Those were the last conscious thoughts before she sat on the bed, fell back and fully dressed, sank into a deep slumber.

Chapter 17

No pressure. I can do it. I can do anything I set my sights on. Coach yelling through the megaphone, "One more lap, Beth O'Brien." That was pressure.

Things-to-do chart came out of the computer desk. In bold letters, she wrote priority list at the top.

#1 call Susie. See how she is.

#2 New business. Make it work. Prepare menu TODAY! And call Lisa.

#3 call Larry Cooper. At least say thanks before possibly bumping into him Thursday at St. Paul. No. No call. *I'd give him an earful about Harold and the scare of my life. Men! Why the hell didn't he warn me?* Maybe an email and Google him. See what he's all about.

Pressure. A simple phone call to someone you gave birth to. Not so simple. Will she be up or down? Do I need a script or do an improvisation, wing it. Oh fuffa.

Beth dialed. *One, two, three. . .Good, she's not home. But the last time we were together turned out wonderful.*

Susie said, "Hello, Mother."

"Hi Sue, how are you and we didn't get to talk but when is your due date?"

"December 6th"

Sometimes like talking to a stranger. Must be hormones

Long silence.

"Honey, I don't want his leaving me to be another barrier between us, please. You're all the family I have now. . .and

Javier, of course, and when the baby comes, well. . .Oh honey, I bought the cutest portable crib."

"Mom, today I have morning sickness so bad, I can barely lift my head. Javier's coming home soon. He'll work from home. I'm hanging up. Will call when I stop heaving."

She's not feeling well. If we were closer on a regular basis, I'd be taking care. Meanwhile, she has a husband who responds to her needs and this is a fine thing. Frank looked the other way when I had morning sickness.

A search for Doctor Cooper's business card found it to be crumpled from the rain. Smoothing it, she used a magnifying glass to get the email address correct. Tacky not to call him. *Chicken.*

Larry, Thanks for the escort. Wish you had forewarned me. The big guy scared me, coming out of the shadows like that. Beth Malone

She checked the gallant doctor's web site and was bowled over. His credits and training were amazing. He not only had a prestigious practice but taught at Columbia University. She scrolled down. . .he wrote books. His latest, "Getting a Grip" was on the best seller list for ten weeks. She read further. . .something, something about his sense of humor. She never could figure out what reviewers were talking about.

Oh my. I forgive him for being a doctor and where did he find time for St. Paul's soup kitchen?

An email popped up. Dr. Cooper himself. *This is fun.* She felt a little hum of excitement in her belly.

Beth, So sorry friend Harold frightened you. Shame on me for being short-sighted. Not thinking clearly these days. He's a good soul. Hope to see you Thursday next. Best regards, Larry

A pen pal. Wonder why he's not thinking clearly? Maybe he needs a shrink.

On impulse, she wrote back:

Larry, how come you're not thinking clearly? Maybe the shrink needs to be shrink- wrapped. Nosy, Beth

She hit send and sat back. *Did I really write that?*

A sudden thought to have an extra phone line installed for the business; Beth dialed the phone company. They'd have a serviceman out by the end of the week.

Before she shut down the computer another new message popped up. . . from the shrink.

Cute Beth, very cute. Do you always think clearly? Larry

Typical of shrink talk, Larry. Answering a question with another question. B

So you've also been shrunk. L

I plead the 5th. Now I must get back to work.

On what? What do you do? Larry

To be continued. B

Beth hit send, felt heat in her cheeks and smiled. *Hot damn. Cyber flirting.* Shutting down the computer and closing up shop for a while, Beth smiled.

Good work. I'd like to pat myself on the back. Still a lot more to do to bring the business to life. Lisa said not to rush. I like to get my ducks in a row no matter how early. Compromise. I do feel more relaxed.

A thunderstorm began as Beth, dressed in sweats over a bathing suit, grabbed an umbrella against the sudden change in weather, and followed the path to the pool house. Unlocking the door, she entered quickly and punched the alarm code and reset. As always the tropical setting was a feast for all of her senses. Clogs and sweats peeled off and eyes closed, she inhaled the steamy chlorinated air.

Automatically stretching—scenes from school years appeared, other young strong swimmers in a row—Coach barking orders—wonderful times. *Why did I allow myself to sacrifice special talents to become the happy homemaker? Or in later years, the unhappy homemaker.*

Climbing the steps to the diving board, she sang, "Don't stop thinkin' about tomorrow."

On top, a pause for a deep breath and composure, she sang, "yesterday's gone." A quick run to the edge, the leap and before Beth knifed through the water, she was sure her voice bounced off the walls and echoed back. "Yesterday's gone, yesterday's gone."

Chapter 18

Thursday rolled around so fast, Beth 's head was in a whirl.

Soup kitchen later; how was Karen; business plans moving along—

Beth answered the persistent ring of the telephone. Before she had a chance to say hello, the unmistakable lilt of Sister Mary Margaret demanded attention.

"Beth, our Karen is on bed rest, thanks to your shrewd observation. She told me you are a fine cook and Beth, St. Paul's hungry need you tonight. We have all the provisions for beef stew. Everything is cut up and awaits your attention."

"My attention?"

"Yes, your attention. We need a cook and you're elected tonight. Be here at three p.m. Oh and bless you, dear girl, for offering your service."

She hung up on me. Trying to say no to Sister M&M was like trying to stay dry in a Nor'easter where the rain fell horizontally. What have I gotten myself into?

Like the good Catholic girl she once was, she accepted her fate and prepared to dress comfortably. A white cotton shirt and blue jeans, tennis socks and sneakers and she was set; back to the semblance of building a new life. Knives, seasonings, lucky chef jacket and cap worn preparing successful dinner parties in the past gathered, wrapped and placed in a carry bag, Beth flew out the door.

Impressed with the well-equipped kitchen, Beth made herself at home; spread out her tools, adjusted the cap at a rakish angle and buttoned the jacket. She caught her reflection in the gleaming glass of the dish cabinet and saluted. "Beth Malone reporting for K.P."

The unexpected brogue of Sister Mary Margaret's voice boomed from loudspeakers nearly causing an accident in the kitchen. Beth was in the process of juggling a large heavy colander filled with carrots, onions, and potatoes in order to save time when she heard the voice.

Nothing hit the floor except Beth. She landed hard with a lap full of vegetables as the little nun, in her most endearing Irish sweetness said, "Bless you for coming to the rescue. Help is on the way. You're the kitchen boss today."

Thanks a bunch.

"Recipe is on the counter—meat in the fridge-- you are on the floor with a lap full of veggies, nicely cut up."

Beth said, "Are you omnipotent or is there closed circuit TV?"

Laughter. "A bit of both. Yes, there is CCTV. I like to see into every corner of St. Paul.

Nosy, I guess. If you want me, call out. Speakers are voice activated. Over and out." The nun's laughter echoed through the speakers before shutting down.

Collecting herself and the veggies, Beth realized Lisa was on target about CCTV and made a mental note to investigate dealers for home installation. *Get cooking. No time to waste.*

Lucy showed up to help with preparations and to Beth's surprise, a cleaned up Harold arrived, hair tied back, frayed white shirt tucked in and he knew how to assist. Within an hour, the aroma of beef stew wafted through the church; pots simmered on the range with an occasional stir and everyone high-fived to know the hungry would be well taken care of.

Tonight, dessert was donated from a fancy bakery since Chef Karen was off her feet.

Another mental note for Beth. *Look for simple tasty dessert recipes in case this emergency continued. Operative word is simple because I have my own business to plan and dinners and my own life to live and I won't be here to make a whatever you want week after week so stick that in your uh.. . .CCTV, Sister M&M.*

Lucy bowed out to repair make-up; Harold waved and said, "Harold set-up tables now."

She thanked them both, wondered who the other volunteers were tonight, hoped Larry Cooper was there so she could tell him in person how she almost blinded Harold and called the cops.

"Oh fuffa! Where's the wine?"

Sister's voice whispered over the speaker, "In the fridge, behind the molasses, bottom shelf. Don't tell a soul. And what's fuffa?"

Red-faced, Beth became a tower of jello just like when she was a girl in Catholic school about to be reprimanded. She crossed her fingers hidden in the chef jacket and said, " It's a catch-all word, Sister. Nothing worth repeating."

Sure enough, there was an unopened bottle of fine Chardonnay.

Sister's voice said, "Corkscrew's at the back of the utensil drawer. Come to my office. Bring two glasses, cheese and crackers for a bit of a repast before the soup kitchen opens. Use discretion, Ms."

As she packed up knives and other personal items brought from home, Beth had to laugh. Smuggling wine out of the house was popular in school days. Parents and head mistresses never knew. *Now here I am, fifty eight years old, smuggling wine into the headmistress's office.*

Beth knocked three times and said, "Joe sent me."

"Enter quick and lock the door." Sister Mary Margaret sat at her desk, black stocking feet up crossed at the ankles, shoes off, big smile on her face. Last light from the fading sun hit the stained glass panel behind the older woman casting a rosy glow. For a moment wrinkles softened, she looked to Beth like the young girl from Ireland she must have been. "We're up to no-good then?"

"Your call, Sister. Fun to have a co-conspirator. Been a busy afternoon." Beth used the cork screw, opened the bottle and poured the wine. Crackers and cheese arranged on a small plate were placed first on linen cloths from the kitchen, then on the desk and she too, kicked off her shoes.

"Attractively set, Beth. You take pleasure in lifting even a simple repast above the ordinary with an elegant touch, do you?"

Beth heaved a sigh. "Yes, I do, always have. It's part of my nature. Catering combined with decorating."

"No, I think not. I think it's a whole lot more, Beth. You feel obligated somehow to seek approval, to gain admiration so you knock yourself out giving service."

She wanted to run from the room, slam the door and never come back. But inside, Beth knew she craved acceptance and love and somehow Sister M&M saw into her. Choking back tears, she said, " Am I so transparent, Sister?"

With a tilt of her head, the little nun gazed at the new volunteer who, under pressure, came through and prepared dinner for St. Paul's. "You're a good lass, m'dear. Lots of us walking around needing affection and praise. You certainly didn't hold back when I called, did you now?"

Beth tossed back the rest of her wine and laughed. "Didn't dare, Sister M&M."

Brushing crumbs from her lap, Sister Mary Margaret rubbed her calves and stepped into sturdy black shoes. "Then you've had a chat with our Harold, have you?"

Corking the bottle, Beth hand swept cracker crumbs away and gathered cloth and plate. "Kind of. Last week, Doctor Cooper paid Harold to walk me to my car."

"Oh." An eloquent raise of her eyebrows. "What a nice gesture."

"Nice gesture, my foot. The kind doctor didn't tell me in advance so picture this, Sister. I'm out in the rainy dark night, no one around, my car is parked at the far end of the parking lot. All of a sudden, this huge shaggy man comes out of the shadows, calls my name. I was on the verge of spraying him with pepper spray—but couldn't find it and calling the police but no cell phone at my fingertips and about to scream my fool mouth off."

"And what happened?"

"Uh, nothing. He said he was Harold and Doc Coop paid him to walk me to my car. I Googled the good samaritan with no brains and found out that he's a fargin' psychiatrist."

Sister Mary Margaret half-smiled. "Is fargin' similar to fuffa?"

Oh—my—God.

"Must be the wine on an empty stomach, Sister. Please forgive me." Beth grabbed the opportunity to head for the door. "Time to check on the stew and see that all is in readiness." Over her shoulder, she said, "Is Dr. Cooper coming tonight?"

"Not sure. In fact, I'm never certain about him. He seems to appear and disappear."

Sister paused for a moment and continued. "Beth, I must caution you to be careful about getting attached to Doctor Cooper."

"I hardly know him but I have to ask you, why?" Beth moved back to the desk where Sister Mary Margaret sat up straight and strong.

"He's gone through a nasty divorce recently and his life isn't what you might call stable."

She leaned forward to emphasize her words. "I truly believe you need stability as you re-establish yourself. Take it for what it's worth, dear girl." She smiled and waved Beth away. "Now get on with you. Back to the scullery."

"Thank you, I think," Beth said," and closed the door.

He seems to appear and disappear. What the hell? No time to think about him. Beth walked to the food station line-up. More volunteers were busy setting up long tables for dining, chairs in place, clean trays stacked high where they should be. A festive feeling filled the air as both young and older parishioners worked side by side. *A well run church with heart.*

May as well set the order straight. First station had bread, crackers and rolls covered in plastic. Next would be the beef stew—no soup tonight because stew is similar to soup. *Make sure there's lots of gravy.* Next was dessert. The array was staggering. Chocolate covered strawberries, fruit tarts, crème puffs and traditional brownies and cookies. Pumpkin and apple pies. More than one bakery came through and no sweet tooth would go home dissatisfied.

Lucy had yet to emerge from her paint box in the cloakroom. The bounty at her table would surprise her, or maybe not. *She's a regular volunteer, not like me.* She raced back to the kitchen, checked the various pots simmering, tasted and added a touch of paprika from her own recipe and stirred. Bit into an inch cube of beef. "Mmmm." *Tender as planned. Stew can be tricky.* Poured a glass of beef stock in each pot for extra gravy. Checked the clock. Thirty minutes to show time. *Brush teeth, freshen face if Lucy allows me to share space at the mirror.*

Beth ladled stew as fast as she was able, to the smiling hungry crowd as they sniffed the air and chatted. They were in a festive mood; whether it was contagious from the volunteers combined with heavenly aromas Beth had no idea, but she was having fun. From the corner of her eye, she spied Doctor Cooper's earnest manner as he leaned toward each person while handing them their preference of the fare at his table. Their eyes met during a lull and a smile slowly touched his lips, grew until he flashed a wide grin. Again, he made notes on the small electronic device in one hand. Again, Sister Mary Margaret came out applauding everyone for their good work, lauding Beth for jumping in to prepare the incredible stew and urging all to have a plateful before leaving. She encouraged them to partake of the dessert table and to take some home.

Before walking away, the little nun smiled benignly. She glided directly to Beth, then sank into the nearest chair. Taking Beth's hand, she said, "Well? What's stopping you from volunteering while Karen's on bed rest? T'will only be a couple of month, maybe three."

Inhaling a deep breath, Beth exhaled and said, "I'm starting a business, Sister and I can't make a commitment for such an extended time."

A laugh from deep inside, Sister said, "That's all? I thought it was something insurmountable. There are plenty of extra hands to do your bidding once a week, m'dear. You're a leader. They will follow your instructions. Help us through this crisis and you will surely be helping yourself." She rose and marched off.

"But, Sister. . ." Wasted words as doors parted and the black swirl of her skirt was seen leaving the room. All around, people were murmuring about the beef stew, congratulating and thanking Beth. She didn't feel hungry and toyed with the food, then tasted and soon finished a plateful. *Good, in fact super*. She wrapped a few chocolate covered strawberries in a paper napkin to take home and reached for her bag. Startled by a tap on her shoulder, she spun around.

Harold, a proud look on his big lop-sided face with the clean shave growing back already, handed over folded paper. "Doc Coop ran out."

Beth twisted in the chair toward the double door entrance to the church. Sure enough, she caught a fleeting glimpse of the tall gray haired man, tweed jacket, attaché□ case in hand, as he left the building. In a hurry.

"Regarding my good friend Harold: Again, sorry about not forewarning you. Had to leave as Sister twisted your arm. Harold will be there this evening to escort you, IF you need him. It's important for him to feel needed. Work in progress, Larry ps Best beef stew ever!"

Nice. Very nice. Another gallant gesture. But what's the rush? We've exchanged emails, fun in a way. I don't know what his voice sounds like. He's kind of mysterious. Sister is right. Is she also right about me steering clear of him? This email connection is only fun. Nothing serious. Now, exactly what does 'work in progress' mean? Must ask.

Beth gathered her belongings and dragged weary bones from the comfortable chair. She looked, really saw the benevolence shining from Harold's soft brown eyes. "Thanks for giving the note to me, Harold. I'll get my bag and you can walk me to the car." A little chink in the wall she'd built to protect herself, cracked to accept kindness.

Returning from the cloakroom, Beth found Harold in the same position like a faithful companion. Together they walked out into the warm night air.

Chapter 19

Spread out in front of her were the yellow pages of the phone book. A headache threatened as Beth searched first one section and then another for home surveillance systems. Nowhere to be found. Obviously she wasn't looking under the right heading. Dumb, incapable of doing what Frank, don't go there, would have found in a flash. *Yeah, but he had years of decision making and you've only had a few months. Be kind to yourself, kid. Too much time wasted. How can I cut to the chase and find someone to ask?*

Beth thought about Maverick as she often did. Not just about the sex but how supportive he'd been from the first day. Sure he had benefited from their friendship and business as well. This time she'd call and ask if he knew anyone in the business. He seemed to be established. Beth hesitated before placing the call. Underlying motives or strictly business? Wanting to move away from the sexual side, she made up her mind.

An early call to Maverick Friday morning found him awake and happy to hear from Beth.

"Hi. Beth calling. Are you up?" *Why does everything have to sound like a sexual reference*? "I need a reliable source for CCTV and thought you might have a connection." To Beth's ears, he seemed disappointed in the reason for the call but as always he came up with a solution.

He said, "Miz Malone, you've called the right number." They both laughed. "Just so happens, I'm licensed in New York State to sell and install CCTV and fire alarms and a whole lot of other work. Have papers to prove it." Beth heard him clear his throat. "Excuse me. I needed one more slug of black coffee—not as tasty as yours but it's all I have handy—before we talk business."

Beth said, "If you're available this morning, we can talk when you get here." She pictured him, blonde hair tousled, heavy lidded blue eyes full of mischief. *No more, Maverick. Strictly business. I'm not going to be an older woman in a quickie affair.*

"Available, yes, M'am. That's me. Ten okay?"

"Fine. See you then." She hung up.

After the morning swim, Beth dressed in a navy and white striped tee shirt and blue jeans. Shoulder length brown hair blown straight, a touch of make-up—another touch and she still looked drab. *Brighten up with a yellow scarf.* An inspection in the mirror. *Oh no. I look like a Girl Scout. There must be a better way to tie a scarf.* The door bell rang.

Seen through the peephole, he was the epitome of virility in a worn leather jacket and snug jeans. *Oh my. Keep your resolution.* "Hi." She stepped back and let Maverick walk ahead.

Great butt. "How've you been?" Beth caught up and ushered him into what used to be Frank's library, indicated where he should sit and got right to business. "What I need is a closed circuit television surveillance system in the house and on the property. It must be discreet inside and installed well before September fifteenth." *Just in case I rush ahead with my plans. Of course Lisa will knock my two heads together but at least the system will be installed.*

She sat back and observed his rugged face go from surprise to interest to questions.

Maverick sat silent for a moment, then opened his briefcase and pulled out an electronic device. "That's a tall order, Beth. First tell me why you feel you need the system."

Moment of truth? She took a deep breath and lied—kind of. "I'm alone in a large home on a big piece of property. I'll feel more secure."

He digested the misinformation. "Okay. Let's inspect the grounds first and see how many cameras you'll need. Then we'll work up figures on the inside." He reached for her hand but she moved fast and through the door.

Outside, Maverick was all business. Beth enjoyed watching a very focused side of him. Measurements were made with a special device; he wrote quickly in his little notebook.

It looked a lot like Larry Cooper's. Butterflies fluttered all over the butterfly bushes planted along the walk landing on the tall lavender spikes and flying away.

Late July is a good time for Monarchs and all butterflies; symbols of renewal.

Self-consciously they walked together toward the pool enclosure. *Scene of sex unlimited.*

He examined non-existent birds in the sky giving Beth privacy to unlock the door and shut the alarm. They entered the steamy wonderland. Beth said, "What do you think?"

"I think you look beautiful."

She couldn't resist the hug offered when his arms opened. "Thanks, Maverick. You've been a terrific friend when I most needed one." Untangling herself from the bear hug, she grinned way up at the weathered ruddy face, wide cheekbones from some Nordic background.

"You didn't let me down. But remember the morning in the kitchen when I told you not to expect. . ."

Strong fingers combed back the blonde mane of hair. He said, "Need a haircut," thought for a minute and blue eyes twinkled like the bad boy he was, "that time in the kitchen had a different ending. You didn't forget, did you?"

Put a stop to it. How well she remembered Maverick carrying her upstairs to the mirrored exercise room and

105

delights that followed. In spite of the heat rising to color her cheeks, Beth said, "No. How could I forget? Our time together was special. Now we both have to move on, right?"

Reluctantly he nodded. "Let's talk business."

Making a quick recovery, he pointed out where one mini dome camera would be placed for maximum coverage, sensor lights and two camera outside. Beth locked up, happy to leave.

They entered the house where the air conditioning seemed too cold. He said, "Screwy weather. Hot a few days, then thunder storms and chilly. Glad I diversified my business or by September I'd be in the poor house."

"You're a smart business man, Maverick. I admire that. Coffee? I'm going to make some."

"Sure."

Aware of his footsteps moving toward her, she diverted his attention. "Is there a style of camera not recognizable as such?" Water and coffee measured, she plugged in the pot and turned to him. "I want the cameras inside to be discreet."

"Oh yeah. I have a picture of one. Looks just like a smoke detector. Perfect for your needs."

"While the coffee perks, let's do a walk through downstairs."

Shuffling through the briefcase, he pulled out the picture and laid it on the table. "Not upstairs?"

The blue eyes appeared very innocent but Beth knew better.

"Maybe directed on the stairs but no further. I'm concentrating on security for the outside and downstairs. When you're finished, I'll be burglar proof."

Coffee poured, ready to drink while Maverick punched magical buttons and came up with some calculations. As he worked, Beth set warm bagels in a wicker basket and cream cheese on a small ceramic plate.

He sniffed the air and groped for a bagel. "Between you and the bagel, I'm finding it hard to concentrate." He bit off a manly chunk, chewed and continued to figure.

"Sharpen your adding pencil or whatever that is." Beth stirred sweetener in the coffee and cut a sliver of bagel to nibble on.

Finally he looked up and grinned. "Ah. Big job, Beth. Thanks for calling me. I'll give you my best price. It includes another worker, eight or nine cameras, digital video recorder called DVR with hard drive disc to record activity wherever cameras are located. I can provide a service to check the disc each day or train you or a designated person to check it. Plus all working parts warranty. Plus, when cameras are installed inside there are holes in plaster and re-plastering and painting to be finished. Best price." He wrote a number on a piece of paper folded and slid it across the table. "Delicious bagel," slathering cream cheese on a large slice and stuffing it in his mouth. "There may be additional costs but I won't know 'til I talk with dealers." He wiped his mouth and waited.

"Twenty thousand?"

"Yes. Minimum. As I said, big job."

"And you know what you're doing?"

With obvious pride, he pulled an official envelope from the briefcase and handed it over.

She opened it to find his license from New York State, verifying he had taken and passed the course in installation of fire alarm and surveillance equipment.

"Done deal, Maverick. Please warn me about any other expenses and the big question is when you can start."

One finger in the air indicated wait as he dialed a number. "Marco, tengo mucho grande surveillance job and trust only you to assist. Si. Lunes. Tardes. No. Siete. Si. Mi casa. Si. Adios." With a snap, the phone closed. "Just enough Spanish to be understood. Okay Beth, I'll have to hustle to get all the component parts to start the job on Monday afternoon. Fast enough for you?"

Head in a spin to see him work so fast although she knew what a smooth operator he was in the sex department, "How will you pay for the materials?"

"My credit is good but give me a check for ten thousand so I can deposit it. I'll call through the day as I gather everything. One good supplier should have everything in stock but he closes early today. I gotta get over there right away."

Down the hall past all the rooms, into the desk where the long checkbook lay. Beth hurried back, wrote a check to Maverick Associates, entered it in the register and handed it over.

"Receipt, please?" One was next to her plate. He'd wasted no time.

They shook hands at the door and before she had a chance to protest, his mouth tasting of cream cheese and remnants of bagel, covered hers. Almost irresistible. A voice called from down the hall breaking the spell.

Breathing heavily, Maverick said, "Someone's here?"

Beth said, "Maria, my cleaning lady," not sorry to be interrupted by what might have been a huge mistake. *Huge— another one of those sex words.*

"Call you later, Beth" and he was gone.

"Mrs. Malone, I'm through with morning's work. Have to leave now." She trudged toward the stairs, a basket of sorted laundry balanced under one arm, one hand full of ironing on hangers. Small and round, now graying like everyone Beth knew, Maria hugged Beth and tucked the weekly envelope in her purse.

"I'll carry the laundry upstairs. Thanks, see you next week."

Chapter 20

Alone, after the walk-through with Maverick, Beth had second thoughts about her home.

For lack of a better description, the place looked kind of shabby, out-of-date. *Oh my God. Upscale people coming to an elegant dinner party in these surroundings. Not acceptable.*

She couldn't remember the last time she decorated. Twenty years? Colors, styles, fashions had changed but not Malone's. Frank said he liked things the way they were. *Oh really, Frank? Everything but your wife. I guess I'm no longer in fashion.*

With a vengeance, she hurled his golf trophies in a garbage bag and dragged them to the curb picturing him bagged along with his trash, one foot sticking out. Time to open the trunk in the attic where all her trophies were stored. She'd polish them and place them in the library to remind her of the winner she used to be and the possibility of the winner to be continued.

Time for an emergency conference with Lisa. An hour later they were in the kitchen,

Lisa gulping iced tea. "Let's get to it. Your emergency—my emergency, oh sister." And they began the room-to-room inspection.

"I definitely agree with you. The downstairs décor needs a major perk-up. Textured paint, new rugs, a few pieces of furniture and some doodads. Tall order in three or four weeks but it just so happens. . ." they grinned at the familiar phrase, "I know a decorator, Hilliard. If he's available, business is slow in August, he can do it and do it well. Before I call, let's sit down and regroup."

Beth said, "Regroup?" trying to look as if she hadn't a clue as to what Lisa was about to say.

"I've been through the over-achiever phase several times in my life and it cost me a bundle. Not money, rather mental and physical stress. I've been hoping to spare you some of that wear and tear by suggesting you slow down." She grinned wickedly. "There comes a time when your car needs a tune-up and. . ."

Beth burst into laughter. "Are you suggesting I'm high mileage, younger-than-me?"

An embarrassed flush came to Lisa's cheeks. "Uh, not exactly, yes, maybe, but in remarkable condition for all you've been through. Beth, I'll call Hilliard but why not enjoy the fun of decorating instead of sprinting your way through the process?

"Please call him now. I love you for caring and am definitely taking your advice seriously. I'll owe you big time."

Thoughtful, Lisa placed the call. As the phone rang she said in the most solemn tone, "You introduced me to fat free food." She hit speaker phone when he picked up.

After Lisa explained the job and urgency, Hilliard said, "Yes, I am interested, Ms. Lisa and for you, all things are possible. Will you be there, my banker lady?"

"Yes, Hilly. Be here in thirty minutes."

"Next week, I think."

"No, Hilly. This is an emergency and she's my best friend. Thirty minutes or I call Tommy."

Silence. "Directions please. Ah, Ms. Lisa, you do know how to make a mon bleed."

She flashed a wicked grin to Beth and gave directions and disconnected. "My friend, you're in for a treat."

"Who's Tommy?"

"His roommate."

Beth arranged a plate of cheese and crackers, poured wine and they settled down to wait in the living room.

"How do you know him?"

"Through the bank; my first client trying to get started. I recognized his potential and Beth, in one year he's made a name for himself. You're in great hands, you'll see."

Door chimes rang and Hilliard showed up. And show was the word for him. Taller than Lisa, thinner than any model Beth ever laid eyes on and gorgeous if a cinnamon skin man poured into black leather framed around the neck with a white silk scarf could be called anything else. Whiter than white teeth lit the entrance hall while he captured Lisa in a lover's embrace and beamed at Beth.

In an island lilt, he said, "And you are the lady in decorating distress, I presume?"

Flustered Beth said, "I am."

Handing Lisa a notebook, he said, "Please to take notes, Ms. Lisa."

He glided through each room like an artist facing a blank canvas, murmuring followed by occasional exclamations and a graceful wave of his manicured hand at Lisa. Beth trailed along like a lost waif and wrung her hands feeling out of control.

At last he turned to them. "You have three-four weeks?"

Lisa jumped in. "Barely. Beth's beginning a special type of unattached gentlemen and women soiree's here on September twenty-first. She's been so pre-occupied with arranging everything else that suddenly she realized the downstairs needed redecorating. She called me—I called you—here we are."

Overwhelmed, Beth began to cry with huge uncontrollable sobs. Helpless, she sank into the nearest chair.

"Sorry. I don't know what came over me. . ." and cried some more.

Leather arms enfolded her, crooning, "There, there." A soft white handkerchief dabbed gently at her tears. "We didn't mean to take over but truly it was necessary under time constraints, love." He lifted her chin to meet his gaze. "No matter how pushy I seem, you have the final say-so. . ." a musical chuckle, "with my approval, of course. So there is no time for tears, pretty lady." He planted a tender kiss on her forehead. "Let us get to work, shall we?" And he disappeared to fetch his paraphernalia and portfolio.

Beth caught her breath. "Did you work with him on a job, Lisa?"

"In the beginning. It was so natural. Two giants show up at the door and take over. Every job is a winner and so much fun." She touched Beth's arm. "Didn't mean to shut you out. What I think is that you can trust me enough to loosen the reins and relax a bit. Your plate is full. I told him the September date otherwise it could take many months."

Breathe in—breathe out. My friend is here.

"Okay."

When Hilliard came back, Beth said in a resolute voice, "Listen up. The finished job must--and this is the key word—must—not appear newly decorated."

Hilliard said, "Ah. A challenge. It must appear fresh as cut flowers, current as breaking news, yet comfortable enough to remove all of one's clothing."

Lisa said, "Nicely phrased, Hilly. It's not that kind of party but who knows. It must look welcoming, comfortable and not as if the plastic and price tags were just removed."

Opening his portfolio, he said, "Interesting notion, fine lady. One I have not heard before. You are a true original."

Beth glowed, the work began, and the next day, early Saturday the three of them planned to go on a shopping expedition. In the middle of turning a sample page, Beth checked the time and gasped.

"I have an appointment with my lawyer soon and I must change and get attractive. The last time he saw me, I scared the two of us with my rumpled face, clothes and open wine bottle on the kitchen table."

They glanced up, waved her off and said they'd come up with ideas for her to peruse when she returned.

Hilliard said, "One more thing, Ms. Beth. You have a bathroom or powder room on the main floor, I presume?"

"There's a beauty near the entrance. Frank loved his creature comforts. Take a look. See if a color change is called for. If I'm not home when you leave, shut the door tight. It self-locks."

After dressing, Beth had a few minutes to spare and couldn't resist the pull of the computer to see if there was anything from Larry. Upstairs in the little office, Beth booted up and checked email. Nothing. What did Larry Cooper mean by 'work in progress'? Determined to find out, she typed a message.

Hey Larry, Were you referring to yourself as a 'work in progress' in your note? If so, how come? Nosier than ever, Beth

An email popped up from Larry.

Happy to hear from you, nosier than ever Beth. I guess I'm the work in progress. Always think my "work" is what's in progress. When I'm writing, I focus on the world I create even though it's non-fiction. It calls to me—says "Come home, Doc." And I rush. Insight from the chef de jour. Any time to get together, coffee, drink, movie? Larry

Did he just ask me for a date? I must be leaving a trail of pheromones in my wake. Not too bad for a woman going on fifty nine. Don't forget Sister's warning. Beth hit print and added the email to a growing pile of correspondence from Larry and thought about a response.

Larry, How about coffee after soup kitchen.

Immediately a response came back.

I had dinner in mind. Please advise. L

Hmmm. Condensed version or email later? Lawyer appointment at five thirty—dressed to impress. Lots to do for a woman who used to dig dirt out of golf clubs.

Will do. Have an appointment in thirty minutes. B

Chapter 21

Click, click went the stiletto heels of Beth's new black strappy shoes across the marble floor of the lobby where lawyer Bruce Bradley's local office was. She prayed she wouldn't slip and fall on her rear end; cursed the salesgirl who assured her the expensive little black dress was "a dress you could die for," and the floral pashmina scarf was "poifect, dahling". Costumed is how she felt although a few male heads turned as she made it to the elevator.

Stepping out on the top floor of the fifteen story building and into the plush offices of Bruce Bradley, attorney at law and associates, she trod carefully almost sinking in the deep carpet. "Beth Malone," she said to the young receptionist who looked as if she twirled off a runway to answer the phone.

Wonder if Alicia knows Bruce uses Models R Us as an employment service?

Alicia was one of the snobs who turned chilly after Beth no longer had a husband.

Toothpaste ad Bruce Bradley opened the temple door where he worshipped himself and arms out-stretched ushered Beth in. Murmuring wetly in her ear he said, " Since when are you Beth?" With a practiced gesture he removed her colorful wrap before she knew what happened.

Good thing I wore it. Without the wrap, he'd have my dress off in the blink of an eye. What the hell is going on?

She said, "Beth is an upgrade from Liz," and refrained from kneeing him where it would hurt the most.

He gave her the once over twice. She almost laughed but Beth was there on business; the will, she wanted copies of everything.

He said, "You look fabulous, my dear," and pulled her close. No doubt to demonstrate his 'fine-how-do-you-do'—just like Frank, best buddy since childhood. He was hard and proud of it. Disgusted, Beth pushed him away and sat in a leather chair opposite the ostentatious over-size desk.

Making a show of checking the time, Beth said, "Let's get down to business, Bruce. He nodded thoughtfully, rearranging his agenda. "I want copies of both wills and any other papers Frank left behind. I also want to know exactly what I'm entitled to. He mentioned divorce papers. . ." Bruce almost interrupted but she held up a hand. "I want a copy of them as well. Do you know where he is and if he's alone?" Bruce's poker face almost cracked and Beth continued. Bruce had given himself away. "I don't care. He's dead to me. Please give me the copies now. I have another appointment."

She waited hands folded while he said into the speaker, "Tiffany. . ."

It figures.

At home, Beth felt soiled from the encounter with Bruce. Stripping, she tossed her finery across the frilly pink bedspread in what once was a little girl's room. *Will I ever wear the clothes again? Sleek and sophisticated is not my style. Bruce will report to Frank, the son-of-a-bitch, that I looked hot. Was it worth the effort to appear recovered from the shock of a husband leaving? No.*

Forty years of closeness with Bruce accompanied by first wife, Martha, later displaced by trophy wife, Alicia and Bruce had never given Beth more than a brotherly hug and peck on the cheek. With best buddy Frank out of the picture, he must have assumed she was easy prey—even thrilled to arouse a sexy successful man like him. Beth shuddered with revulsion. *Find a new attorney.*

She gazed around the room she'd been occupying since Frank left. *A child's room.*

Ridiculous. *Move into another bedroom and claim it for my own. Redecorate. Later. Go crazy with color. Add to the to-do list.* Growing up was more difficult than she thought it would be.

Scrubbed clean and dressed in sweats, She opened a small can of tuna, added a spoon of mayo, threw in some greens and ate a solitary meal, interested in the notes and pictures Lisa and Hilliard left. Lots of possibilities there. How wonderful to have the burden lifted by her decorating team. She called Lisa and was disappointed to find she wasn't home. Beth needed someone to talk to. Maybe Larry awaited the next email. Maybe he too sat alone in need of companionship.

Fat chance. An important man like him was probably at this moment, leaning across a small table in a chic café gazing into the eyes of a willowy model type like Tiffany.

Weary, she climbed the stairs to the small office and booted up the computer. Sick of the day starting with Maverick who wanted to get her between the sheets and she didn't want sex with him again. Too young for her; dear and kind and *mmm* so good but she didn't want to be his older woman. Then the fiasco with Bruce Bradley. Larry Cooper set a little spark burning, a flare in the dark and Beth was afraid of getting close to another man. And wise Sister Mary Margaret's warning repeated over and over. Watch out for Larry Cooper. Right.

Chapter 22

"Saturday night is the loneliest night of the week . . ." a plaintive war song from the forties. It's Friday night but who cares? When you're alone, every night's the same. Who recorded that saddest of songs, wondered Larry Cooper. *Probably everyone,* he thought, pressing rosemary and garlic into two lamb chops. He slid the pan under the broiler and turned off the rice. He walked around the mostly empty apartment, sandals slapping against bare floors. Pitiful, he thought. I have freedom from an unfixable marriage; absorbed blame hurled like spears and left bleeding from the one person I love. My daughter Linda. She'll come around. Hope I'm still living when that day happens. Racing back to the kitchen, he turned the chops just in time. One minute to go before dinner. As he poured red wine and filled a plate with two chops and a heap of brown rice, thoughts turned to Beth Malone as they often did. He settled in the old easy chair in the spacious living room filled with technical books next to real life adventures and mysteries. Mr. Blackberry, his connection to Beth, was close at hand.

Hungry, he ate the solitary dinner, sipped some wine and wondered what Beth was doing right now on this, another, loneliest night of the week? Was she in some charming cafe□ with a distinguished man, leaning toward him with saucer-size amber eyes all attention? Curiosity got the best of him and he text messaged to find out.

An email from Larry. In spite of all the protests to herself, her pulse rate rose as low spirits fled. He was home, thinking of her.

B, I'm home. L

Hi. Had to see my lawyer-soon to be ex lawyer. Just got home and scrubbed myself clean.

Beth, why were you in his office or is this too personal?

Suddenly tears trickled down. She reached for a tissue before they splashed on the keyboard, took a deep breath and continued.

Very personal. Are you busy doing something, writing, watching Casablanca?

I'm in bachelor living room, text messaging on a small electronic device I use instead of a laptop. How about you?

Small office in too-large for one person home, not comfortable as you. I'm at a desk with a computer etc. Is that a Blackberry? Heard about it. I'm relatively new to computers so I'm at a desk. Rather be curled up by the fireplace. We could talk on the phone.

What I want most, Beth, is for the two of us to sit in a small café and get to know each other. Let me know when you're ready. Rcv'd another Blackberry as a perk. Will send to you and we can curl up separately together. Do you live near St. Paul's?

Charming. Watch it.

Two towns north of me. I'm 35 minutes from city. Is that where you live? Thanks for wanting to get to know me. It's been a bad time since March-I'm just getting to know myself.

Riverdale. large apartment. Sold house after divorce. Is that why you were at lawyer—divorce related?

Hmmm. Not exactly. Husband walked out with no warning last March leaving only a note: "It's not you-it's me." All legal papers are with his best friend, the lawyer. Now I have copies of everything. So much for Frank Malone after forty years of marriage.

Anxious for his response, she waited and waited. Finally he wrote:

Sorry you went through a terrible time. You seem to be a take-charge woman at soup kitchen. I admire you.

Thanks Larry. I'm a novice at taking charge but understand how a kitchen and food work. What are you doing so far afield of the city-at St. Paul's?

Long story--bone of contention between Sister M&M and me. When we go to that small café, I'll spill if you're interested.

Am I ever interested in everything he says; yet so afraid of opening the door to a real relationship.

Book signing tour several weeks in Midwest lv Sunday with agent. Getting A Grip doing well, time to press flesh/sign books. Will miss soup kitchen. I'll be in touch. Blackberry's on way tomorrow. Lv address.

Kind of you to share the perk. Looking forward to 'in touch'. How can you get away-what happens to your patients? B

August-traditional shrink get-away. Patients learn to snap out of it-get a grip-or go crazy. Don't meant to sound cold but we need to clean out the cobwebs too and August is it.

Oh. Safe trip.

No wonder Jenna isn't going to be available. She turned off the computer, smiling as she did. *Curl up separately together. The man has a sense of humor.*

Rereading Beth's message, Larry Cooper had a disturbing thought about Beth's runaway husband, Frank Malone. Could it be his former patient? A common enough name. He introduced himself as Frank Malone; business card said M.D. after his name but during therapy, said he needed, his word, needed to start fresh. The time frame fit. His practice was north of the city, he'd said. So this was his way of starting fresh. Frank would be surprised to see how well the little woman he'd described to his psychiatrist as an inconsequential empty-headed nobody, was doing without him.

Chapter 23

Late afternoon, Maverick arrived with his associate, unloaded boxes of equipment and began to work. In the kitchen, they poured over a diagram while scarfing down coffee and donuts they brought with them. Maverick's blond head was close to the curly black hair of Marco; they spoke rapidly in broken Spanish/English and understood each other. Finally finished with coffee and agreeing as to where to start, they began. Beth observed from a distance, admired the partnership of ideas and the way they worked. This marked the beginning for her business, to make the home secure even when there were no guests, and when the parties were in progress, the watchful eye of the camera would catch any misdeeds.

Beth worked. All the letters and flyers were next to elegant envelopes and stamped. Not sealed. What if the date had to be changed; way ahead of schedule since the first party was to be September 21st but you never knew, so she'd left the date to be filled in. A huge knot formed in her stomach as insecurity surfaced. A what-if list formed first in her mind and she wrote them down as Jenna suggested.

Question: What if the idea doesn't catch on?

Answer: Start again with new people or take out an advertisement.

Q: Second try brings few responses. Not enough for a real party.

A: Make party small and intimate. Word of mouth will bring in more. Don't give up too soon.

Reading it over, Beth felt the knot loosen. It made sense. Trust her instincts. Something Beth had to learn. Still reeling from Frank's abandonment six months before and the social circle excluding her as well, she was forced to move on. The expression Jenna used was "going to school' from your own experiences. Make them a learning process. Without realizing it, Beth turned what she had gone through into a desire to give other lonely people a chance to begin again. Positive now that most people craved companionship and found it elusive,

Beth was certain unattached men and women of similar age to herself and in her social strata were not going to single bars and dances advertised weekly. She hoped to offer a needed service in her comfortable home. All proceeds going to St. Paul's soup kitchen, she decided. Sister M&M will be pleased.

Bursting with renewed energy, Beth changed into one of the lycra bathing suits purchased recently and ran out into the warm August afternoon. She practiced all the moves learned over years of her love affair with chlorinated water. Coach's whistle blasted in her memory and she dived, knifing clean in the water. Deep she went, arms synchronized, flutter kicks all the way up and waved to the non-existent crowd applauding from phantom bleachers.

After a while, Beth checked on Maverick Associates. Each room they worked in was covered with canvas cloth to protect furniture from plaster dust, true to Maverick's word. Holes in walls and ceilings as previously discussed and already cameras were installed. Working swiftly as a team, the progress was evident. Maverick, usually friendly and flirty at the same time, didn't acknowledge her presence. Beth felt relieved. An email check, just to see if Larry had free time to say hi was rewarded with hello from St. Louis.

B-quick hello from steamy St. Louis. Warm reception last night.8 book shops here and on to

Kansa City. Missing you already. How about joining me? My treat. Sent pkg. L

Oh my God. Her face grew hot. *I never dreamed, never thought. Oh, oh.* Any elation felt moments before was gone. She wrung her hands together. *What to do—what to do. Call Lisa.*

"Lisa Marcus, please, this is, uh. . ." *what's my name?* "Beth, uh, Beth Malone. What do you mean, am I sure? Of course, I'm sure." As she waited, Frank Sinatra assured her 'Love is Lovelier the Second Time Around.' *Thanks for nothing.*

"Lisa Marcus."

"Lisa, it's Beth. Are you busy?"

"Yes, but I'll make time for you. What's wrong? And Beth, take a deep breath or two and tell me."

Beth pictured Lisa dressed in corporate no frills, at a tidy desk, wild dark hair tamed in a chignon. *Breathe in and out, and calm down. Stop acting like a teenage ninny.*

"Okay and thanks. I'm acting like a nut but here goes. The email man, Larry I told you about, just sent a message. He's away for a month and wants me to join him. Says he misses me—his treat, he says. Lisa, what am I going to do?" Silence on the line and Beth wondered if the connection was lost. No, there was a giggle.

Lisa said, "So Beth, you have an admirer. Terrific."

"But Lisa. . ."

"Listen honey, I have to get back to my client. I'll stop at your home between five and six."

"One more important thing, I need the name of a good lawyer." Beth heard a few clicks in the background.

"Elise Bergen. She's located near you. Mention my name. Now hang on to your shorts. Got to run."

Sure enough, Lisa's name paved the way to an appointment the following day, eleven in the morning. The secretary said she might have to wait. Beth was ready to sign the divorce papers .

Beth paced the small office, ran to the exercise room, put on a yoga tape and tried to calm down. Drank chamomile tea to no effect. *What's wrong with me? Yes, I have an admirer and that's nice, I think. But Larry Cooper? I'm afraid of liking him too much, of allowing myself to care for anyone. Right now I have to concentrate on being a facilitator The party is for others to meet. Not me. I'm only a facilitator.*

Beth blinked her eyes and hurrying back to the office, she reached for the dictionary to double check the meaning. *Means to make easier. Right. Why can't I make my life easier, too?*

She sent an email to Larry.

L thanks for the premature invitation. Do U realize we've never talked on the phone, had dinner, nothing but safe emails. Let's not put proverbial cart B4 the horse. When U return-we meet in person-WOW! What a concept! And proceed from there. B

Chimes rang, Maverick answered the door. Deep in thought, she missed the action going on downstairs. Only when Lisa appeared on the stairs calling her name, did Beth realize how out of it she was.

"Hey Beth, I rushed over as soon as the client left. Figured you needed a shoulder."

Lisa dropped her handbag on the chair and kicked off high-heeled shoes. "The hunk is your butler?"

"What hunk?"

"The one who opened the front door. Tall blond built like a brick house."

"Oh, you mean Maverick. He's my uh, friend. He and Marco are installing CCTV. They started today. I didn't hear the chimes."

Lisa laughed her hearty laugh. "Oh baby, he can ring my chimes anytime."

Embarrassed yet tickled by her friend's reaction, Beth kicked the door closed and said, "Keep it down. I think he hears through walls." They laughed together as they always did.

"How old are you, Missy, if you don't mind revealing the number to your new best friend?"

"Not at all, older-than-me Beth. I'm forty one. For what do you need this information?"

"Just thinking," Beth said with a hint of mischief. "Come on downstairs. I want to see if the men are finished for the day." She glanced at Lisa. "Why don't you let your hair loose and take off your jacket. Make yourself at home."

Without waiting for a response, Beth opened the door, descended the stairs slowly and called, "Maverick, are you finished for the day?"

The blond hair and broad shoulders appeared from the library. The rest of his six foot four inch frame followed, a crooked grin on his rugged features as he looked past Beth. Behind her was Lisa carefully negotiating the stairs in high heels, white silk blouse with a touch of lace camisole visible at the low neckline, a mass of curly brown hair framing her sweet open face.

"Almost," he said, eyes never leaving Lisa, "Back tomorrow afternoon. We'll work in the pool house first so you might plan to swim in the morning. I'll cover the pool so dust and plaster don't get in."

He shuffled his big feet as if to leave but didn't go. By now Lisa maneuvered past several boxes and stopped next to Beth. With the most innocent smile Beth had seen east of the Mississippi, Lisa extended a graceful yet large hand befitting her size.

127

"Hi, Maverick. I'm Lisa."

Beth knew from the look on Lisa's face, the hand shaking hers fit just fine.

He repeated, "Be back tomorrow, same time."

Sounds of a truck, his truck, as it peeled away and Beth locked the front door. She turned to Lisa who remained rooted to the same place in the hall where she was before Maverick left.

"Well, what do you think?"

"Can't think. I can only feel and what I feel is X rated, pal." Fanning the air, Lisa said, "Is it hot in here or is it just me?"

"I'll make some iced tea. Just what we need when the temperature rises to 95 degrees in an air-conditioned house." Beth giggled, enjoying Lisa's reaction to Maverick and thrilled to see it reciprocated. "Kick off your shoes and follow me. Let's have an early dinner."

Chapter 24

Scanning legal papers in the folder on her lap, Beth waited patiently for Elise Bergen, the lawyer Lisa recommended. An attractive woman, red hair piled high in a neat bun on top of her head, hurried into the office. "Follow me," she said and Beth did.

It was a spacious room furnished with a brown leather couch, two matching chairs, a cherry wood desk and a bar in the corner. All business and a little pleasure like the mid-years woman across from Beth.

Glasses perched on the bridge of a perfect nose, she said, "You're fortunate to have a friend like Lisa Marcus. Remarkable woman. What's going on?"

Beth told her the whole story about Frank leaving, the note, divorce papers, and on and on.

"And you want me to do what, exactly?"

"It's been six months and I think I'd better sign the divorce papers and move on. I never dreamed I'd be in this position, divorce as a Catholic, but I must." *Don't cry, don't cry, don't cry.*

The lawyer pushed a box of tissues across the desk so Beth could reach, just in case. "Let's see what's in the folder." Elise Bergen held out a delicate hand with long tapered fingers.

Form by form was scrutinized; she looked up after reading the crumpled note Frank left and said, "Scumbag. Even though the deed is in your name, New York law declares it is marital property."

"Oh, you mean I could lose my home?" Beth felt her heart begin to pound.

"Let's take this one step at a time, Beth."

Beth said," Frank would never throw me out."

"Beth, he walked out on you after forty years of marriage, tiptoed out like a thief in the night. There isn't anything he can't do if he has the power. Listen to me carefully, I know this is a lot to comprehend. As I said, the house is considered by New York law marital property so ownership will have to be resolved. New York divorce laws are complex. Next, did he run off with a woman or a man?"

The thought of Frank with a man caused Beth to laugh. "Possibly a woman although there isn't any proof. His friends aren't talking. He certainly was discreet if he was having an affair."

"You can sue him for adultery if you get proof. Adultery is a crime in New York and grounds for divorce."

"Hmmm. I thought since he'd signed divorce papers and I can sign these papers," Beth indicated the divorce papers in the folder, "a divorce would be final. It's what Bruce Bradley indicated."

Elise Bergen said, "Bruce Bradley is his lawyer?"

"And best friend," Beth said.

"Did he give you his fine how-do-you-do?"

"Tried to. I felt like kneeing him where the sun doesn't shine but restrained myself."

"Sorry to tell you this, but he misled both you and his best friend. These papers are worthless. What would you like to see happen, Beth?"

In her whole life, Beth had never been asked that question so many times. She didn't have to think twice before answering. "Frank and our daughter Susie are very close. I don't want to hurt that relationship. I want him out of my life and I want my house and to be financially comfortable in repayment for giving him forty years of support and devotion."

Elise nodded. "Good. This is what I think should happen. When Frank returns and he will, you will threaten him with the charge of adultery." Beth looked as if she were ready to object and the lawyer waved her off. "Just listen. He won't know what you have up your sleeve. Your ace-in-the-hole is your daughter. He won't want to lose her and if she knows he ran away with some young body and left her mother crying at home, he will. The good daddy will be no more. When he returns, don't get in bed with him. Do not. Unless you plan to take him back. A Divorce Mediator is the way to go. I know a terrific Mediator who will do the job. Stay away from Bruce Bradley. I'll feed you a script as to what to say to Frank. Meanwhile, if you can get a handle on where he's been and with whom, we'll be ahead of the game. If you want me to recommend a private investigator, I will. Think about it."

They both stood up and walked to the door. "One more thing. If you meet a man and get into an intimate situation," Beth flushed red, "it happens. Be very discreet. Very."

"Thanks, Ms. Bergen. I'll hear from you then."

"Elise. My pleasure. Best to Lisa."

Beth borrowed the bathroom key and went down the hall, hanging on to her dignity for dear life. Once in, she locked the cubicle and shook so hard, she thought the door would fly off its hinges. She cried. *Private investigator?* The words made her want to throw up. She spun around and did, repeatedly. *How a marriage ends ups like this is beyond me. Somehow I have to salvage my relationship with Susie. And I will.* Repairing her make-up, she rinsed her mouth with cold water and returned the key.

By the time Beth reached the lobby and walked outside into the sunshine, head spinning with so much information, she knew Elise Bergen had given her the best advice. She put on a semblance of confidence and drove home. Business as usual.

By the afternoon, another phone line was installed, and Beth hustled to keep information organized. She worked on a phone presentation she hoped made sense and inspired confidence.

An actual phone call message from Larry was left saying he understood. She'd almost forgotten about him. There was so much to tell Lisa and no time.

Four o'clock came, Lisa's Lexus pulled up as planned the night before. The women were up to no good. And that was good. Still and hot outside as she ran up the front steps in high heel sling back pumps, black silk shirt under a beige suit. No need to ring the bell, Beth opened the door and she was in.

"I met with Elise Bergen this morning, thanks to you. You keep opening doors for me, pal. I'll tell all later." Lisa gave her a thumbs up.

Using a pantomime gesture, Beth signaled Lisa to fluff her brown curly mane and they strolled side by side to what once was Frank's office, now the library. Maverick was putting the finishing touches to the CCTV monitor. He called over his shoulder, "Beth, have you found someone to check on the tape or I can explain how to do it. Or maybe you want a service so you won't be bothered."

"Thanks for asking. My friend Lisa Marcus, you met her yesterday, understands electronics far better than me. If you have time when you're finished, please explain it to her."

He rose quickly, bumping his head on the shelf above and several books plummeted to the polished planked floor. Embarrassed, he gathered the books, stuffed them back on the shelf and grinned. "Hey. I'm through now if you want the first lesson."

Lisa moved over and smiled up at him. "Oh, is there more than one lesson?"

"Many more, little lady, many more."

Beth backed out of the library and shut the door. When Marco came around looking for his boss, Beth asked him if he had driven there himself. He said he had and she suggested he leave, Maverick would be in touch later. Marco didn't buy it, but left with a little smile under his moustache.

Beth made a quick run to the grocery store, feeling like a house mother not watching the kids. By the time she returned, both vehicles were gone. Alone. Again. And it was okay. Her center of gravity restored, Beth locked up for the night. Maverick left a note saying he'd finish early tomorrow. *Excellent.* Lisa's note said she'd call tomorrow and thanks. Signed Love Lisa. Cute.

Busy day, Beth Malone, as thoughts of a private eye hired to investigate Frank danced in her head. After a delicious spinach omelet, she decided to pack it in for the night but no. Three more calls came in from interested people, all word of mouth from club members. Beth explained she hadn't set a date for the first party as yet but she assured them, they would be on the first call back list.

Chapter 25

CCTV installed perfectly, holes re-plastered and painted, Maverick gave Beth the grand tour, explaining the system as he pointed out hidden cameras, dome cameras and warning signs that the home was protected. "Lisa knows how to operate the monitor." His face flushed when he mentioned her name. "Call if there's any problem and thanks for having confidence in me."

Beth handed him a check for the balance. It turned out to be less than the estimate. "I gave you the best deal possible."

"So did I." Beth smiled, they shook hands and he left.

Beth inhaled a deep breath, happy to know Maverick's fire had been lit by a more appropriate lady, especially someone as terrific as Lisa.

And now to work. Menu to plan, flowers to order, music, wait staff, silver and china, linen, maybe a dance floor in one of the rooms. Her head felt dizzy, overwhelmed with thoughts crashing into each other like bumper cars. *Oh, oh. This is what Lisa warned me about. No rush. Take your time and do it right and don't kill yourself making it happen. But if one relationship comes from the effort, it's worth it.*

Isn't it? Not if it hurts me. Please don't cry. Look how far I've come in seven months. One stroke at a time. Stroke? Coach always yelled: "one stroke—now two—now three, you can do it, Beth O'Brien. And I did. Yeah, but I was a kid then.

Beth adjusted her mental blinders to focus and have some fun with the concept. In order to be successful in this first venture, she wanted to put everything she'd gleaned over the years into being a perfect hostess. Twenty guests—twenty strangers. How to put them at ease right away? Television hosts knew a lot about their guests before interviewing them. Of course they had staffs of information gatherers; she was a staff of one, chief cook and bottle washer. What she did have was a strong desire to achieve success; trophy-winning success somehow lost in the shuffle of a forty year marriage.

Renewal time, Beth. Out came the possible guest list. She just spoke with Frederick Harrington. What did she know about him other than he was a recent widower and gallery owner in Tarrytown? Entering his name in Google, Beth was surprised to learn Frederick opened the gallery right out of college and thirty five years later, it was still the place to go. Discovering new artists was his passion.

Notations made and she went down the few on the call back list. Where someone wasn't to be found Beth was certain a well-placed phone call would be another way to gather information.

Effort, time, memorizing and well worth it. No rush with all the planning, decorating, soup kitchen and other activities. Lisa is so right. Probably the first or second week in December gives me enough time to do it without having a breakdown. Or maybe sooner, depending on how I feel.

Most of all at this moment, she wanted to hear from Lisa, didn't want to call her at work but so tempted. The phone rang. Hopefully, another response or Lisa.

"Hey Beth, Got a minute?"

"Lisa, I've got as many as you want. I'm so happy to hear from you. How was, uh, your evening?"

"Just as you might expect. Went to a truck stop for dinner, watched mud wrestling, got all steamed up, had sex in the back of his truck. You betcha."

"Huh?"

"Thanks Carolyn, tell Mr. Blackwell I'll call back in five minutes. Beth, you there? Where were we?"

"You were giving me a vivid description of last evening ending with 'you betcha'."

They had a fit of the giggles. Lisa said, "I don't have much time to tell you how dear a person Maverick is. Sweet, funny and kind, like that." She paused then talked fast. "We're having dinner Friday night. Must run."

"Wait and pardon me for asking but did you . . ?"

"Not on the first date, silly. He didn't even press his long lean. . .Oh God, I really must hang up. 'Bye."

Not on the first date. Just like when I was young but then it was don't kiss on the first date and don't ever go all the way 'til you're married. Times have changed and changed.

There was one more call to make before settling down to work; a call before Sister M&M called her—beat her to the punch so to speak. She dialed St. Paul's. A thin high voice answered, "St. Paul's. Top of the mornin'."

"Sister Mary Margaret, this is Beth. Is that you pretending to be a youngster?"

Hearty laughter came through the phone as the voice dropped an octave "You've found me out, Beth dear girl. My way of screening calls when no one else is about. What's on your mind today, as if I didn't know."

"I'm checking to see if you have a chef for tomorrow." She could picture the scheming Sister, feet up on the polished desk, tapping arthritic fingers together.

"You're a sweet lass you are to once again offer your culinary skills to our humble kitchen. I thank you and the Blessed. . ."

Beth laughed so hard tears fell. She begged Sister M&M to stop. "I give up. What's on the menu and what time shall I have the pleasure of interrupting my very important things to do?"

"A fine donation of chicken breasts and veggies arrived early today. Got me up before breakfast. I'll leave it up to your creative side to whip up a delicious and bountiful feast to feed the hungry souls who depend. . ."

Beth tuned out as Sister went on and on. Waiting, impatient but polite not saying a word, she doodled notes to herself. So caught up in an idea about the party, she almost missed Sister Mary Margaret calling her name.

"Beth dear girl, have you gone to sleep on me? I do tend to get long-winded sometimes and lay the blarney on with a heavy shovel. Truth be told, I miss your fine company."

"I miss you too, Sister Mary Margaret. I must work and slave today in order to give proper attention to the hungry souls so I'll say goodbye for now. See you about three p.m. tomorrow. Please save time for our afternoon repast."

Chimes rang out. She wasn't expecting anyone. Maria answered the front door, called to Beth something about a package to sign and she hurried downstairs. True to his word, Larry Cooper had sent the promised package.

"Thanks, Maria. Are you finished for today?"

Maria came back with purse in hand, coat already buttoned. "All set, Mrs. Malone. See you Friday morning. That Maverick, he's a nice boy. He and Marco did a good job cleaning after themselves. No extra dust."

Oh God, she thinks Maverick is a boy. If she knew what he and I were up to in the pool house and once upstairs. . . I must have been out of my fargin' mind. Hmmm. Come to think of it, I guess I was. Back then.

A few quick snips with a scissors and the package was open. Beth tore through wrappings, came across "Getting a Grip," Larry's current best seller. *How sweet is this*? Signed *Yesterday's gone, think about tomorrow, Larry. He's wrong. Yesterday's not gone yet.*

The next wrapped gift was the Blackberry with directions. A post it note said "now we can curl up together separately. *That's what you think, Larry. From now on, we talk; in person or on the phone like real people.*

She left the goodies on the kitchen table and floated to the cabinet where numerous cook books were stored. Somehow, Beth knew she must focus on a menu for the soup kitchen

138

tomorrow when all she really wanted to do was lie down with the new book. Hell, she'd been cooking chicken for years. Who needed a recipe? And dumplings she could make with one hand tied behind her back. It was almost dark, not yet but in a few hours and she definitely needed rest from all the excitement.

What excitement? Uh. Hey I don't need excuses to relax with my very own signed copy.

She poured a glass of Chardonnay, set crackers and Jarlsberg cheese on a tray and kicked off her clogs. Barefoot, she tucked the book under one arm and with a silly grin on her face, sauntered toward the family room.

Reading lamps were turned on and Beth snuggled under a beige and red plaid throw, head up on matching pillows in the cool room. She read the first page.

When you were a kid, bent out of shape about one thing or another, did your parents ever say: "Put your shoulder to the wheel and nose to the grindstone?" And you thought they didn't understand you and what the hell were they talking about and parents suck and you should run away but you only had thirty cents in your pocket and dinner was on the table at six every night and it would be dark. What they meant was, listen carefully because you're going to be tested on this and by guess who, readers? Why your very own kids some day. They meant--simply put: Get a Grip! Get Over Yourself. Get a job—earn money and find out how great it is to pay your own way.

And that was only the first page. *Wow.*

She dialed St. Paul's. Sister Mary Margaret said, "Yes, Beth."

"Sister, sorry to interrupt you but I forgot to ask if Karen has a chicken recipe on file and my other question is do you have an ample supply of potatoes?"

"Is the Pope Catholic?" The little nun hung up.

Questions asked and answered. Beth laughed out loud. She didn't have to research a recipe so she hunkered down and turned the page. Half way through the book, sleepy from wine and indulgence, the phone rang. It was fully dark now, the room too chilly. Beth reached out with lazy fingers and picked up the phone.

"Hmmm?"

Lisa said, "Beth, is that you?"

"Who else answers my phone?"

"You sound weird as if you're high or you just woke up. Everything okay?"

"Peachy. Larry, the shrink, sent me a signed copy of his latest book, 'Getting a Grip'."

Lisa loved the title from the laughter in her voice. "He also sent the promised Blackberry with directions. You'll have to hold my hand on this one. Maverick said you knew your electronics."

"He did, did he? About these gifts, does this mean you're engaged or what?"

"Or what. It scares me, Lisa. It seems like a mating ritual thing and I'm scared."

"Do you want me to stop by tonight?"

"Very kind but you work all day and I'm half way through his book and enjoying the writer."

"Beth honey, you said and I quote—"enjoying the writer."

Beth was silent, trying to recall what she said only seconds before. "No, I said 'enjoying the writing.'

"Sounded like a Freudian slip to me and on that interesting note, I'll say so long, friend. If you want me, call. I'll be home in a half hour and for you, I'm open twenty four hours."

That ended Beth's reading for the night. She needed a major swim, dinner and bed.

Chapter 26

A few calls trickled in regarding the Singles Salon. The word was spreading. One woman was a customer of Frederick Harrington's gallery. She divulged more information than Beth wanted to know at the moment and wanted assurance she'd be in on the first gathering. All right. There was a need and Beth Malone would fill it. She felt great. She didn't want to think about Larry but there he was looking attractive on the back cover of the book and in her mind. And he showed up on her email a few times asking where she was, did the package come and he'd miss soup kitchen tomorrow. He also mentioned leaving a message on her phone. He hated when that happened because he never knew if the person got the message or what.

She took a few minutes to send him an email saying she received his phone message, sorry to have missed him; she liked the sound of his voice; the book came and thanks so much for Mr. Blackberry.

Maybe he'll call again.

Hurrying to the church door, hands full with a carry bag of her own utensils and a couple of recipes plus the starched chef jacket and hat, she was met by Harold. His face was a world of woe. Grabbing her bag, he mumbled, "Lucy hurt bad."

They left her things in the kitchen and Harold holding Beth by the coat sleeve, almost dragged her to the door of the women's locker room.

She pushed through the door, calling, "Lucy, are you here?"

A muffled voice sobbed, "Uh huh."

Stretched out on the lounge bench, Lucy held a wash cloth to her face dripping pinkish puddles on the carpet.

Beth rushed to her side, spoke calmly, tried to soothe Lucy before removing the cloth to see what damage lie underneath. "Who did this to you?"

One eye was bruised, cheek lacerated and swollen. She tried to shake her head and moaned in pain.

Oh shit. The cut may need stitches. Beth said, "Harold, please get some ice and a clean towel. Hurry. Tell Sister Mary Margaret we need her."

Clearly agitated, he wrung his large hands in distress. "Sister M&M not here now." Beth knew he wasn't speaking as well as usual.

"Harold, I need your help. Doc Coop says you're a good helper. Please come in here after you get the ice. I must get a doctor or have someone drive Lucy to the hospital." She watched Harold respond. He nodded and she heard big feet pound on the marble floors. Again she asked Lucy who hit her. "Tell me or I'll call the police." The magic words.

Struggling to get up, Lucy made it to a sitting position with Beth's help. "No police." She held her head, rubbed the temples and whispered, "Boyfriend. Had one too many; when I told him to bring me here for soup night, slammed me in the kisser. Never laid a bad hand on me before. Not like the last guy." She started to cry and stopped. Lucy squinted at Beth.

"How's my mascara? Streaked, huh? We gotta get dinner cookin'."

Patting Lucy as she held her up, Beth inhaled a combination of whiskey, strong perfume, sweat, and coppery blood. Her boyfriend wasn't the only one drinking too much in the afternoon.

No time for a sermon. Not my job. I just came to cook and serve.

Harold peeked in. "Not s'posed to be here. Got ice and towel. What else?"

"First Aid Kit." He ran off. Beth assumed he knew what she wanted and where to find it. Sure enough, he was back in a flash. The big fella waited while Beth looked for something to cleanse the cut. "Okay. Lucy, bear with me. I know some basic first aid and maybe you won't need stitches once I get a better look." The well equipped kit had everything anyone would need for simple emergencies. Once the cut was cleansed, Beth applied antibiotic cream and a butterfly band aid. Leading Lucy to the mirror, she said, "It doesn't look too bad."

Lucy gasped at the swelling, the discoloration. "I want you to rest for an hour or more with an ice pack on your cheek. Ten minutes on and ten off. Careful to keep it low, away from the bandage." Turning to dependable Harold she asked him to find a blanket and cover Lucy.

"Thanks, Beth. You're okay." Her eyes closed.

"So are you. I've got to start dinner right now or we won't be ready for the hungry crowd. When Sister comes back, I'm sure she'll want to see you." She left a bottle of water next to the sleeping Lucy.

An inauspicious way to begin the work ahead but somehow, with a few church volunteers, a massive feast of stir-fry chicken and vegetables in a chicken broth sauce and mountains of whipped potatoes were in the final stages of preparation. With fresh fruit cups and cookies and pies donated by a bakery for dessert, Beth was positive no one would go home hungry. She prepared a repast of fruit and cheese for Sister, told the teens who came in to help that their job was to dice the fruit and fill little cups, and she smuggled herself out of the kitchen and over to the office. The Chardonnay in her bag clinked against two heavy wine glasses. Beth said, "Hush," and knocked on the door.

"If Joe sent you, come in." The little nun sat swallowed up by the black leather chair, black stockinged feet crossed at the ankle propped on the desk.. Instead of looking relaxed in the reclining position, she seemed weary and almost disheartened. Even the sun diffused by the stained glass window did nothing to soften her features as it did the week before.

Setting the snack on the desk, Beth opened the chilled wine bottle and poured two glasses. A silent toast to whatever was on their respective minds as they had a bit of fruit.

Sweet juices of melon and strawberries mixed with bananas restored color to Sister's cheeks. She broke the soft silence. "Our visiting doctor saw Lucy and said whoever tended to her should be commended so I thank you. Beth, you have a knack for taking charge of a situation." She sipped some wine. "I'm saddened by the physical abuse of dear Lucy and fear for her safety. This person she calls her boyfriend has led her down a path of poor choices. And it's not the first abusive boyfriend."

Beth started to speak and Sister shook her head no. "I know Lucy is a grown woman past fifty years in age and she should know better. But like so many of our flock, she's lonely and first she put up with verbal abuse thinking that wasn't too bad. Now this. I've prayed knowing it was bound to happen but my prayers were not strong enough."

Gnarled fingers clasped each other and she bowed her head over them; white hair usually in a neat bun, hung in wisps around her face. Faded blue eyes gazed at Beth. "What do you suggest I do short of putting out a contract on that slime bucket?"

Embracing the lady she'd come to admire in a short time, Beth smoothed her white hair back in place and thought before speaking. "Sister, I told Lucy I'd call the police and she said no. That's the first option. Now you and I must come up with a viable plan to stop this bully." Beth pulled the visitor's chair closer and Sister bent her head to listen. "One thought is for us to go to the bar he frequents and confront him. Wear your habit, maybe full regalia, I can dress kind of the way you're dressed."

Puzzled, Sister said, "This is your viable plan?"

144

"Yes. They fear the wrath of God no matter what they say. And you are a representative of God. We go in dignified, speak our piece in front of everyone, shame the little shit. Sorry Sister."

Sitting back in the over-large chair, Sister said, "And what if it doesn't have any effect on him?"

Warming to the idea, Beth said, "Then we hit him with a pool cue and run like hell."

"Beth, dear girl, you are naive□. It would be suicide to try a stunt like that. However, you've certainly grown and changed since you walked into St. Paul's a month ago."

"I guess I got carried away. What can we do?"

Finishing the fruit and wine, Sister said, "I've already called Melanie at the Women's Shelter. She's on her way. Lucy agreed to counseling to boost her self-esteem and a place to stay for a while." She sighed, removed her glasses and polished them.

"Would you mind if I got in touch with Larry Cooper? As a psychiatrist, he certainly has insight to similar problems."

"Ah, I didn't realize you two were so friendly."

When Beth tried to object, Sister shook her head and smiled a worn-out smile. "Be cautious, lass. I mentioned before that he's a troubled man."

"Thanks, Sister. I will keep your words in mind. If you ever want to play nuns and robbers, I'll be your faithful novitiate."

Beth glanced back before closing the door. Sister Mary Margaret's eyes were shut, deep breathing filled the room with a light snore. Sometimes the nun, small in stature, seemed to be six feet tall with authority and wisdom; tonight she was merely worn out with attempting to solve everyone's problems.

And I have two hundred dumplings to make.

Once again, soup kitchen was a success in spite of the drama, the hungry folks went home satisfied.

Chapter 27

The next day, weary after two hours of talking herself through the Blackberry directions, Beth plunged in to the maiden voyage. Lisa wasn't available to show her the way. Her advice was to follow instructions as if it were a recipe—one step at a time.

Hmmm. Easy for her, difficult for me. Text messaging. Everyone seemed to be doing it. Here goes nothing.

Larry, sorry 4 not getting back 2 u. hope message comes thru-this is first text message. R books flying off shelves? If u need plain citizen to write blurb 4 back cover next book-I'll do it. Luv this 1-so far half way thru. Lucy at St. Paul, beaten up by boy friend. She's the 1 at dessert table. Sister sending her 2 Shelter but I wonder if you might suggest someone to counsel her. Feel sad about this situation. B

Beth-happy 2 hear from u and Mr. Blackberry. Looks good. Sorry 2 hear about Lucy. Melanie at Shelter-fine therapist. I couldn't do better. Will b back 2day. How about din. Sat if better 4 u. Want 2 sit in small cafe□ w/u. It's not 2 soon, B. Just din. L

He's right. Just dinner. Not moving in; not making moves. I like him . . .a lot. So what's the big deal? Say yes.

Thanks. 2day good. Advise what time. not 2 confident about night city driving. U'll have 2 come 2 the boonies. Small cafe¢s locally. Time?

8 2 late?

Live in country-not a bumpkin. 8 fine. c u, B

She hit end on the Blackberry and pressed it against the warmth of her cheek. The way Beth felt right now, she could have heated the state of Rhode Island. She tried to recall any time in her life when she felt quite like this and drew a blank. Hard to be cautious when she felt like this. Time to find out how Larry Cooper was in person.

Wait a minute. Did I say okay for tonight? What was I thinking?

Already it was noon. She'd spent the whole morning with the Blackberry; no exercise, planning for the multitude of projects on her mind. And now a date. No, she corrected herself, a simple getting-to-know-you dinner. *Sure. First things first. What to wear? Call Lisa? No. I'm a grown-up who hasn't gone on a date since uh, 1966 give or take a few years. Oh my God. Call Lisa.*

"Lisa Marcus."

"Emergency call from Beth. What do women wear on a Friday night to have dinner with a man the first time."

Not missing a beat, Lisa rattled off, "Beige satin jeans, rust and beige jacket ruffled trim with beige camisole underneath—maybe a little cleavage—not too much. Nice for September."

"Sounds perfect, except for the cleavage. I don't have anything approaching that kind of look in my wardrobe."

"Oh. Who's the man?"

"Larry Cooper."

"Uh huh. Better go shopping."

"No time."

Hearty laughter through the line. "Since when does a woman not have time to shop for clothes? Go now. I have one hour. Meet me at Dusty Rose in town. They have the most current fashions."

"But..."

"Right, get your butt in the car and meet me. The clock is ticking."

Beth grabbed her keys and purse, opened the front door to find Maria about to ring the bell. "Oh Maria, I have to run out for an hour. Please look at the list in the kitchen. Thanks. If a delivery comes, have the man bring it to the pool house." She called over her shoulder, "Lock the door."

"I do, Mrs. Malone. Remember, today I go home at five."

The tinkling bell on the door at Dusty Rose added charm to the lovely shop. In the early years when Beth tried to be fashionable, this was where she shopped. True to her word, Lisa was not only there but already she searched through the racks for Beth.

"Look, these are the pants I described." She held up beige jeans made of stretch satin.

"What size are you?"

"I think six or eight, maybe."

A double take from Lisa. "To me you look like a four." Another search produced the pretty jacket she'd described over the phone. She plucked a light camisole from a stack, glanced at sizes and pulled another. "Here's small and one in medium. Try on and see if you like the outfit."

Bewildered, Beth said, "How do you know about these particular clothes?"

"Because they're exactly the ones I'd love to wear but I'm too big. Now go."

To Be Continued

A few minutes later, Beth peeked out to beckon her friend. Lisa hurried over to the dressing room. Beth stood on a small platform near the mirror wearing the new outfit, brown hair askew in a ponytail, wearing socks. She had a silly grin on her face as if to say 'do I look nice or what?'

"Beige shoes will finish it off. You'll razzle-dazzle him, Beth."

"I, uh just want to look up-to-date, you know?"

Lisa hugged her. "Got to run. Enjoy the evening and call."

"Thanks." This shopping was fun. She'd get home in plenty of time to swim and, and. . . She couldn't think of another thing except the evening ahead.

At home, Beth tried on the new clothes once more, cut off the tags thereby making them hers. She thought the look was attractive, youthful and definitely comfortable. After a shampoo, she'd blow-dry straight and add some shine spray. No goofy pony tail tonight. At four o'clock, she was ready for a swim. In the library Maria polished furniture and wiped the last bit of dust from the CCTV installation.

"I'll be in the pool house so when the delivery comes, send the man to the back and tell him to ring the bell. And thanks Maria. Your envelope is on the kitchen table."

Maria smiled. "I leave at five today, Mrs. Malone."

Stepping out into the darkening day, Beth was surprised to hear thunder and see lightning followed by huge raindrops. Too preoccupied to check the weather forecast, she wondered if Larry's flight would be delayed and if he'd be able to drive north to see her. *Oh fuffa!* Or maybe it was just a passing storm and no big deal.

As always, the chlorine scent drew her like a magnet. Worries seemed inconsequential, aches and pains non-existent, all was right with her world. Beth swam her repertoire of strokes, imitated the graceful moves of Esther Williams doing the back stroke lifting gleaming shoulders from the water. Delicious fun. The loud buzzer interrupted her pleasure. Damn, damn. Must be the chemical delivery. Late for him. Five fifteen.

Climbing out of the pool, she flung her cap to the floor, wrapped a towel around her waist and strode the indoor carpet to the door. She unlocked it and said, "Working late tonight?" She stopped. "Larry? Uh. Larry. Come in." He was dripping wet, pushing a hand truck with several boxes of pool supplies covered with a tarp. And Beth was barely covered with a soaking towel. Not the outfit she had in mind on their first date.

He dragged the truck over the threshold, removed the tarp from the boxes and grinned.

"I'm a little early. Sorry." He didn't look sorry at all to Beth's eyes but she let him go on as she dripped. "Flights east were canceling so I flew out on the last available flight, rented a car at the airport and drove right here. Called and Maria said to come. When I pulled up she was leaving, said you were in the pool house. The delivery guy didn't know what to do with the packages so I said leave the hand truck and," he stopped to catch a breath and smile directly into her suspicious eyes, "the rest is history."

"Well, Larry. You've caught me in my element," she gestured to the pool, steam rising with bubbles now that she was out. "I was almost finished with my workout."

"Please don't let me interfere. I'll wait outside . . .in the storm . . .with thunder and lightning for company."

That made her laugh and he joined in.

"Make yourself at home. There's a coffee machine and coffee in the kitchenette and some energy bars in a drawer."

Beth threw off the towel, ascended the ladder and dived.

He never did make the coffee, spellbound by her expertise as she went through all the dives that won medals and trophies so long ago. He gave her a standing ovation when she climbed out of the pool and handed over a white terry cloth robe.

151

"If I had a medal to bestow, I would do so. Instead, allow me the honor of planting this for now."

The gentlest kiss touched Beth's forehead; she felt his warm breath down to her wet feet. "Thank you, Beth Malone."

Nice.

Beth made coffee and answered Larry's questions about the structure and tropical setting.

He pointed to the dome camera in the ceiling.

"Good idea. Is this the project you mentioned, securing your property?"

They sat in lounge chairs and relaxed. "Yes. I was advised to have CCTV installed when a friend, she's a business consultant, heard my plans to have parties here. Most of the guests will be strangers even though they'll be sanctioned. The house has some valuables and lots of rooms were added. It would be impossible for me to keep track of everyone." She glanced at Larry. "Too much information?"

He threw his head back and laughed. "Not nearly enough, Beth. I enjoy seeing this side of you. I'd like to hear more about the parties, if you're willing." He climbed off the chair, took their empty cups to the kitchen and Beth heard the sound of water as he washed them. *Very nice.*

A quick change into sweats, jacket and boots and Beth was ready to check out the weather; find out if the cafe¢ was open; if not, what to cook? Plan B.

Waiting by the door was the welcome sight of Larry. His face lit up.

"I thought you ducked out to go shopping."

Beth laughed. "I did that this morning."

She opened the door to find the rain slowing down although the wind was fierce.

"Quick." Pulling him outside, Beth secured the door and they hurried to the back sliders. Once in the house, Beth said, "Weird weather. I'm going to take a shower and dress for dinner. I'll put your raincoat in the dryer. Good thing you had it with you. Make yourself comfortable. Cheese in the fridge, crackers in cabinet to the right. Browse. I'll be down in thirty minutes."

As she ran up the stairs, she heard the refrigerator open and a smile spread across her face. *Larry's comfortable in my home.* Beth's high heeled shoes coming down the stairs were slower than the ones she took going up. Larry must have been listening for her return because before she reached the landing, he was there waiting. No mirror reflected her image as well as the expression on his face.

"Thanks, Beth. You're worth waiting for." Coat on, he seemed eager to leave. "How far is the café and what time is the reservation?"

"About fifteen, twenty minutes. The reservation is for 8:30. It's only 7:30 now. Would you like a drink before we go?"

"Not before we get in the car, thanks. Let's go. The roads may be slippery."

Beth started down the hall toward the front door, Larry close behind. She turned, shot a worried look at him. "Is something wrong? You seemed so pleased when I came downstairs; I was very happy to see your reaction. I've never worn clothes like this."

"The trouble is that all of a sudden, I'm pleased looking at you. It's not the clothes, Beth, although you look like a model in them. But even soaking wet in your bathing suit, I felt the same way and I don't want to scare you off; make you want to run and hide. I just. . .like you . . . a lot. Great wordsmith, right? I sound like a teenager. I figured if we hurried to the restaurant, had dinner and talked, I'd calm down and feel normal." When he grinned, Beth saw the young man he once was. "So nothing's wrong. Where's your coat or do you have an umbrella?"

When his hands lingered a moment too long helping her into the new raincoat, Beth didn't mind although an echo of Sister's words found a way into her head. *Be cautious.*

Chapter 28

Calling too early for Beth to think straight, Lisa said, "So how was he? Larry. Your date last night."

"Nice."

"How nice?"

"Very."

"Beth, I woke you, didn't I? Sorry, I couldn't wait one more second. Go back to sleep and call me."

"No."

"No what?"

"Don't hang up, I'm awake." Beth yawned and stretched.

"The twins called with a surprise. They're taking the train down this morning. And Beth, Maverick wants to meet them, hang out, play ball, do stuff. What do you think?"

"Enjoy every moment, Lisa. Call if you need me." She hung up, laughed out loud just for the fun of it and started the day.

Sitting in the kitchen, Beth enjoyed the view. Rain had a way of washing the world super clean; the sun attempted to burn away morning clouds. Tall sunflowers needed staking as did a lot of the flowers. Lots of repairs to keep her busy. She sipped coffee, picked at a bagel with cream cheese reliving the best evening—except for the beginning and end--she'd had in years.

La Petite Auberge, the French restaurant they went to was filled with a lively Friday night crowd. Calling at the last moment because the cafe□ she planned to take him to was closed, she was happy to snag this particular reserved table toward the rear in an alcove. Very secluded.

Several people swiveled heads to watch Beth with a date. "Country club nosy bodies," she said to Larry. Nodding hello she moved on. At last, the table for two. Just as she pictured it in a daydream but then she thought of Larry with some gorgeous young model and here he was with her.

Larry leaned across the table through the tapered candles. "You've set the place buzzing."

"How so?"

"Looking glamorous as if you own the place, an unknown man breathing down your neck."

"Is that why my neck feels damp? I thought it was from the rain."

Am I the least bit amusing? Frank never thought so.

He squeezed her hand then examined and turned them to look at both sides. "So small and delicate. For such a capable person, I expected a larger hand."

"Not too delicate, Larry. These hands are strong."

The wine steward appeared, an antique key dangling from a velvet cord around his neck.

Larry held up his hand. "We'd like to see the dinner menu first, *si vous plait*. Only then will we select a wine." A knowing smile from the wine steward who beckoned a waiter with a menu.

In answer to Beth's curious gaze, Larry said, "I like to match and blend taste. Humor me, please."

Beth nodded, interested in learning more about him. Sister Mary Margaret referred to him as the mystery man and here he was, revealing the mysteries.

"This cafe☐ is elegant. I assumed we were going to a simple place with candles in raffia wine bottles on checkered tablecloths, pasta of every kind on the menu."

"Sorry, I deceived both of us. The cafe¢ I referred to is closed for renovation. Since I haven't been dining out in many months, I figured I'd call at the last minute. So here we are. It's not too shabby for the sticks. Lots of city people come up for the local color; see the natives at work and play, some of us wear shoes—use forks, you know, quite civilized." Shaking out the black linen napkin, Beth spread it across her lap and smiled. *I'm having fun and I do believe I'm flirting.*

"You made your point, funny lady. Even if the cuisine isn't up to snuff, being here with you is the best time I've had in a very long time."

They were quiet for a while, eyes engaged 'til Larry broke contact and studied the menu as if it were something profound. "Fine French restaurants are well known for sauces and superb presentation of specialties." He touched his forehead, imitating a psychic. "You prefer salmon without sauce to spoil the purity of the fish."

He opened his eyes and grinned when she blinked in astonishment. "So far—on target?" Beth blinked yes. "I prefer..."

A quick scan of the menu and Beth said, "Beef medallions in vegetable puree¢ with sliced mushrooms in a burgundy butter reduction."

Delighted, he said, "Yes," and signaled the waiter while humming, "You were meant for me. . ."

All I need is Ginger Rogers and Fred Astaire to come waltzing in. Pinch me, someone. Larry.

Two hours passed in camaraderie and when they left La Petit Auberge, the feeling clung to them. At Beth's door however, Larry reverted to earlier behavior when he grew restless and ready to bolt. He reached for his suitcase left in the entrance hall, thanked Beth for a wonderful evening, didn't try to kiss or hug or even shake hands. Mumbled something about seeing her at soup kitchen Thursday... and was gone.

"Well, I had a wonderful time too, Larry." She yelled at the closed door. "Would you like to come up to my daughter's childhood room and get naked with me? Or I have lots of rooms we could do it in. Take your pick or what the fuffa?"

Climbing the stairs, she began to strip. *He said he liked me a lot and the evening was amazing. It's just as Sister Mary Margaret said; Larry is a troubled man. I need to be around healthy people. Sorry to say but it's so long Larry. And good luck. Would've been nice to at least kiss him. Being single is not for Sissies.*

Chapter 29

Tan and fit after a month hiatus, Jenna Stanley, clinical psychologist, welcomed Beth into her sun lit office. Pausing to adjust the blinds on this mid September day, she gestured for Beth to take a seat. They sat in the now familiar arrangement facing each other, small table between. Jenna smiled, folded her hands and waited.

Beth shifted uncomfortably in the chair not knowing where to start. After a few minutes of silence, she began to speak. Like a broken water spout, words poured out." I've been on this merry-go-round of pushing myself to work, to succeed and finally my friend, Lisa, I told you about her, suggested I slow down, hold up on the singles parties I'm planning while I redecorate and make sure everything is in order before the party happens in order to be successful which is so important to me and in my head I keep hearing my swim coach telling me to do one more lap and I just now realized I'm not that kid anymore. And the man who likes me, I think and I liked him. It's so juvenile. Larry Cooper—he's a psychiatrist, maybe you've heard of him, he wrote "Getting a Grip." Well, we emailed back and forth after meeting at St. Paul's soup kitchen where we both volunteer and oh, Sister Mary Margaret cautioned me against getting involved with him because she said he's a troubled man. Anyway, when he asked me for a date and we went out for dinner. It was great, wonderful but he acted weird afterward because he said he liked me a lot and didn't want to scare me off and I haven't heard from him since."

Jenna handed her a box of tissues. It was then Beth felt the tears coursing down, soaking the front of her shirt. Mopping up, Beth said, "I'm a mess. And then I saw a new lawyer and she suggested I hire a private investigator to locate Frank, the missing husband. She says it's important to get evidence that he left me to be with another woman. Adultery is a crime in New York. And this is what my previously uncomplicated life has turned into. A mess. Now I need your counsel. Please."

Leaning forward in the earnest way Jenna had, she said, "What do you think is a good path at this time?"

"Oh no. Answer a question with a question. Shrink talk." Beth focused on a narrow path, a swim lane, her lane. "Okay. My plate is full right now and with the business ahead, a grandchild coming and as chef the next couple of months at St. Paul's, that should keep me out of mischief for a while. Regarding Doctor Larry Cooper, I would tell my daughter not to chase after a guy. Not that she ever listened. Let him sort out his feelings and come running after me. Otherwise, it's his loss. As for Frank, the first chance I get, I will definitely find someone to discover where he's been since March and with whom."

She searched Jenna's face for approval and received only a nod. Beth headed for the door. "Thanks, Jenna."

"Your time isn't up, Beth."

A wave from Beth and a click of the door was her response.

For the first time in years, on the way home Beth pulled into a drive-in and bought a hot fudge sundae. *Mmmm.*

Chapter 30

Organized work and enjoying her projects was the key. Beth had plenty to do with soup kitchen every week and Thanksgiving coming up in two months; but the big change in her thinking was to have the first party in mid October. By then decorating must be finished.

Another meeting with Hilliard and Lisa this week. They were so much fun. She was half in love with the amazing decorator who was an evening entertainment all by himself. She still hadn't talked to Susie about the Thanksgiving soup kitchen first and home dinner after. Better tackle that now. In the past, Susie always needed to ease into changes.

"Suzette-mother-to-be," said the cheerful voice.

Her daughter never sounded like this before.

"Hi honey, what a nice greeting. Are you as happy as you sound?"

"Hi Mom. Yes I am. We're having a girl. How adorable is that? Come shopping with me, Mom. Baby girl clothes are the cutest."

Sitting down to absorb the news, Beth pictured holding a granddaughter—like her own daughter, a new start; a whole future she'd be part of. She choked back tears, not wanting to spoil Susie's moment. "Of course, honey. We'll have a great time getting ready for the baby."

"So what's on your mind, Mom? Is it about Thanksgiving? I know you like to plan way ahead."

"Yes. First of all, my friend Lisa Marcus is coming with her twin sons who'll be home for the holiday from college. Did I mention that I volunteer at St. Paul's Church soup kitchen on Thursdays?"

"No."

Don't like the sound of that. "I've been doing this for a while now and, of course, Thursday is Thanksgiving so their dinner is at two , same time as ours."

"So."

Oh—oh. She's not taking this too well. "And their cook is pregnant, due soon with complications and has to be off her feet 'til delivery so I'm kind of the only one who can take charge."

"Which means?"

Acting like a brat. "It means I need all the help I can get for a couple of hours before coming home and having our celebration. Now Lisa and her boys will help me and I was hoping you and Javier will come too. You know, like one big happy family." Beth hoped the thing about Lisa and the twins was true.

"Hold on."

After an interminable amount of time, Susie came back. "Okay. I talked it over with Javier and he said fine. We'll help any way we can. Tell me what time to come over and we'll travel together. It should be interesting and fun. I'll set the table before we leave. And Mom, when can we go shopping for baby stuff?"

"Are you free tomorrow after school or are you too tired then?"

"Too tired to shop?" Her daughter's bell-like laugh rang in the phone. "Never. I'll be at your house by three. You drive, okay?"

"Yes. Okay."

Stunned, Beth made plans with her daughter and sat for while wondering where did she go right the past few months. One thought tickled the back of her mind while she nibbled on a salad lunch. *What to do about a real bedroom of my own? If*

I knocked out a wall between two smaller rooms upstairs, a large room accommodating a new king or queen sized bed and a balcony would be perfect. No more child's room for me and I'm going to labor over this. Call Maverick about the carpentry? Why not? He's moved on happily to Lisa and could probably use the money.

Late afternoon Lisa called. "The twins are home for a few days but have to leave Sunday. We'll postpone our meeting with Hilly and finish up Monday. Kenny and Todd said yes to helping at the soup kitchen." Breathless with excitement, she rattled on. "Right now, they're playing ball with Maverick—shooting hoops at the athletic center here. It's wonderful to see them together, Beth. Beth? Are you there?"

"Of course. I'm getting a kick out of your happiness. You've loosened up so much since we met. What's Maverick doing for Thanksgiving?"

"Well, I hate to impose but it would be kind if you'd invite him. He's grown very dear to me in a short time."

"Lisa, I don't want to sound like an old biddy but please be careful of giving your heart away too soon."

"Thanks for the advice. I haven't given away any part of me so far except for my friendship. How 'bout that, you old biddy."

"Oh my God. I could have used some advice from you before. You're a lot smarter than me, young lady. On another note, I've been sleeping in the room my daughter grew up in since Frank left. Now I'm grown up and want a bedroom all my own with no memories. Would you mind if I ask your Jack-of-all-trades- if he does carpentry or knows someone who does? I need a wall knocked down, I think."

Laughing, Lisa said, "When they return and have hot chocolate, I'll ask my boys. The oldest one, that is. Call you later."

So, they weren't intimate. Amazing. They were becoming friends first, enjoying each other's company like in the olden

163

days. Lisa's smart. Wise might be a better word. She's setting a good example for me.

Beth checked for text messages. *Nope. Nothing from Larry.* She went swimming.

A jubilant message from Lisa was on the answer machine. "Maverick will be over at nine a.m. if that's all right with you. He'd be happy to look at the project. The boys are coming along. They have experience in building since their Eagle Scout days. More to follow."

This last bit of information caused Beth's eyebrows to raise. Eagle Scouts? Kenny and Todd seemed too good to be true. She better get to sleep early tonight to be bright eyed and bushy-tailed for Lisa's trio of strong men.

Nine o'clock sharp. Door bells chimed. Three smiling faces appeared at Beth's door.

"Hi men." Tall. They were all tall and the twins were identical. Rosy cheeks, not too much blonde facial hair, maybe they shaved twice a week, but long and lean. Maverick looked fine as always, maybe better. "Anyone hungry?"

"Not right now," said Maverick. "Right, guys? We want to check out the job first. Oh, this is Kenny, blue parka and Todd, brown jacket. Mrs. Malone."

"Beth to you. Your mom and I are close friends."

Removing their gloves, they shook hands and grinned in stereo.

Beth led the way upstairs after making sure everyone wiped their boots on the mat.

Through the wide hallway upstairs, she led them to the rooms she thought might be expanded into one. "What do you think?"

She watched as Maverick consulted with the twins, knocking on walls, checking to see if any were load-bearing and what might work. He asked if there were blueprints. She had to think about that question. If you were a blueprint,

164

where would you be? Logically, Frank would have kept it filed in special home papers, of course. She excused herself and went to the study. After an intense search, Beth located the rolled blueprint and hurried back. The men/boys were seated in a circle on the floor drawing, each one with an idea worth listening to. The harmony was almost overwhelming for Beth to take in. *This is the way a family unit should be.*

She handed the roll to the first hand to take it. Todd, maybe. It didn't matter. Unrolled, they searched for load-bearing walls, pipes and more she didn't understand; they talked quietly among themselves and finally Maverick smiled up at her. "We can do it. At least make a start.

The guys only have a few days but they'll be back in November. Let's have something to eat and we'll talk about your expectations and what we can accomplish."

To her delight, they took over the kitchen. Kenny, or maybe it was Todd, seemed to be the chef-in-charge and the other two were designated assistants. Beth backed out saying she'd already eaten and had work to do.

In her small office, she checked email, Blackberry, and as a wild card, checked her phone messages. Still no word from Larry. Instead of taking it like a—*what's the expression Lisa always used*– 'like a lox on a plate,' Beth straightened up, turned off the computer and went swimming. She didn't plan to win a prize and if Coach showed up, she'd tell him she was too old to be his Golden Girl anymore. She was going to enjoy her pool; the only thing in her marriage she fought for and won. And later she'd go shopping with her daughter for the baby.

Today, concentrate on joy.

Chapter 31

By the time three o'clock rolled around, Maverick and the twins were gone. They'd be back in the morning. Beth baked oatmeal cookies with wheat germ and raisins for Susie as a pick-me-up, smiling the whole time. When a weary Susie came in, the first thing she did was sniff the air like a puppy and followed her nose right to the kitchen. Dropping into a chair, she reached for two cookies and the waiting glass of milk.

"Oh Mom, you didn't forget. My faves and so delicious."

Beth stifled the urge to gather Susie into her arms and never let go. Instead she sat and enjoyed a sight she didn't expect to see for a long time. A beginning at last. "You can take the batch home with you after we shop. Javier might like them."

Laughing, Susie said, "He's pregnant right with me. When I get heartburn, so does he. He also felt nauseous the first few months. I hope he doesn't go into labor when I do." She finished two more cookies and the milk. "Hit the spot. I'll go to the bathroom and let's split. There's a terrific baby store a few miles south in the big mall."

At first Beth drove as if she was carrying a dozen eggs on the front seat until Susie said, "Move it, Mom. I'll deliver before we get there the way you're driving. I won't break."

The mall wasn't too crowded and Beth pulled into the parking place Susie indicated was closest to the shop. The noise level was Las Vegas without the slot machines. Oblivious, Susie barreled ahead Beth in tow and soon they barged into a wonderland of miniature clothes. There were very few pastels like ones available years ago, pale pink, baby blue, soft yellow, pastel green. Beth grabbed a cart and tracked

Susie, the wild woman as she held up camouflage cargo pants with ruffles, a similar skirt and tights to match. They giggled and Susie threw them in the cart. Tie dye shorts and tank top in pink. In with the pile. Beth steered toward nighties and what Susie called "Ones-ies," tiny t-shirts that snapped in the crotch. *Cute and oh, the colors!*

"Stimulates the baby, Mom."

Stimulated the mother as far as Beth could see. The most fun Beth had in a long time and to see Susie like this was incredible. There were mothers with babies in strollers and Susie stopped to talk to everyone asking questions about sizes. Beth heard snatches of conversation with words like Similac and breast pumps, labor pains and dilation and moved on before anything else was said.

She called to Susie, "How about diapers, bottles, necessities, blankets. Let's make a list."

"Javier wants to shop for what we call baby needs. You and I just want to have fun together." She threw in three pair of tiny shoes; pink sneakers, suede boots with Velcro straps, and beach sandals.

Blinking, Beth said, "Babies don't walk for a long time, honey."

"I know that, Mother. I want our baby to be fashionable," adding red patent leather Mary Jane's to the cart.

"Right, honey. It's getting late, though. The cart is full and I'm tired. Happy but tired." *I'm not tired but I know she is and when the adrenaline wears off, she'll crash.*

"Oh, sorry Mom. Can we do this again soon?"

"Yes, honey. Sit down while I check our purchases through. I may even get a credit card here. The sign says you get a discount with a credit card."

What a day. At home, Beth packed Susie into her car with many bags and said she'd call Javier to alert him that she was on her way home. He'd carry everything in the house. Maybe even Susie.

Chapter 32

When the door closed on her daughter and Beth was in the quiet, too quiet of her home again, she felt let down—deflated. The excitement of work going on upstairs and shopping for her grandchild with a renewed closeness to Susie stripped away and she was alone. Confused about Larry, Beth found her resolve not to contact him weakening. So she made a chart of pros and cons—good points and bad points; and when she finished, it didn't take very long, Beth discovered she'd built a romance out of smoke and mirrors. No substance.

Examining her clean face in the mirror after a refreshing shower, Beth decided it was a good face with a fine future. Gone was the mourning over men who walked away. Wherever Frank was with his trophy didn't matter. It hurt sure but he wasn't worth it. And what the fuffa was Larry Cooper to her? No one. Just silliness while she got through a bad spell. Someone to occupy her thoughts. *Well Beth, move on. You're too smart to waste precious time.*

Wandering around the big house, Beth stopped at the entrance hall. Her imagination caught fire picturing hopeful guests at the door. One by one, what would be the nicest way to welcome them? She read somewhere that the White House welcomed their guests with a tray containing pre-poured white wine, champagne, and water. They entered with something to drink in one hand. Assign one of the wait staff. Music soft and rhythmic to stir the blood. Maybe the bossa novas–she had several arrangements. It worked at other parties she'd given long ago.

Why not? One bite size hors d'oeuvre. No mess or toothpicks to get rid of. Garnish tray with herbs or parsley.

She scooped up a pad of paper and a pen and wrote fast. Dinner music. Mozart. After dinner go for smooth jazz or old standards sung by, her mind ran through the catalog, Fred Astaire and Gene Kelly. Wonderful voices without the polish of famous singers. Back to the food. Simple food beautifully prepared scratching her original idea to go trendy or fancy. The plan was to keep it comfortable without resorting to chips and dip. Beth felt a smile tug at the corners of her mouth and she laughed. Alone in the house and laughing.

The flyers and letters were printed, had been for weeks. All she needed to do was write in a date. She pulled over a calendar, selected the Saturday before Halloween giving her time to get everything finished. Already word-of-mouth guaranteed nine women and eight men. She'd start calling them now and finish tomorrow to confirm availability. Gather wait staff, finish with decorating, and plan menu.

Lisa was right. It took careful planning in order to be successful. Beth wasn't successful yet but she felt it in her blood, in the air she breathed. Good things were coming her way.

Chapter 33

Somehow two hectic days passed with Maverick and the twins working on the bedroom enlargement. With all the hammering, drilling, and whatever-ing they were up to, Beth found herself cooking pots of chili and beef stew; the food list went on and on with three working men to feed. Never in her life had Beth been so active and she loved it. Laughter from the guys, music ranging from classical to country to rock brought vitality to her quiet home. Old shag carpeting pulled back revealed hardwood floors in perfect condition. Beth remembered an area rug she admired at a specialty shop when, during the shopping safari with Hilliard and Lisa, they discovered a platform bed. Perfect. They knew where the best and most unusual pieces of furniture could be found. In one year, Lisa was friendly with merchants where Beth knew no one; her life had been so limited. No more.

Todd—or maybe it was Kenny—suggested a built-in sound system and television and how about a gas-fired fireplace? He sketched a corner with the fireplace and a flagstone hearth and smiled up at her. "We could build this over Thanksgiving."

Maverick examined the drawing and nodded. "It'd look nice right over there," gesturing to a corner. "Mind if I add something, Todd?"

"Sure but you'll do it anyway, boss man." The guys grinned and punched each other in the shoulder.

A rough sketch of furniture placement, tall windows, and everything they talked about appeared on the page. It was the kind of creative process Beth thrived on and it was happening right here in this old unused section of the house built so long ago. When it was finished, she'd call Hilliard.

Walking to the windows at the very back, she looked out at the pool enclosure. This would be her first view of the world every day. Beth turned to the expectant faces and smiled.

"Bells and whistles, guys. That's what I want."

Before leaving them to huddle over new plans, she turned in the doorway. "As a special thanks for all the work you've done this weekend, I'm inviting you to a pool party this afternoon."

Whoops of delight followed Beth as she hurried off to ask Lisa if they had other plans.

She stopped when a voice called her name.

"Beth, how about brick instead of flagstone, more, uh feminine. What's that? White brick, says Maverick."

Closing her eyes, she pictured pastels, Impressionist watercolors, white brick. Yes. "I like it. Thanks a lot, Kenny or Todd."

"Kenny, the older and smarter one."

Laughter rang out as her thoughts raced ahead. *Stop. Don't race. Enjoy every moment.*

Pausing, Beth caught up with her thoughts and breathed deep and slow. Then, in spite of her own warnings she hurried to the phone.

Chapter 34

After the usual reaction to the enclosure, Beth said, "Listen up, men. I haven't had guests in my pool before and I'm assuming you know how to swim."

She felt eager eyes watching every move she made. Transformed from nice lady into swim coach, Beth sprouted horns. She watched, surprised as the twins jumped in the water, one feigned drowning and the other did a great job of rescuing him. From two lounge chairs on the side, Lisa and Maverick sat grinning.

"Australian crawl, anyone? Push off, stay in an imaginary lane and show me something good."

It became a race, of course; twins battling to see who could swim two laps the fastest.

Beth said, "It wasn't a race, men. Since you turned it into one, Kenny wins by a nose."

Todd pulled himself over the edge of the pool and dripped a path to Beth. "Not fair."

"Why?"

"Kenny's nose is bigger."

With a laugh, Todd dived off the side and did a nice exhibition of the various strokes he knew. After that, it was a free for all with Beth demonstrating moves the boys picked up quickly and then they dived. The enclosure rang with laughter for the first time and Beth realized how selfish she'd been keeping it all to herself.

Eventually, Lisa, looking almost svelte in a black, high cut in the leg, suit and Maverick in surfer trunks, slid off the side into the moderate water. They waded a bit then swam side by side and seemed to play tag, laughing close together. Beth and the boys slowed to observe them from a distance, Beth with a finger to her lips.

She cut through the water like a fish, popped up in front of the boys and said, "How about pizza?"

They grinned. Kenny said, "What about Mom and boss-man?"

"Let's not disturb them right now, okay?" and gestured for them to follow her.

The tall young men made a Beth sandwich on the way back to the house. They lifted her up and swung Beth as if she were a child again. This was high on the list of one of her best days of an awful year.

Between mouths full of pepperoni and sausage pizza delivered twenty minutes later,

Kenny and Todd in dry clothes now, thanked Beth for being a good friend to their mom. "She was lonely, yeah, for a long time, and now whenever we talk to her, she's so, uh, so happy. Right."

They talked in tandem, beginning or finishing what the other was saying.

"I feel the same way about your mom. She's my best pal."

They saved a few slices for Lisa and Maverick and cleared the table.

"I appreciate the way you pitched in with Maverick and I'll pay you for your work just as I would any carpenter. Don't say no."

The boys looked surprised. "Say no? We never say no to money, food, or . . ."

Kenny said, "Whatever."

One happy family waved goodbye and Beth was alone. This time she welcomed the quiet. Satisfied in the changes to her home and herself, it would be nice to share it with a companion. For now, Beth was happy with her life.

Chapter 35

Wrapped in a towel after the evening swim, Beth strolled back to the house after locking the enclosure. Her mind focused on dessert for the first party. Three flavors of crème brulee served in small ramekins along with everyone's favorite, tiny chocolate chip cookies, or? *No, leave it be.*

Before entering the kitchen Beth paused to gaze at the sky. Peppered with a generous dose of stars, a dash of billowy clouds and one sliver of golden moon. A recipe if she ever wrote a cookbook for romance. She reflected on the darkness, losing one minute a day until daylight saving time. Clocks fall back in one month. Survival one season at a time. So far—so good.

Locking the sliders, Beth turned to see a body peering into the refrigerator.

Oh my God! I'd know that ass anywhere. Jaw dropped, Beth froze.

Frank Malone straightened up, cheese in one hand-- tomato in the other, a huge smile on his whiskered face. "Lizzie," he said, arms outstretched as he advanced. "I heard about Susie's pregnancy. We're going to be grandparents. Can you believe it?"

He moved to embrace her, food still clutched in both hands. Beth ducked under the tomato and said, "Get out."

"Ah Lizzie, I must've been having a mid-life crisis and now I'm back."

Face contrite, ever the performer. No wonder his patients loved him, she thought. He could appear boyish, serious, sympathetic, sexy, kind; whatever he believed his audience required.

No more, Frank; show's over; long run ended when you walked out.

Again she said, "Get out, Frank."

Ignoring her he sliced the tomato and some cheese, placed them between two slices of whole wheat bread already coated with mustard and sat down. He bit into the sandwich, chewed and swallowed and took a long pull of beer. "You know sweetheart, I was sure I'd get a warmer welcome than this."

Soulful eyes peered up at Beth where she remained frozen to the same spot at the sliders.

Another bite, another swig.

Time for action. She hurried to the phone, hit 911. "This is an. . ." Frank twisted the phone from her grasp and hung up. They were very close now.

Smiling down, he shook his head. "Honey, you don't really want to call the police."

Slick and seductive, just his style, Frank led his wife to a kitchen chair and continued with the bedside manner perfected over years of practice. "Wine?" When she didn't respond, he opened a chilled bottle Chardonnay and poured a glass setting it in front of her. "You're wet from the pool. I love when you're wet, remember?"

Blinking, Beth stared at the husband who walked away in March and out of who knows where, just turned the key in the lock she'd forgotten to change and walked back in.

"Get out Frank. Now. Take the sandwich and beer and get out."

For a moment he appeared startled. "But this is my home, our home. I have nowhere to go."

"Wrong. This is my home now. Maybe Susie will take you in or your buddy, Bruce. For the last time, get out and give me the key."

Bewildered, Frank plodded toward the front door, glancing left and right as if taking a quick inventory of changes made since his departure. Pausing at the door to what used to be his office/trophy room, he opened his mouth to speak.

Beth cut him off. "Keep moving. It's my home."

At the door, Beth held out her hand. "The key."

He made a big show of removing it from tight jeans and slapped it in her hand as if it were a surgical instrument. The door closed behind him with an audible click of the lock.

Heart pounding, back pressed against the door for support, Beth said out loud, "Just when you thought it was safe to go into the water. . ."

Even though Frank appeared to deflate as she marched him out, Beth knew he'd pump up soon enough. She hadn't seen or heard the last of Frank Malone.

Finally Beth had gotten into good eating and sleeping habits and Frank was back plummeting her into a sleepless night. Pillows on the floor, fitted sheets in a tangle, the single bed she slept in a total wreck. The too early ring of the phone wasn't welcome.

Groping for the phone, Beth said, "What?"

Susie, nose totally out of joint, yelled, "Mother, how could you throw Daddy out of the house? I told you it was a mid-life crisis. He heard about the baby and hurried home to be family again."

No amount of deep breathing is going to fix this.

"Honey, I can't go into this right now. The most important thing for you to do is stay happy and healthy for your little family's sake. Let your parents work out their problems. On a happy note, I loved shopping with you and look forward to the next trip. Now I have to run. Bye." She hung up on Susie calling out, "But Mother."

Locks changed by the local locksmith, shiny new keys replaced old dull keys. Is this what Frank thought he was doing when he left? Beth wondered; exchanging his dull old key for a shiny new one? And what happened, Frank? The shine wore off fast.

Cross-legged on the entrance floor, Beth held a new key in one hand, old key in the other. One represented possibilities and a fresh start; the other--her old life. It took courage to move on alone to the unknown. The old life wasn't great but it was familiar. Again she allowed tears to fall. Sun coming through the clerestory windows warmed the metal keys in her open palms. Tight fingers closed into a fist. Slowly Beth got to her feet. Choices. *Hang the keys next to each other as a reminder before I do anything stupid.*

Call Lisa was on her mind when she voted no to the thought. Lisa, happy for the first time in years, didn't need any distractions. She called Lisa.

"Hi, it's early but I had to talk to you."

"Just going to call you, partner. Signed us up for doubles tennis. Starts next week. We'll practice at my condo with some guys. Okay? Don't say no. What's up?"

"I forgot about the tennis but okay. I'm rusty but I'll catch up. What's up is, are you sitting down?"

"Oh, oh."

"Frank showed up last night." Beth proceeded to tell the whole incident and Lisa alternately squealed and gasped.

"So what's next?"

"Locks are changed and I need you or Maverick to check the video to see if he's snooping around. I'll get a restraining order if I have to."

"Okay. What a shocker. Will you have to change the party date? Remember we have the last shopping to do with Hilliard later. I'll pick you up at five."

"Party date is on. I am so ready. Menu planned and almost a full list of guests. I smell success."

Chapter 36

After relating the story to Jenna Stanley, her psychologist, Beth said, "And then I said get out and give me the key." Gulping water, Beth mopped tears, sat back and waited for the inevitable.

Leaning forward, Jenna said, "How did you feel?"

Angry, Beth bolted from the chair and paced. "How do you think? Furious, scared, what's next? Just when I was doing so well, he shows up. Almost back to square one. I don't know what to do."

"And your daughter?"

"That's a laugh. We've been bonding. Nothing like shopping for baby clothes to provide family cement. He tells her about his mid-life crisis. I wonder if that's the girl friend's name. Susie falls for poor dad's story. Now she blames me for not taking him back." Beth ran out of steam and fell into her chair.

Jenna said, "What do you want?"

Glancing around the quiet of the psychologists office, the peace it stirred in her, she found answers. "I want peace, harmony, Frank gone. I want to find my own way. I have all the papers, the letter and his will. He left me in comfort."

"Make a list of your goals and don't worry about others. Focus on what you choose to accomplish. You foreshadowed his return when you said your new lawyer told you to hire an investigator. Time to do it, Beth and get those blinders on. You're in good hands."

Blinders on so securely, Beth passed the ice cream drive-in without stopping.

Chapter 37

Punctual as usual, Lisa showed up radiant and worried at the same time. The fierce hug she gave her friend almost lifted Beth off the floor. "Let's talk about this latest development in your most interesting life, Beth Malone. Never a dull moment."

"Who, me? I'm just this little homemaker abandoned by *ad nauseum* and trying to survive."

"And doing it quite stoically with an occasional burst of hysteria," Lisa said, leading Beth down the hall to the newly re-furbished family room.

Right out of a decorating magazine but with a broken-in look, the walls had faux texture in pale to walnut tones. A few area rugs warmed the buffed-to-a shine hardwood floors, and the comfortable couches covered with a nubby beige fabric had some unusual hand-stitched velour throw pillows scattered about. Patterns of colors flowed one to another; lavender, soft yellow next to a strip of orange, a hint of sage green; each one like a painting, and in a corner a signature. *Hilliard.*

Beth said, "The tables and lamps are coming tomorrow." Collapsing on the couch, a pillow clutched to her chest, she sighed.

Hands on slimming hips, Lisa surveyed the room. "A few more touches and this room is *fini*. What do you think?"

"Hilliard should bring in whatever he thinks will work. I'll make the final selection and he'll do whatever he wants to do. I can't take any more time to decorate."

Chimes rang out. Lisa glanced at her watch. "Right on time, thirty minutes late. You sit, I'll get the door."

Pleased to have Lisa take some of the burden off tired shoulders, Beth leaned back and closed her eyes. Muffled voices at the entrance and quick steps down the hall got her attention. She opened her eyes to find Hilliard, Lisa, and a pert blond cop standing in front of her.

Intimidated by the sudden company, Beth rose and said, "What's going on? Is this about Susie? Was there an accident?"

"Not to worry, Beth. This is Tommy, Hilly's roommate. She's a policewoman about to become a detective."

Surprised, Beth shook Tommy's firm hand. Tommy said, "Hello," displaying dimples, green eyes, and a friendly smile. "If you don't mind, I'll have a look around at Hilliard's work." She turned, glanced over square shoulders, a mischievous grin on her pixie face. "I don't need a search warrant, do I?"

Hilliard balanced on one booted foot and then the other as he watched Tommy scrutinize his work. Poker face set, she strode back and on tip-toes, reached up, grabbed him by the leather lapels of his jacket and pulled his head down so their lips met. The room sizzled for a minute.

"You did it. This is the best. When you get the pictures up and. . ." They almost danced down the hall to see the living room.

Lisa beamed at her surprise guests and Beth tried to gain composure.

"I thought he was. . ."

"I thought so too until I met Tommy. She's irresistible for him and tough as nails."

"You rotten wretch. You didn't warn me."

"Didn't want to spoil the surprise. So many times it was on the tip of my tongue." Lisa sat next to Beth and said quietly, "Do you have a secret you want to 'fess up too, good buddy, so we can clear the air?"

Beth searched her soul and knew truth was the only way. "I had sex with Maverick two times. Before you met him. It was foolish and stupid."

"And great." Lisa patted her hand.

"That, too."

"And you introduced him to me and we're so good together. So it's okay. Just don't do it again."

"Never." Beth held up her hand in a Girl Scout's salute. "Scout's honor."

Their eyes met and they laughed until tears fell and Beth grabbed Lisa by the hand and with some effort, pulled her off the couch. "No crying on the new couch. Let's find the kids."

They found them in the kitchen, rummaging in the fridge.

"Call the cops, Lisa. Strangers are robbing my refrigerator just like Frank did the other night."

This brought a reaction from the young cop. "Who's Frank?"

Lisa said, "Do you want me to tell, Beth?"

"Sure. I'm not up to it.'"

Quickly Lisa gave a thumbnail sketch of what happened up to Frank's sudden appearance in the kitchen last week.

"Did you report it?" Tommy said.

"I tried to but he stopped me."

"How?"

Hilliard said, "Let's order Chinese food, my treat. This sounds fascinating."

Gesturing to a drawer, Beth said, "Menu's in there. I like chicken, broccoli in white sauce. They deliver." She brought out the Chardonnay and a bottle of Merlot with glasses and set up at the kitchen table.

"I'm off duty. This'll hit the spot." Lisa and Hilly joined them as Beth filled in the story of Frank leading right up to where she threw him out and how the next day the slender thread she was mending with her only daughter shredded when Susie, after hearing about Daddy's mid-life crisis, said Mother, no longer Mom, was cruel not to take him back. Beth emptied her wine glass and groped for more.

During the recitation, Tommy removed a spiral notebook from her shirt and took notes.

"Cop short hand. I have a few questions and some observations. Back in March, how did he leave the house without you hearing?"

Pained to recall, Beth said, "He must've slipped a little something into the champagne so I'd sleep soundly after sex."

"No way to prove it. Next, did he take money and what's the financial situation?"

"He left me very well off. Even signed divorce papers although later my new attorney told me the papers were worthless. She advised me to convince Frank to see a Divorce Mediator and if I can prove he committed adultery, threaten him with a law suit. The bank assured me I am financially in fine condition. His partner bought him out of their medical practice when he so-called retired."

"Okay. But everything you have is marital property. And the only link to you is your precious daughter he intends to blackmail you with."

"Blackmail? Well Susie's pregnant with our first grand baby. Oh, that's the first thing he said when he backed out of the fridge. He heard about the baby and hurried back. We're going to be grandparents, he said. That's when I told him to get out and tried to call the police and he took the phone out of my hands and said I really didn't want to do that and he seemed so beaten when he left. And forlorn."

The food was delivered, talk interrupted while Beth ladled out portions heaped on plates and chop sticks went into action. Beth needed a fork. Lisa gave up and needed one as well.

Between forks full, Lisa said, "Does this remind you of soup kitchen, Beth?"

"Kind of. Only I didn't do the cooking. Only the ladling. Nice for a change."

Hilly said, "You volunteer at a church?"

"Yes, St. Paul's in Northtown. They have a kitchen you could die for. Their soup kitchen dinners are well known. Are you two planning to get married?"

Tommy and Hilly choked and laughed at the same time. "It's on the agenda," she said.

"It's a gorgeous place, if you want to be married there. I'll be your chef, treats on me."

"Thanks. That's very nice. Back to the scumbag." Tommy scanned the notebook. "He'll hold the baby and daughter hostage over your head in an effort to re-establish him back into your life. Okay if I make this a personal investigation? This kind of scenario happened to my mom and she let the s.o.b. back in the house. Life was never the same. I'll have to pull in favors but I know where some bodies are buried and I'll dig."

Beth took a deep breath. Another crack in the armor she protected herself with broke and let sunshine in. "Fine with me. What do you need?"

"Where has he been since March and who with. What's the name of Ms. mid-life-crisis? There must be phone records, credit cards, cell phone calls. What's the name of lawyer?"

"Bruce Bradley, his best friend. Another scumbag. Tried to make out with me in his office."

"Okay. This may take a while but you keep your chin up and don't get stupid. Any questions, call. Don't, under any circumstance, let him in your home. I want to get the goods on him to be able to prove to Susie that Daddy dear gave up her Mom to run off with some trophy. When it didn't work, he came back, sure you'd fall to your knees, grateful." With that, she gathered the dishes, forks, chopsticks and swept everything into the sink. "Forget shopping tonight, Sweetheart," she said to Hilly. "This cop has work to do. I'll go with you tomorrow after the ceremony, when I get my shiny new badge and we can play cops and decorator."

A quick wave and they left. Hilliard called out that they'd be back tomorrow night and thanks again for her generous church offer.

"She's a marvel, isn't she?" Lisa said, clearing the rest of the table.

"They both are." Beth sat still, hands folding and refolding a paper napkin.

"Should we scrap the doubles tournament?"

"I feel like –first a question-who rose from the ashes? It's either Biblical or mythical."

"Beats me. Can't think clearly at this moment after all that's going down. Hey, I sound like a cop."

"Anyway, I feel like I've risen from the ashes to build a new life and I feel very strong. So we'll practice tennis with the men at your place and then march on the courts and play to win. Teach me your strategy and we'll show the bitches."

"Well spoken, partner. Tomorrow after work, is the first session. See you then."

Chapter 38

Beth decided to screen all the house calls and respond only to the party calls on the new line. The first party was full. Frederick Harrington was coming. Good. She already did homework on this guest and felt confident on keeping a conversation going. James-call me Jim-Corrigan, New York State congressman—divorced, was easy to Google. Grant Morgan—Connecticut banker—widower. Many of the men would be easy to research.

The women surprised her. She expected most of them to be kind of sedentary, stereotyped stay-at-home ladies. *Shame on me.* More than half were still employed, four CEO's of corporations unrelated to cosmetics or fashion but computers and publishing. Dynamic women, divorced or widowed seeking companionship. Two actors and two doctors, one dancer, one principal of a high school and one a professor at a local college. And where would they go to meet someone? Certainly not to a singles dance or bar. *That was the #1 response to my letter and flyer.* This should be an exciting mix.

She walked through the rooms to be available to the guests. The living room looked splendid, more formal than the family room yet welcoming with sage green velour couches, the sculpted cushions combined with pillows by Hilliard gave them a custom appearance. Walls were covered in palest sage natural silk. Draw draperies in ivory and ivory woodwork. An exotic flowered shawl draped over the piano was elegant. What a difference. And Hilly said something about a picture, a painting he was bringing tonight.

She moved on to the garden room at the back of the house. Similar to a Florida room with jalousied windows, white rattan furniture, the old cushions replaced with a fresh design from Hilliard's private collection. He called it his cottage industry, farming his designs to trusted skillful seamstresses for the finished product. Plants hung everywhere, thriving on the light. The floors were hardwood, left bare for dancing.

My team of friends, she thought. *Each of them helping me to get through this time.*

Chapter 39

On the way to the club Monday, Lisa repeated her mantra, "We play to have fun and to win."

"I never had fun on the court before. It was always so tense, everyone judging you if you made a poor shot."

"No more. Not with the strategies we worked out. Remember the signals and the fun. When you're at the net, hand goes behind your back to let me know if you're going to poach across. I'll quick move to the other side and come to the net. Always keep them guessing. Lots of smiles between you and me. High fives and such. You're a great lobber so lob over the net person's head and I'll put away the next shot. They'll go for you thinking you're the weakest. I'll be there if you can't handle it but chances are, you can."

"I love our outfits. Lycra skirts with shorts underneath and tee shirt tops. White's good."

"Like Wimbledon. We look like pros. Let's do it."

Arriving at the club just in time to sign in and get the court assignment, they waved to women not seen for months. Lisa had lost twenty five pounds, Beth's hair was long, highlighted and they strode with confidence to the locker room.

"We've got them buzzing about us, now let's pour the coals on as we take this first round," Lisa said. She glanced at Beth as they walked to the courts. "Nervous?"

"Sure."

"Good. Use that nervous energy to win."

Beth shot her a skeptical look and said, "Sure."

After the match, when Beth and Lisa posted their winning scores, old acquaintances came by to congratulate them on the win. Big smiles all around and with a wave goodbye, the team left the club grounds.

"How sweet it is," Beth said and they high-fived.

All the way home, the bubble never burst. Reliving every shot, every mistake, was the best. They laughed, gossiped about the reaction of the bitches to them as a team, and moved on.

Lisa cautioned that today was possibly the easiest match. Next time, they played at another club and the competition might be more difficult.

Beth said, "No problem, partner."

Hilliard and Tommy pulled up right behind them, in a rental truck. They looked gleeful, the cop and the decorator, as they began hauling out tables, lamps and very carefully, two large wrapped canvases.

Beth said, "Why didn't you let the store deliver?"

Hilliard shrugged. "Didn't trust them."

"Wait while we change. Don't want to dirty the winner outfits."

Lisa and Beth hurried up the steps, Beth unlocked the door, reset the alarm and left the door open. They heard grunting as they changed into sweatshirts and jeans and ran down to help. Already tables were in place in one room and lamps on floors were set down as more items were brought in. Tommy put the women to work right away and before long, the truck was empty. Beth was curious to see what lay behind the wrapped canvasses. Hilliard ran out and carried the smaller one to the family room; ran back and the larger one was brought to the living room. Now the women followed as if he were the Pied Piper and they were the townspeople.

Something wonderful was about to happen. "Drum roll, please," called Hilliard, the master showman. With a graceful flourish, he unwrapped the canvas. Beth and Lisa gasped. It was an underwater scene done in oils, thick gobs lifted in different directions to create moving water, and the figure of a woman swimming, one arm stretching out, the other arched back to stroke forward, legs powerful. Beth moved closer. "First Love" was etched on a brass plate. Bottom right corner, the signature, *Hilliard*

"I thought it would look well here." Hilly indicated a strategic place on the wall where, as you entered the room, the painting would catch your eye first.

"Yes." Beth said, "Yes, yes. It's beautiful."

"When Lisa told me about your swimming ability, I had the idea and started painting. It's my gift to you, my lady no longer in decorating distress."

Beth laughed and cried and thanked him as he hung the painting and the women helped with the tables and lamps and this room was definitely finished.

The living room was next. Everything fit as expected and before Hilliard unwrapped the painting, he said, "If you don't like this, I'll kill myself. No pressure, Beth."

Erotic was the word that came to Beth's mind at first sight. Not in an overt way but subtle. A woman seated on a park bench reading a book, unaware of the breeze lifting her skirt too high. A man's hand across her lap helping the breeze or patting the skirt down? Rendered in watercolors, framed in a carved gold wood frame about 3 feet by 3 and a half feet, it evoked a different era yet looked as if it was happening right now. "Hello" etched in brass, signature *Hilliard*.

"It looks like a museum piece."

"This is my first show."

"I'm honored, dear Hilly."

Lisa said, "Sure adds a bit of heat to the living room. And now kids, let's call Maverick and celebrate Tommy's promotion."

Tommy grabbed her man by the arm and said, "No way, but thanks. We have to return the truck and go home to play cop and decorator. But tonight you be the cop, okay?"

"So where are the handcuffs?" he said. Laughing, they ran out.

"Wait," Beth said. "Where's the bill? I want to pay you now."

"I'll be by tomorrow. Invoices in the kitchen."

Chapter 40

"What a month, huh?" Lisa watched as Beth tried to put the finishing touches to her make-up. "Here, let me do that." She pried the brush from Beth's quaking hand and ran a light blush over Beth's high cheekbones. "You looked so calm about an hour ago. In fact all month you've been on top of everything. We won all our matches, no further annoyances from Frank. Tonight's organized to a fare-thee-well and the weather's perfect. What more can you ask for?" She zipped Beth's simple black long dress with sheer sleeves, cut low in the back, high in the front and patted her shoulder. "There. You look fine."

"I could ask for a kind word from Susie to begin with."

"Tommy said she'd have information today or tomorrow. She's about completed the file on the secret whereabouts of Frank Malone and company. Tonight we focus on a new beginning, not just for you but possibilities for twenty guests taking a chance by coming to your gracious home."

This was the long awaited date, October 24th. All the effort, planning, agonizing over and the fun. Don't forget the fun, Beth thought. It's Party time. Time to slip the blinders on and focus only on tonight.

"And look at you, chief of the wait staff in disguise. Mighty impressive in your white starched shirt, black tie and gold and black plaid vest. I do like these colors better than the red and black plaid. Those pants look nifty. Losing the last fifteen pounds did the trick."

Lisa strutted around the room. "Okay. I'm in charge of the wait staff; make sure food is served in a timely fashion as instructed; keep an eye on every fargin' thing I can think of while not tasting a morsel. That's my job while not earning a nickel. Right?"

"What's your point, my partner and best pal?" Beth added one last brush stroke of blush to her cheeks.

"The point is tonight you're acting like you're wielding a whip"

"What?"

"Yes. Bossing me around as if I'm your slave."

A worried frown crossed Beth's face then vanished. "Well, my friend, tonight you are."

Lisa thought for a minute and shrugged. "Oh. Okay."

They grinned at each other. Beth reached into her jewelry drawer, withdrew a narrow velvet box and presented it to Lisa.

"What in the world?" Lisa said and opened it. A diamond tennis bracelet lay nestled in the satin fold. "Wow! I can't accept this."

"A long time ago Frank gave me a tennis bracelet. I had it sized, loved it and wore it all the time. Last year, he surprised me with this one forgetting I already had one. Not wanting to upset him since he was so pleased with himself, I left it in the box. In retrospect, he must've felt extra guilty that day, huh? So now we each have one to wear to matches as we win the tournament." She fastened the bracelet on Lisa's wrist. "What would I have accomplished without a friend like you, Lisa?"

"Cope. You'd cope. But together is more fun. Thanks. So much." They hugged and hurried down the stairs; Beth to greet the first guest; Lisa to start the music and do her job.

An actor/waiter who once played a butler on one of the soaps, escorted the elegant Frederick Harrington to the living room. His eyes lit up appreciatively as he first gazed at Beth who walked toward him, hand extended in greeting; then at the beverage tray another waiter offered. He selected champagne and entered the room.

In a rich baritone voice he said, "This welcomes me to your home as did the parking attendant when I arrived. I don't mind being first tonight."

A great start.

After that, the guests arrived one at a time, commenting similarly. Inside, Beth was exhilarated. Frederick paused before the painting titled Hello. He scrutinized it from every angle doing everything but taking out a magnifying glass for a closer look. He signaled for Beth's attention before popping a bite size stuffed mushroom in his mouth.

"If you please, Beth. Who is this Hilliard, the artist? I haven't heard of him."

Excited, she composed herself and smiled. "He's a remarkably talented young man. There's another Hilliard in the family room, if you're interested. Dinner will be called in twenty minutes."

"I am indeed." He tucked the arm of Fern Rosen under his and they walked off in search of the room talking like old friends. Fern was the CEO of a computer corporation; the chemistry between them obvious the moment Beth made the introductions.

It was a lively gathering, people chatting and tapping toes to the bossa nova rhythm. No one seemed to be shy. Beth watched for signs. Probably the champagne and wine loosened any stiffness and the music and one bite hors d'oeuvres did the trick. Beth casually walked among guests, using the information she had to break the ice. When a few of the men congregated separately from the women, Beth lured them into mingling. The educators were destined to sit next to each other at the table; as were seating arrangements for creative types and so forth. She tried to match careers when possible and hoped the mix worked.

After an hour of playing getting-to-know you while settling into the surroundings, a small bell tinkled announcing dinner. Beth led the way down the hall to the dining room as she pointed out the various rooms and the bathroom facility. A polite chuckle came from the group and some of the men actually raised their hands to be excused. That brought a huge laugh and a lot of comments. The ice was definitely broken. Music changed to Mozart as they approached the dining room.

Lit only by tall white tapers in crystal holders lined up like soldiers down the center of the table, the dining room was eerily beautiful. Appreciative *oohs* and *ahs* came from the upscale gathering, surely accustomed to fancy dinners. Beth's heart was full listening to the praise, knowing stark simplicity created the stir. Silently she thanked Hilly and Lisa for their help. She hoped it wasn't too dim to read the place card but everyone found their places and continued to chat.

Beth sat at one end of the table; the other end had no chair. Ten guests on either side.

Men in suits or sport coats with ties; the women were either dressed way up or very casual but they all presented well. No sequins, a few sparkles on a dress, all wore outfits in traditional fall colors of rust, gold, brown and hunter green. Beth was the only one in black and pleased about her choice. She wanted to be background, a shadow, the facilitator, didn't want any of the men to be interested in her.

The wait staff entered with the first course and a hint of aromas wafted in. Contained 'til now by fans vented to the outside, Beth didn't want the house to smell like cooking before it was time to serve. Lisa led the way with arugula, half a poached pear, and chopped walnuts served in shallow glass bowls. Ramekins containing blue cheese were there for those who desired a sprinkle on top. The wait staff placed each one on a china plate and asked the guest about dressing and cheese. Oil and vinegar or balsamic, also in containers, were ready to be poured by request. Black olives, carrot and celery sticks on crushed ice lay in shallow bowls down the center of the table.

Beth observed Lisa as she leaned over the banker from Connecticut, Grant Morgan. He spoke a few words to her and whatever he said caused Lisa to grin. A becoming blush rose to her cheeks.

There was a lull in the conversation as guests ate the delicate salad and bit into small hot biscuits; a noticeable rhythm like a quick in-coming, out-going tide because as soon as the salad course ended, conversation swelled. Plates cleared efficiently and suddenly a parade of main course dishes were marched in. Guests nodded, chatted and they all seemed at home.

In my home.

The choices were broiled salmon with or without a special sauce, or beef tenderloin medallions in Béarnaise sauce with mushrooms. Beth had asked the guests to make a selection prior to the party adding allergies so there wouldn't be any last minute confusion. In this day of sugar free, fat free, gluten free diets, everyone's needs were taken care of without embarrassment. Vegetable de jour was a guaranteed favorite. Everyone loved savory Yukon gold potatoes mashed lightly with yogurt, low fat milk, chicken broth, parsley, chives and seasoning.

Glasses were filled with wine, champagne or water as requested while nods and murmurs went on through the main course. Beth made the rounds to touch base and encourage as much friendship as she could. As the table was about to be cleared, she hit her glass with a knife to get some attention.

"While the exceptional wait staff," everyone applauded, the wait staff bowed, "clear the table and before we have dessert, coffee and tea, I wonder if you all would like a seventh inning stretch?"

Laughter and clapping as the guests rose with more than a few grateful groans. "You might want to continue conversing in the family room or head back to the garden room. The floor is made for dancing. I'll show you the way." The music beckoned with Fred Astaire singing,

"Dancing in the Dark." Beth gave a surreptitious glance at her watch. Nine forty five. The party would end at eleven. *Don't rush the guests. Keep the mix going. Mingle.*

197

To Be Continued

Entering the softly lit garden room made Beth feel the most comfortable. Almost but not quite a greenhouse, it brought the feeling of outside indoors. She was drawn to the windows looking out on the pool house. The full moon shone down bathing the area with a yellow shimmer. A warm hand pressed her bare back.

"Is that what I think it is?" A husky masculine voice whispered in her ear.

She wanted to pull away, smack him, but no. She was the hostess. "I'm not a mind reader so I don't know what you're thinking. It's a pool enclosure."

Turning, she found the author of children's books, Joe Andrews, standing too close.

Forced to let go, he gave her a toothy grin.

"Joe, we haven't spoken very much this evening. There's someone I'd like you to meet." Beth steered him to a wicker love seat where Corrine Barnes, owner of a pre-school was sitting alone for the moment. Plump and pretty, curly gray hair fluffed around her face, she brightened as they approached. Beth made the introductions.

"You two have much in common." Corrine tilted her head as if to say, like what? Joe adjusted his tie and did some male posturing. "Joe is a well-known author of children's books and you, Corrine," Beth paused, a mischievous look on her face, "were once a child." It provoked a chuckle from both of them. Beth moved on. Glancing back, she saw Joe take a seat and become animated using his hands as he spoke.

The dancer, Joanne Barry, pulled the Congressman away from speechmaking and they danced to "Singing In The Rain" sung by Gene Kelly. Several others joined them in the makeshift ballroom.

A tap on Beth's shoulder, quiet consultation regarding dessert service. Lisa said, "Going great guns, pal. Do we set up in the dining room or less formal, the family room and maybe this room?"

198

"This room and the family room. A table with coffee and tea and mini crème brulee, three flavors. Just flame the tops fast and out. Don't forget the miniature chocolate chip cookies."

"How do you make food so small? Stuffing mushrooms that little must have been a bitch."

"Later."

Detached at this point of the festivities, Beth felt like the chaperone. She observed guests dancing, others in eager conversation, set apart from their games. Anxiety from months of planning ebbed away and she was left with what? she wondered. Deep inside was emptiness in this Noah's Ark of a party. Ten women—ten men and her. What she wanted was to play getting to know you.

"One hundred dollars for your thoughts," said a husky voice near her ear. The comment brought laughter before she turned to see the man speaking. Sam Taylor. The sports agent she'd had contact with in the early stages of gathering the guest list. What she'd found out about him was impressive. The man in person was even better. He crackled with contained energy, dark brown eyes had a way of gazing at her. No, not at. More like they shared a joke—some special knowledge. *Or am I reading more into meeting him like some teen age nitwit?*

"You already paid your dues but my thoughts aren't worth it."

He held out his arms for a dance and as if they'd made this move for years, she entered the circle and they danced. Gene Kelly sang "You Are My Lucky Star." After a few turns, one hand on the bare skin revealed by the low cut back of her dress, he said, "Remarkable muscles, Beth. Swimming and diving, right?"

"My love affair with chlorinated water." She gestured toward the lit-up enclosure.

"Ever think of going pro?"

Beth did a double take and re-examined his face. He didn't seem to be flirting. Those dark brown eyes looked as if they always talked business. "Sam, I'm not a kid anymore, in case you hadn't noticed. I competed and won but that was a very long time ago. I swim every day for myself."

He shook his head and dark hair streaked with gray tumbled nicely across his furrowed brow. "I'm considering the possibility of gathering talented mature swimmers for competition and exhibitions. Think of it. A way to promote health and beauty for senior women." His gaze was intense, energy contagious.

No longer dancing, they went over to the windows. "I'd like to see you swim. Are you available tomorrow?" Beth felt a surge of excitement. Coach's voice shouted, "You can do it, Liz O'Brien. Go for the scholarship. A free ride, free ride." She turned it down back then to put Frank through medical school. *Don't turn down another possible opportunity.* Her face lit with the reflection of the moon through the window and an inner light long extinguished caught fire. "One o'clock works for me, Sam."

He handed over a business card.

"Can't read without my glasses and this dress doesn't have pockets."

He said with a grin, "I can see that."

She smiled in return. "Leave the card in the guest book at the door, please."

"I wanted to assure you I'm legitimate."

"You were vetted before you arrived." She squeezed his hand, hating to break the connection and returned to hosting, announcing to the guests, "Dessert is served, kids."

Lots of laughter and comments when Beth said "kids" as the mature guests congregated around the dessert table, snagging cookies as they waited for beverages.

With a new lift to her step, Beth moved down the hall to the family room to find dessert in progress, Lisa in charge. "You look like you have a secret," Lisa said.

"Mmmm. Show and tell later. This is definitely one of the most satisfying experiences in my life."

Tea in one hand, a plate with chocolate, strawberry, and vanilla crème brulee in small ramekins in the other, Beth searched for a place to sit. She perched on a comfortable chair and tasted her special recipe.

The art dealer and the computer CEO sampled dessert under Hilliard's painting "First Love." They looked as if something good was cooking between them. Beth overheard positives comments about dessert. If she could sing worth a damn, this was the moment to burst into "Some Enchanted Evening."

The banker, Grant Morgan called out, "Here's to our charming hostess, Beth Malone." He raised his coffee cup and sipped. "I understand that everything we dined on was created from your recipes and that you either cooked and/or supervised every detail of this great party. Is this true?"

Applause from the guest and the others strolled in from the garden room and joined the toast.

"Guilty as charged. A labor of love, let me assure you. And the proceeds go to St. Paul's soup kitchen fund in Northtown. You will receive a charity donation receipt in the mail."

"But Beth," the banker continued, "a dinner like this has a monetary value much higher than the one hundred dollars you asked for in the flyer. That's not a good way to conduct business."

Not pleased to be discussing business in front of everyone, Beth was embarrassed. "This is my first business venture. I still have to figure things out. Thanks, Grant."

Lisa hurried over to Grant Morgan's side and spoke privately to him. He nodded. He said, "This evening is the highlight of what has been up until now, a dreary time for me.

I thank you from the bottom of my heart for extending your hospitality and friendship."

"Hear, hear," a woman's voice called out and a communal spirit surrounded Beth.

And soon the evening ended. By eleven thirty, the last goodbye and thanks for a lovely evening was said. Beth kicked off her shoes and faded into a chair. Maverick strolled into the family room and settled on a couch. Lisa stuck her head in the door. "The slave is overseeing the clean-up in the kitchen. Then I'll frisk the kids and come in."

Maverick said, "Then we'll play surveillance man and the maid and I'll frisk you."

Beth said, "How did the party look through the monitor?"

"Amazing. It's all on tape. You threw a wonderful party tonight. I caught a few possible match-ups."

"It's like buying a lottery ticket. You never know. At least with this one, I had an educated chance to make things happen. Did you have something to eat?"

"Of course. I have an in with the maid. Food was the best, Beth."

"Unzip me Lisa, please. I must change into sweats before we do a quick recap and you go home, okay?" Zipper down and shoeless, Beth padded to the stairs. "I may never smile again. My face is tired."

Lisa surveyed the finished clean-up of the wait staff. They looked as though it were party time. "Wonderful job, gang." She handed each one an envelope. "We'll call on you again. Thanks. Do I have to frisk you?"

The shortest one called out, "No, but I'd love to frisk you."

"Ask my boyfriend. He's the big guy in the family room."

Laughing, they all left. She handed envelopes to the parking guys who shook hands and drove off.

"Alone at last," Lisa said, locking the door.

Maverick licked the last ramekin clean and gazed at her. "Boyfriend?"

She climbed on his lap, snuggled up and said, "Yes. Aren't you?"

"I want to be more than your boyfriend, Lisa."

The air between them became electric as if a new current turned on. Lisa kissed him. "Like what? What do you want to be?"

Unable to meet her eyes, he unbuttoned her plaid vest one button at a time speaking slowly. "I want to be your carpenter," one button, "painter," two buttons, "electrician," three buttons, "plumber," four buttons, "lover," and guided her arms out of the vest and let it fall to the floor. "And what else." Maverick stroked her back up and down, side to side. "Tell me what else."

When he spoke, his voice was choked with emotion. "I want to be your husband for life."

Now Lisa lifted her face from the warm familiarity of his strong neck and tasted tears from the big guy's eyes. "Yes."

When Beth finally came downstairs, she was alone in the house.

Chapter 41

Thinking she'd sleep late, Beth didn't set the alarm but old habits never die. Up early as always, seven in the morning looked wonderful to her. She danced around in sweats, making coffee in the clean kitchen, nibbling on a few cookies recalling moments from the party. Eager to watch the video to see if anything memorable was captured, unable to operate the damn machine, she'd have to wait. Beth sat down with the guest book to see if any of the guests had written anything special.

Sam Taylor not only tucked his business card in a page but wrote a personal note thanking her for the extraordinary evening. He looked forward to seeing her at one o'clock today. She felt a wicked smile begin. *Interesting man with a plan.*

Several people requested their names be placed on the guest list for the next Singles Salon.

If at first you don't succeed. . .

Grant Thomas asked forgiveness for talking business in front of the company. He left his card and also said she should talk to Ms. Lisa Marcus about business matters. He wanted her to know that he made a date with one of the lovely women. Didn't say which one.

Beth Malone, matchmaker.

The art gallery gentleman, Frederick Harrington was definitely interested in Hilliard's work. Please call him after six today. He and Fern Rosen would be back from their outing by then.

How delicious is all this?

Closing the book, she set it aside. She had an audition to prepare for. A warm-up swim was in order and stretches and some pasta.

Climbing out of the pool, Beth flung her cap to the side aiming away from Sam Taylor. She didn't want to make a bad impression on the intense person watching her every move. He didn't stand, hand over a towel, clap, smile or do any of the usual things people did when they watched her swim. Well, she was a fine swimmer. No one else had to confirm what she already knew.

Wrapping a towel around her hair, she slipped into a terry robe, turned off the various lights and started the pump.

"Back to the house. I have to shower and change." He followed her out and waited as Beth locked up. And they walked in silence in the late October air, so crisp it was like McCoun apples mouths watered for this time of year.

"I'm usually not at a loss for words Beth, but watching you truly knocked me out."

She felt her body loosen up a little hearing his words. "Thanks. After I change, would you like some lunch and maybe tell me more about the women's team you mentioned?"

"Confession. Before I saw you, a swim team never occurred to me. All I thought about was a reason to see you again."

Beth stopped in her tracks trying to process what he'd just said. "Why? Why didn't you just ask? Do you have an any idea how much effort goes into an... an...audition?" Without waiting for a response, she barreled on. "Anticipation, stretching, a warm-up swim, practice dives—a fargin' bowl of pasta for breakfast!" She shook her head so hard, the towel fell off and Sam caught it before it landed in a pile of leaves.

"I'm cold," she said and stormed toward the house, Sam in close pursuit. Unlocking the sliders she marched ahead. He followed. Hands on hips, Beth faced him.

"Why didn't you just ask?"

"I didn't think you'd accept a date because you were the facilitator of this event. I'm an agent. This is how I think-- there's always an angle. I yanked it out of thin air. Please. I'm a good person. Ask my mom."

"So who are you right now? Good person or agent?"

Without hesitation Sam Taylor, there under false pretenses, spoke looking directly into Beth's eyes. "I'm divorced, two terrific grown kids and three grandkids. Business is fine. I have all my teeth, most of my hair, in good health with papers to prove it, and I was drawn to you. Out of an attractive bunch of women, you're the one I wanted to be next to so I made up a story. Not a terrific way to begin a friendship. I'm sorry."

Beth turned to the refrigerator. "Tea, soda, juice? I'll be downstairs in thirty minutes. Newspaper in the family room, no sport magazines."

When she returned after giving much thought to Sam Taylor, she even thought about calling his mother, she decided to give him a chance. Take a better look. She cleaned up real good, her own mom used to say. The loose boat neck coral cashmere sweater over stone washed black jeans fit "poifect, dollink" as her favorite sales girl said. Short heel black leather boots completed the outfit. Gold hoops almost as big as sewer covers in the ears. *Why did I fall for earrings that size?*

Sam spun around when she sauntered in. He'd been examining "First Love."

"Do you like it?"

He kept his eyes on her as she moved closer. "What?"

"The painting."

"Amazing."

"Yes, he is."

"No. You are."

Beth laughed, a real belly laugh. "Are you good person or agent?"

Sam said, "I'll be paying for this fatal flaw for a long time. I hope. Good person when we're together, Beth. Deal?"

She only smiled and shook her head. "We'll see. Lunch? I'm expecting some friends this afternoon so I can't go out."

"Any leftovers?"

"Don't know. Lisa and the kids put everything away."

Beth felt his eyes on her as they made their way to the kitchen. "You'll have to lend a hand. Pay for your supper, so to speak."

"Again?" He was so close, she inhaled spice cologne. "You sit, I'll poke around. Do you mind?

"Before last night, I would have said I do mind." She sat, stretched out weary legs and waved. "Have a go at it and keep in mind, you're on probation."

For the first time, Sam displayed a deep dimple in each cheek and looked like the good person he claimed to be. Humming something Beth couldn't make out, he opened the fridge and removed covered containers. A bunch of them.

"What are you looking for?"

Sheepishly he grinned at her. "Crème brulee. I didn't get to taste any. Too distracted."

He held up a container. "Got it."

"That's your idea of lunch?"

"Appetizer."

He found two spoons and napkins and in companionable silence, they finished last night's dessert. When she put her spoon down, he noisily scraped and licked the ramekins like a kid.

Beth enjoyed his company. Together, they made a light lunch. Chef salad and fruit and he suggested they eat outside. "Before we know it patio meals will have to wait until spring."

Beth liked the idea, liked that he preferred the outdoors. Maybe even liked his easy manner and sense of humor.

"Will your friends think you've gone out?" Sam caught a red and gold leaf from an oak tree as it blew past. He didn't talk much as they dined, concentrating on food and surroundings.

Another thing Beth liked.

"No. They'll barge in wherever I am. If you're still here I might introduce you. They're an interesting bunch."

"What do you mean by might?" Serious, brow furrowed again.

"If you promise to behave as in good person all the way. By the way, so far, I'm enjoying your company. The plus side is you have teeth, most of your hair, you speak with pride of your family."

Spontaneous laughter from Sam caused Beth to join in. And at this moment, Tommy and Hilliard rounded the corner of the house and right behind them came Lisa and Maverick, holding hands.

"Lunch," Hilliard said, "and the party lady didn't invite us. Call the cops."

Tommy flashed her shiny new detective badge. "You're under arrest for mistreatment of good friends and who is this accomplice?"

Sam's laughter died on his lips but Beth jumped up to embrace first one and then each of the others before introducing him.

"This is Sam Taylor, a guest from last night."

Tommy's jaw dropped. "I arrested a couple of your clients last year DUI and you bailed them out. Two bad boys."

"Officer Tommy O'Malley. They said after you finished with them, they swore off drinking and driving. I pictured a burly Irish cop and there you were."

"Patrol woman then, now Detective."

They shook hands. Tommy said, "Hey gang, Mr. Taylor is the big sports agent."

Maverick and Lisa kept smiling, hands locked together, looking for all the world as though they had news to spill.

"You two seem very, what's the word, smug?" Beth said.

Tommy said, "Uh, secretive?"

Hilly stalked all around them, sniffing the air. "Ah, I detectify orange blossoms and rice."

Caught up in the fun, Sam said, "A cake with two tall figures on top?"

"We proposed and we said yes. Last night. In the family room."

By then the women were in tears, Hilly and Maverick shook hands. Sam hung back as the observer, then gathered the few dishes and glassware and headed to the house. A few minutes later everyone piled in, full of joy and mischief.

Offering congratulations, he told Beth it was time to leave. "When can I see you again?"

Flustered, Beth said, "I'll check the schedule. My book's upstairs. Can you wait a minute?"

"Sure. For you, I'll wait as long as two minutes. Clock's ticking." He put on a dark brown cashmere sport coat and waited at the bottom of the stairs.

I can't think of a reason not to see him again. I like the way he stands straight, comfortable in his own skin.

Beth ran down the stairs, appointment book in hand, and there he was smiling up at her, standing at ease yet with an authoritative bearing. He tapped his watch. "Five minutes, Beth."

She opened the book, thumbed through until she found the current date. "Okay, what night do you have in mind, Sam?"

"Tomorrow night, the next night, the night after, the following night. Say when." Again the dark brown eyes were serious.

Beth did a quick assessment and hoped she could pass a test like this. About five foot ten, he wasn't as handsome as Larry or rugged like Maverick or dashing like Frank. But he had a strong, honest face. *Funny since he lied to make sure I agreed to see him.* Good cheek bones, interesting eyes, and two delicious dimples. Nose a little crooked. Contact sport injury, she guessed. Wavy hair expensively cut, athletic shape for a man around sixty and clear skin. *And he likes me.*

"Flatterer." She traced a finger down the dates. "I play tournament tennis Monday morning with Lisa, my partner."

"You have to eat dinner."

"True."

"Have dinner with me and we'll play getting to know you, if you'd like. Is seven too late?"

"No."

"Okay, I'll pick you up at six thirty." He leaned close, not too close and brushed her cheek with the sweetest kiss. The spicy scent was just enough to make her want to smell more.

They walked to the front door.

He said, "Goodbye Beth. You realize I don't want to leave." He was gone. *Wow.*

She practically skipped back to her friends where they waited with a bottle of champagne, ready to celebrate the engagement and Tommy's promotion. They all took one look at Beth's glowing face and Lisa said, "What's going on?"

"Beats me, kids. We met at the party and tomorrow we're having dinner. And th-th-th that's all, folks. Oh Hilly, a big art dealer is interested in meeting you. I have to call him this evening."

Tommy jumped in his arms, he looked panic-stricken, and everyone said it would be wonderful so they opened the champagne and toasted. Leftovers came out of the fridge and when all was quiet, Tommy announced her news.

"I have the full report on Frank Malone. Are you ready, Beth? This should give you the closure needed to get on with your full life."

Suddenly Beth was chilled, then overheated. Her heart raced and she grabbed Lisa's hand to steady herself.

"Deep breaths. Take deep breaths," Lisa said.

Tommy had everyone's attention. She withdrew a sheath of paper from an inside pocket of her suit coat and began.

"Following the credit card trail: March 25^t Four am-filled tank in SUV at Midtown Garage. 11 am checks into Boston Savoy-penthouse suite; brunch and dinner charged four meals; March 26 checks out after brunch. 11 am. Fills car in New Hampshire. Checks into The Maine Inn on the coast. Rents fishing yacht with crew. At sea two days in rough weather. Credit card use up to this time-calls to his lawyer, numerous calls to theatrical agents in New York City and female friends of traveling companion."

"I knew it," Beth said. "Felt it in my bones. An actress-bimbo-trophy. No wonder he didn't feel comfortable in his own skin." She wailed. "He wanted to get into her younger skin."

Inappropriate laughter burst from her pals. Lisa said, "Sorry, couldn't help it, Beth. The way you expressed yourself was so on target and funny."

Tommy said, "Continuing with the credit card trail, okay Beth?" Beth nodded.

"March 29 Drives south to NY directly to La Guardia. Long term parking. Flies west to Seattle--first class--overnight stay and flight to fishing paradise next day. Lasts 3 days; February 4 Many calls to lawyer, agents/producers in New York and LA. Flies to LA. She meets VIPs at studios. She shops on Rodeo Drive.; February 10 Check out of Beverly Hills Hotel, fly to Greek Islands 5 days. He fishes. Fly to French

Riviera. Stay in villa owned by lawyer.; April 10 fly to Oregon. He fishes. Many calls to agents New York and LA."

Suddenly Beth interrupted. "Tommy, where did he meet the bimbo person? Do you know?"

Consulting her notes, Tommy looked up. "Here it is. Frank was seeing a psychiatrist in Manhattan. . ."

"What?" Beth clutched her heart. *Frank had a secret life. Forty years together and I'm clueless.*

"Yes. Goes back to July last year. Doctor Lawrence Cooper. Monday appointments."

Lisa said, "Isn't that the name of your email buddy?"

Dumbfounded, Beth nodded.

Tommy continued. "The plot thickens. The bimbo, as you so nicely called her, worked as a waitress in the building coffee shop." Another look at the list. "Lana Martin. Tall, shapely blond, estimated C-cup, long wavy hair, big blue eyes, short uniform. In her twenties." *Carbon copy of me. Sure.*

"There's more. After see-sawing between fishing trips and New York and LA shopping and phone calls, in August, Lana gets a small part in a big movie to be filmed in Mexico. A call from lawyer friend in September and he leaves Lana to the movie, flies to La Guardia, picks up SUV and drives directly here. Case closed."

Drained yet relieved to know the whole story, Beth sat back before thanking Tommy.

"Two words for Frank and it ain't Happy Birthday. More champagne, anyone, everyone?"

Tommy declined. "I'm working later. Club soda's good." Hilliard unfolded from the couch and poured some.

Maverick, who'd been sitting quietly during the recitation, said, "That explains Doc coming home to pay me Monday's, then rushing off dressed to kill."

Lisa said, "You have the goods on him, Beth. Now you can get Susie back. Mid-life crisis, my butt. He had plenty of time to think this over. Months to plan. So Lana got what she wanted and left him empty handed in a cold bed."

Shaking her head, Beth said, "I don't know how to deal with this. I don't want to damage the love she has for her father but most important, I want my daughter back."

Tommy moved over next to Beth. "Think about it for a while. Digest the events. You'll know what to do."

Hilly said, "Take her baby shopping."

"Sounds about right. Now Hilly, brace yourself, the eminent Frederick Harrington wants to meet you. Time for that call." Beth punched in the number and an appointment was scheduled for the next day.

As they left, calling out mutual thanks, Beth heard Tommy say, "Don't worry honey. I'll go with you."

Maverick and Lisa cleared dishes and leftovers. As they left, Lisa said, "I'll pick you up tomorrow. Get a good sleep, if possible. Another match to win before the finals."

Locking the door, Beth barely made it up the stairs. Too tired, too much information topped off with Larry Cooper as Frank's psychiatrist. How bizarre. She'd never sleep.

She slept.

Chapter 42

"We almost lost, partner. Not that they were better but you didn't keep your focus and..."

"Yeah, yeah, yeah. Cut me some slack, Lisa."

They were almost to Beth's home after the tennis tournament, Beth in no mood to post mortem the game.

"We won by a whisker and now we're in the finals. We survived in spite of me learning about Frank's misadventure, in spite of finding out the man I was pining over was Frank's psychiatrist, and in spite of trying to figure out damage control to my daughter. I miss her so much, miss watching her shape grow and feeling the baby kick."

Lisa pulled into Beth's driveway. "Sorry for being insensitive. I feel for you, you know I do. If you want to discuss a plan, I'll stay. Otherwise, I have to get to the bank. By the way, when I served salad to Grant Morgan, he asked if I had a twin sister also named Lisa Marcus or was I moonlighting. So my cover was blown during the first course."

They grinned at each other. Beth said, "When you and Maverick get married, will you keep your last name?"

"Oh my God. I don't even know his last name."

"Good time to find out." Beth grabbed her tennis bag and waved. "I have a dinner date tonight with Sam Taylor. To be continued."

Ready at six thirty after an hour of trying on first date clothes, not knowing where they were going but after all, it was Monday night and a lot of restaurants were closed, and Sam had seen her in a long black dress and soaking wet in a bathing suit and who cared. *I do*. No more pony tail. Shoulder length hair framed her face and her taste in clothes had improved since Frank left. At last, Beth pleased herself and wore a favorite lavender cashmere v-neck sweater with gray pants, a gray short cord jacket and gray suede ankle high boots. She was set to go.

The evening was chilly, not cold yet for the last week in October. When the chimes rang out, she strode to the door to greet her date. Warm and eager was the look on Sam's face when the door opened. Beth smiled in response, extending her hand. A gust of chilly air blew some leaves in and to her surprise, Sam's hand's shot out capturing them before they fell to the floor.

"Football?" she said.

"And wrestling. Hands have to be quick. Are you ready?"

"Yes." Keys and bag in hand, they were outside after the alarm was activated.

Sam released the leaves into the air, watched as they twirled spinning away, and opened the door to a shiny black Porsche.

"You're pretty in lavender. We're going to a small café four towns south. I've taken clients there. Food is fine, atmosphere tops. Petite Patoots is the name. Do you know it?"

"No." She glanced at him. Dressed in tan cord pants, tweed jacket with suede elbow patches over a crew neck tan shirt, he appeared to be a country squire not a sophisticated sport agent. A worn polished cowboy boot pressed the gas pedal and they were off.

Music played through the speakers. Bossa nova. Sounded like the disc Beth had on during cocktail hour at the party. She swayed in the car seat enjoying the rhythm and wondered if Mozart was on the agenda during dinner. They didn't speak much during the drive and she was comfortable in the silence.

When he asked about the tennis match, she said, "We won. I didn't play my best, Lisa chewed me out. We won."

Sam asked how she felt about not playing her best.

"Bottom line, playing my best is important to me. Always has been. So now you know something about me a lot of people don't know and probably don't care."

They were at a stop light. She turned her head to find him looking her way. "Now you have to tell me something about yourself others don't know."

He drove on. A few minutes later he parked and Beth saw the colorful sign, Petite Patoots.

"Funny name."

"Petite refers to the size of the restaurant of and Patoots is the term of endearment for the owner's wife. She's the chef. Their son went to college with my daughter. We've stayed friends through the years."

Sam parked, hurried to open Beth's door and escorted her into the café. Mozart played on their music system. Too much of a coincidence, she thought, and again felt a smile coming on.

Ten tables, small and intimate. Sam was greeted by the owner, Tony Domingo. Short, round and puffed with pride, Tony snapped pudgy fingers for attention to his honored customer. The tables were filled except for one off to the side. *Charming* was the first word to come to Beth's mind. Stucco walls, beamed ceiling, white tablecloths and floral napkins combined with little clay pots of colorful chrysanthemums on each table. *Yes, charming.*

Tony held the chair out and Beth sat. Instead of sitting across the table, Sam sat next to her.

"Anything to drink?"

Beth said, "Chardonnay." Sam grinned at Tony.

Sam picked up the conversation begun in the car. "During an early wrestling match in my long career as a jock, I made an illegal move the ref didn't catch and won the match. I never forgave myself and vowed always to play fair. In my profession, there's a lot of maneuvering with clients and prospects but I tread a narrow path with myself. Then I meet you and the first damn thing I do is make up a story to get your attention." He averted his eyes and opened the menu.

Following his lead, Beth opened hers. As if she read from the menu, she said, "You must realize I had to get up early, workout, take a preliminary swim, and prepare for the pseudo audition."

He hung his head.

"And I was excited and ate carbs I wouldn't normally be eating in the morning. You do realize that, don't you?"

He nodded.

"So how come we're out for dinner?"

"I don't know," Sam said. "I can only hope you have a forgiving heart. But, how come?"

She lifted her head from behind the menu and shrugged. "A hunch, maybe. Something about your bearing. Military, right? And your scent. Spice."

Tony whisked their menus away, brought Beth's Chardonnay and a martini for Sam and asked what they wanted to eat. "Anything at all. My Patoots will fix. Sam, the usual?"

Beth noticed another secret grin between the two. "Filet mignon medium with sautéed mushrooms, steamed spinach and a small salad, lemon for dressing," Beth said.

"Appetizer?"

"Shrimp cocktail."

Mozart changed to Fred Astaire singing "Dancing in the Dark" and Beth glanced at Sam who looked everywhere but at her. She couldn't stop the laugh bubbling up from deep inside and she punched him in the bicep. "You big lug. That's the sweetest form of flattery, you know."

Rubbing his arm, he said, "What?"

"The music. You recreated the music selections I played at the party and gave it to Tony."

His ruddy face took on a kid's puckish grin. Freckles she hadn't noticed before marched across his rosy cheeks and crooked nose. Beth touched his nose, traced where it must have been broken. "Wrestling?"

"Football. I'm a walking bruise."

Now Gene Kelly sang his heart out and they searched each other's faces and enjoyed the companionable silence between them.

Tony cleared his throat and broke the spell. Beaming at them like a proud father, he presented a cut glass shrimp dish with four jumbo shrimp arranged around the top, lemon slices and a red sauce on the side. Sliced mozzarella and tomatoes over greens for Sam with oil and vinegar dressing. Tony backed away, a pleased look on his round, creased face.

Sam said, "Thanks, Tony," and lifted his glass to Beth's. They clinked glasses. "This is our first dinner together, alone. To many, many more."

"I'll drink to that."

Half way through the main course, Sam with his small porterhouse medium rare, Beth loving the Filet Mignon, Sam asked her to reveal another something from her past no one else knew about. She almost choked and pictured Sam applying the Heimlich Maneuver and thought how pleasant that might be.

"Don't censor your first thought. When you're ready, come clean."

She finished the spinach, hoped none stuck in her teeth and said, "Okay. In high school, I smuggled two bottles of wine out of the locker room after swim practice. The whole team went behind the bleachers, someone had a couple of joints and we all got stoned and drunk and threw up and it was awful. But no one caught us or ever found out and after that we won every meet for the next three years. Unbeaten." She chewed a few more pieces of steak and sat back. "There."

Sam cocked his head and said, "So you think the drinking and smoking bonded the team?"

219

"Well, yes. I believe so. It was the shared experience, the misadventure."

The music played on. Bossa nova. Full circle. Melodic tinkling of cutlery against plates unheard as Beth and Sam got used to sharing a space. New customers came and went, Tony left them alone and a mature waiter brought lemon sorbet to cleanse their palates before coffee and dessert.

"Nice touch, the sorbet. I'll have to use it for my next party. Now it's your turn."

Sam's face drained of expression. "I'm not censoring my first thought so here goes. Vietnam. I was a young pilot—helicopter, endless mission the day before. I was on the schedule again but couldn't lift my head. Everyone did drugs, smoked pot, whatever. No excuse. Best friend couldn't wake me so he took my place. Didn't come back." He took her hand, held it tight. "No one else in the whole world knows. Only you."

Only me. He tells me about this significant part of his life and we hardly know each other. Moved beyond words, Beth reached out and placed her hand over his. At that moment Tony came over for the dessert request. Beth shook her head no.

"Sam, coffee, espresso or cappuccino? Whipped cream?"

Sam, sounding upbeat, said, "Who can resist? Beth, you'll love their cappuccino." She nodded and sent a smile of thanks to Tony.

When Beth asked to meet his wife, he gave a vigorous shake of the head. "She doesn't leave the kitchen 'til the last dish is clean. Next time, you come later and meet her."

In the Porsche, buckled up for the ride home after many thanks and compliments to the owner of Petite Patoots and noticing no check or credit card ever made it to the table, Beth turned to Sam.

He said, "You wear your whipped cream very well, Beth."

220

"Oh, where and why didn't you tell me sooner."

"Here." He reached over and licked the whipped cream off the corner of her mouth.

It wasn't a cold night but suddenly the small car heated up. Just a little lick and Beth found she wanted more, much more. *Oh my*. There was heavy breathing from the two of them as if they were teens doing some heavy necking, one tiny chaste lick to set them on fire.

"Sun roof or open windows?" Sam said. They both chuckled.

"Sun roof sounds good. Home, Sam."

Chapter 43

The drive home was quiet, each one lost in private thoughts, maybe the same thought. Too soon? Sam opened the passenger side almost before Beth realized the car stopped moving, so smooth was the ride. She turned to ask if he'd like to come in and from his intense look, knew he did.

Beth said, "I'd offer cappuccino but we just had some and I'm out of whipped cream."

"Whipped cream is nice."

"You've seen the downstairs, and the pool enclosure. Is there anything else you'd like to see?"

"Sit." Sam pulled Beth to the third step of the stairway leading upstairs. "We're not strangers, you know."

"We aren't?" *Where is this heading?*

"Not at all. We met about a month ago when you mailed a letter and flyer to me regarding the Night of Possibilities. That's the first time we met. Meeting two is when I called to respond. You explained about the evening. Number three was the call from you to me confirming the date of the party. The party is number four. My phony audition at the swimming pool is number five. The drive to Petite Patoots is six and dinner is number seven. Seven is a lucky number."

"You make a convincing case, as if I needed convincing. I don't know why, but I feel as if I've known you a long time and it feels good."

He stood up and held out a hand. Beth slipped her hand in his, a delicious warmth spreading through her.

"There are nice rooms upstairs and some renovation going on

"Can't wait."

"This is where I've been sleeping since the husband walked out."

"He walked out." Sam stopped and waited.

"Yes. Last March." Beth breathed deeply allowing his scent to fill her. Facing Sam she looked up into those dark brown eyes. "I've been making a whole new life since then after scraping myself off the floor."

Sam's arm tightened around her and they were quiet for a moment.

Beth clicked on the light displaying the pink ruffled room with the single bed. "The room my daughter grew up in." The light clicked off. "And this is my exercise room."

"I'm impressed. All the latest equipment and you show the results." Their eyes met and they laughed at what sounded like a commercial. "Don't punch my bicep again. It's dangerous getting close to you."

"You think?"

He pulled her close and said, "No, I don't think. I can hardly think straight at all, especially with you here next to me."

Beth cleared her throat, tried to see through the sexual haze. "I don't suppose you'd be interested in seeing my office."

"Right."

"Um, how about the renovation of my new bedroom?"

A slight pressure of the hand holding hers indicated Sam's desire to be led in that direction. She felt a little shaky as they walked toward the back of the house. Beth flicked on a low light; they entered the new room. Maverick and the twins had left the room clean, no sawdust or plaster anywhere. Just the big open room with the new platform bed in the middle, packaged sheets, comforter, new pillows waiting to be opened. Beth remembered she had purchased scented candles and unwrapped them to give a fragrance to the room. Spice.

She started to point out where the fireplace would be and the balcony and the view of the enclosure when Sam covered her mouth with his. A perfect fit. Their heads tilted just right and the way he cupped the back of her head was unbearably sweet. They breathed harmoniously and when they finally broke apart laughing like kids.

Sam said, "All this and we're still standing up."

And they laughed some more and hugged until Beth said, "Why don't we break open the new sheets? See if they work."

The plastic wouldn't give and in her hurry, Beth bit into one and ripped the packaging.

Watching her, Sam said, "I told you, you're dangerous."

He unzipped the comforter, pried open the pillow coverings and together they rushed to make the bed. And paused, looking at the inviting bed, knowing what came next. Beth broke the spell by lighting new candles and the spicy scent wafted through the room."

"I must have known you were in my future."

"How?" Sam said, removing her jacket.

"Spice is your scent and I bought the candles before I met you."

"Is that right?" he murmured, lifting her sweater up until it was over her head. He dropped it on the floor next to the jacket. Beth sat on the bed and unzipped her shoe boots. Sam slipped them off and slid them across the floor near her growing stack of clothes.

"I have a great idea," Beth said. "While I can still think, and have a few stitches of clothes on, and you seem to be fully dressed by the way, why don't we take a shower? I really love clean skin and clean sheets. What do you think?"

Sam sat next to her and in a minute, he stripped down to bare feet and bare chest, clothes in a heap with hers. "Just one time out."

He pressed her back down on the bed and caressed her neck and shoulders, breasts and belly with gentle hands. She sighed and reached up for him, for his face and lips and they strained to be together. By mutual consent, zippers came down, pants somehow landed on the floor in a heap. Warmth of loving contact, hot moist flesh opened to be filled in an urgent union. He was strong, pulsing in and out, and for the first time Beth felt alive with the joy of being with a man, this man she felt she could love forever. She gave herself up in glorious relief and opened her eyes to find Sam gazing down at her with the same rapture she felt. He cried out her name. They held each other and after a while, were still.

She gazed at her lover's face in wonder; his eyes closed and breathing deeply as if asleep; while she felt energized enough to win Gold medals at the Olympics in diving and swimming or cater a crowd and run for President with one hand tied behind her. She tried to calm down, to steady her breath to no avail.

"Sam?" she whispered.

"Hmmm?"

"Tell me a secret."

In the flickering candlelight she traced scars on his chest wondering if they were sports or war related. She'd ask him next time. *If there was a next time. Please let there be next times.*

He stirred, didn't open his eyes and said, "This is my secret. It may sound premature but I believe I'm in love with you."

"Oh my." *Don't cry, don't cry, don't cry.* She cried.

"Honey, why are you crying?"

"Happy. I love your secret." She climbed on top of him kissing his face, the dimples from the grin spreading across to light up his serious eyes. Nuzzling his neck, she whispered, "I don't know if this is possible but I believe I love you, too."

Wrapped in each other's others arms, he slept for a while but again, the energy wouldn't let her rest.

Nudging him, she said, "Sam, you up?"

226

Sam stretched, opened an eye and peered at Beth.

"This is just like "The Manchurian Candidate" when. . ." Beth said.

Sam interrupted. "Wait a minute, Beth. I'm trying to catch up." He propped up pillows and leaned back pulling her next to him. "Okay. I'm awake now."

Excited now to have his attention, Beth continued. "Janet Leigh and Frank Sinatra are in a taxi and she says that after she met Frank on the train, she went home, called her fiancée and broke up with him. See?"

"See what, sweetheart?"

"It's like us. We knew right away that we were meant for each other. You don't have to go out for a month, a year, or whatever, especially at our age, to know."

They were quiet for a while, snuggled together, wrapped in the warm quilt. His breathing grew deep and steady.

"Sam, you up?"

He chuckled and reached for her hand. "Definitely up."

"Sam, let's not shout it from the rooftops yet. There are lots of things I have to tell you; I have to sort out this problem with the husband and patch things up with my daughter but Sam, if there's such a thing as soul mates, I believe we've found us." Finally running out of steam, Beth grew quiet.

His hands turned her face toward him in the semi-darkness. Softly, he said, "Yes. Oh yes, love. We've been waiting for each other for a lifetime."

"Kiss me so I'll know it's not a dream, Sam."

Chapter 44

"Bye dear, have a nice day," Beth waved and laughed, watching her lover drive off shaking his head and laughing. *Oh my God. The party meant to bring lonely people together blossomed into wonderland for me and for Sam . . .for us.*

A few minutes later, Lisa called. "How was your date?"

"Great. We went to a truck stop for dinner, watched women's mud wrestling, got all steamed up and made out in the back of his Porsche, I mean pick-up truck. You betcha."

Silence on the line. Then Lisa burst into laughter. "I deserved that, you devil. I'm serious. How was the well-known sports agent on a date?"

Lisa, remember how you and Maverick were hit by a thunderbolt when you met?"

"Who could forget it?"

Beth felt her heart beat faster recalling the evening and night with Sam. "Somehow we've found each other, like soul mates and we're in love. I mean really, deep love. I'm overwhelmed with this feeling, Lisa. And do you remember the movie "The Manchurian Candidate?"

"I think my mother liked that old movie. What does that have to do. . ."

"Forget it, Lisa, you brat. Just stick with the thunderbolt and soul mate."

Laughing, Lisa said, "Explain it over lunch one day. Meanwhile, I'm so surprised and happy for you. Off to work now. Lunch today, maybe?"

"Don't know if I can eat. I'm going to do my quiet stuff at home today. Sam's coming back to take me out for dinner later. This morning when he left, I said, "Bye dear, have a nice day and we laughed so hard."

"Oh Beth."

Beth hung up, laid her head down on crossed arms and sobbed with joy and a twinge of sorrow for time lost.

"Top of the mornin' to you from St. Paul's," said Sister Mary Margaret.

Beth felt a smile tug at the corners of her mouth. "It's Beth Malone."

"Of course it is."

"Are you available for a brief visit this morning?" Beth pictured the little nun swallowed up by the leather chair, sturdy shoes kicked off, feet in black stockings crossed at the ankle up on the desk.

"Oh, let me check my busy schedule." No pages rustled and Beth knew she relaxed at the desk, eyes closed, counting seconds before saying yes. "I have some emergencies that can wait a bit while we visit, dear girl. Hustle over and bring some of those chocolate chip cookies I fancy."

Beth wrapped the box of cookies hidden from Lisa and the gang and now, deep breath—Sam, yes, Sam-- grabbed her purse and keys and headed for church.

St. PAUL WELCOMES YOU said the sign and Beth felt quite at home here after months of working in the soup kitchen. Pushing through the carved wooden doors, she hurried straight to Sister Mary Margaret's office and knocked three times. "Joe sent me."

"Come in. Did you bring m' fix?"

"Smuggled it in over the border. Fooled the chocolate-sniffing canines stationed at the gate."

Sister Mary Margaret tore through the wrapping, pried open the ornamental tin with gnarled fingers and popped a cookie in her mouth. "Ah," she sighed. "Ambrosia for the soul. Thank you, sweet lass and may the blessing. . ."

Beth leaned over the desk to hug her friend. "My pleasure. I saved these for you. Now if you can spare me a few moments of your precious time, there's something I want to discuss with you."

Slowly Sister Mary Margaret straightened in her chair. "Only if I may continue to nibble on cookies and sip some coffee. Pour another mug for me. There's a dear."

"I have a question about soul and soul mate." Again she felt the smile tug at her mouth. "I met a man, something about him drew us together, I mean, he says he was drawn to me and I well. . ."

Sister stopped eating and leaned forward. "A lot of attraction goin' on at first sight."

"I'm overwhelmed with this feeling of love. I feel it shining through my whole body and I see it in him and we just met and I'm lit up and something inside says we're soul mates. Is there such a thing?"

Nodding, Sister Mary Margaret said, "I believe in soul mates. The one certain someone meant to be with you. It doesn't always happen but when it does, don't let go. You'll wind up bent and old."

She spun her chair to look through the window behind the desk and sat there for a long while. What was a sunny, brisk morning turned cloudy; dried leaves blew past signaling a cold snap. Her rusty voice spoke sending chills through Beth.

"I was sixteen, a wild daughter and the youngest of ten. Nan passed on and Da didna care by then what to do with me so he said I was to enter the church. But I had other plans." She spoke slowly as the story played out in front of her. "There was a lad, my Casey. We were crazy in love. He was the center of my soul; all I ever thought about and hormones raged and we were carried away with the lust. I was the only child at home so it was easy to keep the secret under full skirts and big sweaters and when the time came closer, we ran away in the night. Casey took his brother's car. 'Twas a stolen car. We traveled for many hours and we were tired. He drove too fast."

Her ragged breathing filled the room. She continued. "I lost everythin' that night. When I awoke in a hospital far, far from our village, I was the sole survivor. I knew nothin' 'cept I was empty and alone, had no name, no identification, not even in the car burned beyond. . .The Sisters took me in, gave me a home, showed me the way and years later, when an opportunity came, they sent me to America. New York. I had the education to fill a good position right here. And here I've stayed. Little Miss No-Name. Through the years, bits and pieces of m' life returned but I left it all behind. Yet every day and night, I pray for Casey and our babe." She turned back and with effort she got up from the desk. Heart aching for the little nun, Beth crossed to her and they embraced. "This is my secret and now I share it with you."

Beth felt Sister's strength and frailty at the same time. Closing her eyes, she said a prayer for long life and good health for all of her loved ones.

"I'd like to meet your young man," Sister Mary Margaret said with humor, her voice strong once again. They chuckled. "Bring him to our Thanksgiving dinner. See you Thursday. Our Karen is hanging on. She'll probably carry to thirty eight weeks with the twins. If you hadn't stepped in, she would have lost them."

In the empty parking lot, Beth sat in the Mercedes too limp to turn the ignition key. Stunned by Sister Mary Margaret's story, she thought of her own problems and they seemed small by comparison. Their paths had crossed and a special bond formed.

Overwhelmed by the enormous amount of trust Sister placed in her, Beth felt grateful and proud.

She'd sort out how to put Frank in his place, finalize the divorce, and somehow salvage the relationship with Susie.

Time to go home. Tonight she planned to play getting to know Sam, part two.

Chapter 45

Like an eager teen waiting for her boyfriend, Beth watched through a window with a view of the driveway. When the purr of the Porsche engine caught her attention before it came in sight, she ran to the front door and down the steps to greet Sam. He talked fast as he steered Beth back in the house, hugging and kissing at the same time. His jacket came off and was dropped on the small bench next to the door. Placing hands on both her shoulders, he drew her close and told her what happened at the office.

"I've been watching this kid since he was a freshman in high school. Remarkable potential in football. Made friends with the parents and the boy—this is upstate New York. Watched him continue to grow as an athlete and a person. So today, they're all in my office. The parents and the kid cleaned up for a visit to the big city; the kid's got offers from pro teams first draft and free rides to top colleges. My four year investment of time, energy and," he stopped to catch his breath, "the contract that makes me his exclusive agent is on my desk, pen's in the kid's hand and Beth, all I could think of at that moment was you. Dripping wet, in the shower, in the pool, and I excused myself, went to the bathroom, splashed cold water on my face and returned to my desk."

"Then what?"

"He signed the contract and now I can begin negotiations for his career."

They stood there grinning at each other. Beth broke the silence. "Did you have a nice day, dear?"

Planting kisses all over her face, he said, "Yes, dear. How did the dishes go today?"

He ran as Beth chased him upstairs calling, "Dishes? Did you say dishes?"

Much later, wearing nothing but a lazy smile, Beth straddled a naked Sam in the unfinished bedroom, lit only by moonlight. "As I was saying, I do much more than dishes."

He reached around her waist, flipping her beneath him.

Breathless, she said, "That was an illegal wrestling move. You said you'd never do that again."

"No, Love. I'll show you the rule book. It's perfectly legal." He stretched out next to Beth and said, "Let's make this whole thing legal. With a contract and stuff. What do you say, hmmm?"

"Oh Sam, how lovely but there are some obstacles we have to overcome first."

She started at the beginning when Frank left in March and talked until hunger overcame them and Chinese food was ordered. The story unfolded through egg rolls and barbeque ribs and Beth's favorite chicken and broccoli and Sam's shrimp fried rice. Sam's chop sticks went still as Beth told him about the night Frank walked in and raided the refrigerator. When she said Tommy and her sources managed to build a profile of where Frank had been and whom he'd been with, Sam began eating again.

"Have you consulted a divorce lawyer?"

"Yes." Then she filled him in on the advice from Elise Bergin.

Dressed in a robe now, Sam gathered containers and utensils from the makeshift table upstairs and set them aside. They sat cross legged on the bed.

"It sounds like you have all the ingredients for an attack. Have you thought about how to put it together and make it work to your complete advantage?" Sam said.

"You must be a killer in business."

"You have a situation here and want to resolve it quickly and in the most beneficial way to you. Do you want my help in laying out a plan?"

"Yes, I do."

"I like the sound of those three little words, my sweet love. Let's move into your office."

It didn't take long, an hour or less, and a plan came to life.

Chapter 46

With the help of Tommy, Frank's new phone number and address were found. She also found a business phone number. He had moved into a condo south of town and was opening a high tech fitness center nearby. *Well, well, Frank. All the bodies you want at your disposal.* Beth dialed the business number first.

A young female chirped, "Build Better Bodies. Dr. Malone's office, Sheree here."

Beth almost laughed. "Doctor Malone, please."

"Who may I say is calling?"

"Tell him his wife is calling."

A stutter and a gulp and then, "Hold the line, please. I'll see if he's available."

Rereading her notes for the twentieth time, Beth waited and centered herself with calm deep breaths. When he picked up, she was ready.

"Lizzie, how are you?" Frank's voice boomed out. "Wonderful to hear from you. What's on your mind?" His voice lowered to what he must have thought had a sexy edge. "Are you ready for me to come over?"

Fuffa you, Frank. "Are you available to meet for coffee today at say, three?"

He laughed and made a show of checking an appointment calendar. "Three is good. I have a window right then. I'll be over."

"No, Frank. Let's meet at Kozy Kitchen in town. Three o'clock, then. Bye." She hung up and sat back for a minute, heart racing. *Dress for success. Take a briefcase with notes. Get this show going.*

But first a hard swim, the only thing that kept her from losing her mind all these months. Beth and the water. Yes, she'd made a wonderful friend, started a new business, chef duties at soup kitchen and her relationship with Sister Mary Margaret, and closed the gap with Susie, and Sam, thank you to the powers that be for Sam. But the water: the pounding, cleansing water would get her through a cup of coffee with the man she had lived with for forty years.

Clink, clink went two quarters in the parking meter, and Beth Malone strode into the Kozy Kitchen, head held high. A quick glimpse of her reflection pleased her. Shining brown hair highlighted with light streaks, yellow cashmere turtleneck and black jeans under a black suede jacket and short black boots. She looked carefree and energetic. *So far, so good.*

She spotted Frank in a corner booth and walked over, swinging her briefcase, wanting to swing it into his handsome face. He rose, made a move to kiss her but she slid across from him and said "Hi." He got the hint and sat down.

"You look well, Frank. What have you been up to?"

He pouted for a minute and whined about the condo he had to rent when she sent him packing. She ignored the comment. "I heard you were opening a fancy fitness center, very high tech. Is it open yet?"

He beamed, displaying teeth whiter than white. "Almost ready. My office is complete and potential members are lining up. All the latest gear, machines, clothes, and instructors. It will be a huge hit. Other doctors are calling about investing already."

The waitress came over and Beth ordered black coffee. Frank was drinking what looked like hot chocolate.

"Wonderful, Frank. You were always clever in business." *Flattery.*

Sitting forward, he put on an earnest look. "I've missed you so much, Liz."

"Beth."

"What?"

"That's my name now. No more Liz. No more Lizzie. Beth is my name." Beth smiled.

"Oh. Did you call to tell me you've changed your mind, uh Beth? About us?"

The Kozy Kitchen was not too crowded just then. Late for lunch, early for dinner and Beth was glad about this. No one from the old crowd was visible. It would be easier to talk. Coffee came, she stirred sweetener in and waited until the waitress was out of earshot.

She smiled her sweetest smile. "A detective friend traced your path from the time you walked out until the time you returned to my kitchen, Frank." She opened her briefcase and placed a copy of Tommy's findings in front of him.

He scanned the damning evidence as color drained from his face and suddenly he looked older.

"This is proof that you had an adulterous affair for months before you left and afterward. Adultery is a crime in New York and if I choose, I can sue you on those grounds with the proof I have." Continuing to smile, she said, "Susie wants me to let you return. I told her when you left, I would never take you back. I didn't know about the adultery then. Susie kept calling it a mid-life crisis. So the question is, how would our beloved daughter feel if she knew that the father she adores left her mother for another woman?"

Frank opened his mouth to speak and shut it. His head shook back and forth.

"Do you want to lose Susie and probably the grandbaby as well if she finds out you abandoned me for another woman? She doesn't know anything about your affair, as yet, because I don't want to damage the love she has for you. It's bad enough that our small family tie is broken." Beth sat back and sipped the coffee, wishing it were wine; hoping she was doing well.

He tried to drink but sputtered the chocolate drink and wiped his mouth. The arrogance he thrived on dissolved in the face of cold evidence. Beth waited for him to grab at straws, put up a fight, threaten her with something but at first Frank Malone seemed to cave in.

"We must think of Susie," Frank said. "Keep this information between us and tell me what you want. I'll think about it and get back to you." His shoulders slumped. Almost gone was the confident son-of-a-bitch he'd always been.

"I want the house and property and want to live in comfort for the rest of my life in recompense for giving you forty years of my life. In return, you have my silence and I won't sue you on charge of adultery which would be a mess. A Divorce Mediator will draw up the necessary papers and we will be legally divorced. It takes about a year. I've seen a divorce lawyer who counseled me on everything I've just told you. The sooner the better, Frank. Our daughter and her fine husband are about to have our grandchild, a baby girl. Let's not spoil their lives." The words came out the way she'd rehearsed them.

At that moment, Beth's former best friend Sharon walked by and greeted them. The scene from the club when Sharon told Beth their friends didn't have room for singles replayed in Beth's head.

"Well hello, you two." She reached over to hug Beth who pulled back and then she leaned over to plant a juicy kiss on Frank's mouth. It seemed to revive Frank. A sparkle came to his eyes. "Good to see you together again. Let's do dinner. I'll call." She waved a few fingers and moved along, swaying her hips.

"Liz, uh Beth. You're not friends with Sharon anymore?"

"No, Frank. Once you walked, I wasn't welcome in our old pals circle."

"Oh. Sorry."

She waved away the apology. "There's nothing further to say, Frank. If you agree, we'll move along. If not. . .you'll hear from my lawyer." She stood up. *Please agree. Please, please.*

"Sit down for just a minute."

Out came the cell phone, Frank turned his head for a whispered conversation with Bruce Bradley, no doubt. An argument with his best friend from what Beth could make out. A long argument and at one point, Frank's voice rose. From what she could make out, Frank said something about everything being in Bruce's name. And the words "Don't forget it." Frank hung up. He took a big swallow of the hot chocolate, probably cold by now.

"Bruce advised me against the plan but I have my doubts as to his ability as a divorce lawyer. He was really instrumental in the whole affair, Beth."

"You're a grown man. Take responsibility."

She watched a transformation take place as he straightened in his chair, fists clenched so hard that white knuckles showed.

Frank leaned across the table, eyes narrowed. "How was The Night of Possibilities, Beth? Did you meet a special someone that night or one of the other nights since you've been alone?"

She maintained composure though a sharp chill raced through her. *Breathe. Gossip in a small town. Of course someone told him. Be very discreet with Sam.*

Hands clutched together in her lap out of his sight, she said, "You abandoned me. When I put myself back together, I realized I wanted to reach out to other single people and I did. Successfully." Avoiding eye contact, Beth gathered her briefcase and handbag and rose to leave. "Goodbye, Frank. Call if you change your mind."

To Beth's surprise, Frank followed her outside.

"No lawsuits, Beth." His voice was low and contrite. "Get in touch with the mediator and set up a date."

She nodded. "We'll both have to sign papers agreeing to what we just talked about and penalties if either of us breaks the agreement. She'll be in touch with you. Goodbye, Frank."

Heart pounding, Beth strode to her car. She liked saying "Goodbye, Frank."

Chapter 47

A month later, the amicable agreement was signed at a meeting with the Divorce Mediator. Beth and Frank walked out together. She paused at the door to button her coat against the mid November cold.

Pensive, Frank moved beside her, the bounce temporarily gone from his step. When they approached Beth's car, he said, "Now what?"

She almost felt sorry for him and swallowed the impulse to pat his arm.

"Now we get together with Susie and Javier and tell them we've decided to divorce; assure her of our love and you can get to know our son-in-law who is a talented young man who adores Susie and believes in family values. He's been very kind to me since you left." Beth opened the car and slid in.

"Do you have time for an early dinner if Susie and her husband are available?"

Frank shivered in the cold, eyes watering. *Tears or the cold? He seemed unbearably sad. True or false.* Beth nodded yes. He flipped open his cell phone and speed dialed their daughter. It was on speaker phone. His hands shook.

"Hi, Daddy. How are you?" Susie's voice rang out clear and sweet, filled with happiness to hear from her father.

"Hi honey. If Javier is home and you're both hungry, your mother and I would like to meet you for dinner soon."

"You and Mom?" She squealed in delight. "Not tonight. He's working late and then he'll be away for a few days. How about next week? Monday looks good."

Frank looked miserable. "Just a minute, honey." He asked Beth if she was available Monday next. She thought it through and asked to make it early. Kozy Kitchen.

"Great, Daddy. Where?" He made the arrangements and disconnected.

Good food, early enough before the dinner crowd, she thought. Probably no place for Susie to create a scene.

Frank didn't like when things weren't going his way. He drooped from head to toe, gave Beth his sad little boy look. "May as well get it over with."

"This is where we were headed a long time ago, Frank. I just didn't know it." She started the car and drove away.

"Daddy," shrieked Susie, waddling with arms outstretched to greet her beloved father. Beth, happy to see the restaurant relatively empty at this hour, was hidden from view. She walked right behind Frank. A little smile and wave from her to Javier at the table brought him to his feet and he planted a respectful kiss on her cheek.

"Mom," Susie greeted Beth with a hug and they all sat. "Well," Susie beamed, "here we are, all together for the first time."

A waitress hurried over with menus, poured water, asked about drink preference. Javier ordered caffeine-free cola for Susie and Heineken beer for himself. Beth wanted—needed a glass of wine and placed her order, sure any effects would wear off with dinner. Young, perky and eager to please, the waitress turned to Frank. In a sweet voice, she said, "And you, sir?"

Beth could read his mind when he looked up and gave her the full treatment. *Oh my God.* His longish hair fell away for a minute and Beth saw a surgical scar behind his ear. *No wonder he appeared to be at least fifteen years younger than his true age. A face lift. And right in front of their daughter and Javier, he was flirting with this kid. Get me out of here fast.*

244

Still mulling over the rocket science question the waitress asked, Frank murmured, "Martini, very dry with a twist."

A giggle from the waitress. "Kozy Kitchen doesn't serve that. Only beer and wine and soda."

Frank sat up, checked out her left breast where the name tag was pinned. "Oh, all right, Candy. Make mine a Heineken's."

When mercifully Candy swayed away, Beth felt relief wash over her. Frank was painful to watch; she hoped Susie and Javier didn't pick up on his antics. Let the games begin, she thought.

Their table was off in a corner toward the back, private enough for quiet conversation. Already a few diners had come in for the early bird special, seniors taking advantage of the lower prices. Beth hoped once dinner was ordered, Frank would stop preening and cut to the chase. Above all, she wanted Susie to understand the situation and not run screaming into the street after dumping a plate of spaghetti on Beth's head.

Small talk followed until dinner was served. Beth, relieved no one ordered pasta, listened with half an ear to the conversation. Frank continued to delay so Beth kicked him under the table as Susie prattled on about the baby, school, Javier's designs. They exchanged a sharp glance. From Javier's reserved manner, Beth knew he suspected something was up. One more threatening look from Beth pushed Frank to the edge. He had to speak now or Beth would take over and it would be easier for Susie to digest the news coming from him.

He cleared his throat and began. "Your Mother and I have something serious to discuss." The table fell silent. "We've decided to get a divorce."

Susie burst into tears. Javier slid his chair close to her placing a protective arm around her. Frank's eyes beseeched Beth to bail him out but she knew, no matter what, the words still had to come from him. Javier blotted Susie's tears while murmuring comforting words in her ear.

"Susie, your Mom and I never intended to hurt you in any way so please listen, okay?"

Sniffling into a napkin, she nodded, big eyes suspicious.

"When you said I was having a mid-life crisis, to some degree you were right. I, uh, needed to uh, find myself."

What a crock of shit, Beth thought.

He took a long pull of beer. "And out there, in the wilderness, fishing and alone, I did."

Pardon me while I puke.

"But I kept in touch with you , baby." He smiled his Daddy smile. She bought it. "And realized it was time to come home and start a new life. So I won't have a medical practice but I will be able to take care of injuries that may occur at my fitness center. You both have lifetime membership, of course and the nursery will be perfect for the baby. What's her name?"

Elizabeth Francesca," Javier said. "My mother's name is Francesca and Elizabeth, of course, is for Mother Beth." He squeezed her hand.

Beth knew Javier understood a great deal of what lay unspoken.

It was a don't cry moment for Beth and she didn't. Not then.

Frank tested the name. "Beautiful. Francesca could also be for Frank." No one replied.

Dinner was served. Beth's appetite was in gear now that the divorce was in the open and she dived into chicken parmesan, one of the specials. She kept waiting for the other shoe to drop with the unpredictable Susie who hadn't asked many questions yet. *Cat's out of the bag so enjoy this meal and don't stop thinkin' about tomorrow.*

Silver clinked at other tables, laughter rose and fell as the restaurant filled. Young Ms. Candy came by frequently to check on water, drinks, asking "is everything okay?" too many times. Their table was quiet.

"What happens next?" Susie said, close to tears again. "When is the divorce final and what about holidays like Thanksgiving and Christmas and. . ."

"Next year in answer to the divorce question. Regarding holidays, at this time we feel," Beth said, with a meaningful look at Frank, "the holidays should be separate. Thanksgiving early afternoon, you and Javier are helping out at St Paul's soup kitchen with me. Afterward, you can make arrangements with your father to have dinner with him. In fact, I can cater it with the dinner from St. Paul's. Whatever you all decide on is fine with me." She smiled at everyone, finished the last of the chicken parm, and dabbed at her mouth with a napkin.

A bus boy cleared the table, Candy returned asking about dessert, coffee, whatever. It was lost to Beth as she excused herself and left for the ladies room. Susie had already made two trips there during the hour. Suddenly the door opened and she appeared walking straight into her mother's arms.

"Mom, I'm not a fool. I love Dad but now I know he lied. To me, every time he called with his sob story about finding himself and to you. Oh Mom, he abandoned you. He must've run off with some girl and it didn't work out."

Beth held her, stroking her back. The only thing she told her daughter was that no one is perfect and everything would be all right.

"Did you see the way he flirted with the waitress?" Susie said.

Holding her at arm's length, not easy to do because of the large belly, Beth said, "Don't speak ill of your father, Suzette. He's been a wonderful dad to you."

"I'm not Suzette anymore, Mom. Just call me Susie." They laughed.

Walking back to the table, Beth said, "Thanks for naming the baby after your two mothers." Beth felt another chip in the

247

armor she'd protected herself for so many years, fall away. "It means so much to me."

"Javier and I flipped a coin; you were tails so you came first." She giggled.

There but for a flip of the coin. . .Oh well. I won the toss.

On the way home, Beth replayed the one-way conversation she overheard when Frank talked with Bruce Bradley. She never liked Bruce, never trusted him and his ethics were suspect. What if he orchestrated more than Frank's philandering? What if the greedy Bruce was involved in some shady deal and that's the reason Frank agreed to give in to her demands. No. Too melodramatic. Happens to other people not to people she ever knew. But what if? She shook off the foreboding and hurried home. *Divorce. I never thought it would come to this but here I am. Starting over.*

Chapter 48

"And we have to be discreet," Beth gasped as Sam entered her. "Oh my."

"Shush. . ." slowly he thrust up and down, "sure."

His eyes were filled with passion and tenderness as they moved in the now familiar rhythm of love-making. When Beth sensed his urgency, she reached for the joy of orgasm. Together they had the shuddering release where nothing existed in the world but this moment and each other.

His car parked out of sight in the three car garage was his concession to discretion. She thought they needed to take more precaution. Not for a whole year, he argued. After all, she and Frank signed a legal agreement. Guaranteed Frank wasn't going to stop womanizing and she and Sam were waiting for her to be free to get married. They came to a decision. His apartment in the city was business so it wouldn't be a cozy getaway. His house upstate, a log cabin A-frame with all the modern conveniences, wasn't too far north and perfect for them.

"We can both conduct business up there. I have high speed computer network and I can install another phone line for you." He traced a finger over her fine cheekbones and pert nose. "What do you think?"

Beth faced him, loving every little nick from years past, the serious dark eyes, every part of this man who had walked into her life. "My pool? What about swimming, diving every day?"

"Oh yes. The pool. My rival. The upstate house is only an hour north. I'll have a driver take you back and forth if need be. And there's the lake."

"Lake?"

"We're on a lake so in the summer, if we spend a few days, the lake is wonderful. I have a pier and a couple of boats."

"Oh. Do you fish?" She thought of all the miserable boring times on lakes with Frank fishing.

"Sometimes, but you don't have to unless you really want to."

She kissed him thoroughly until they were both out of breath. "I'm so happy you came to The Night of Possibilities. Next party I'll raise the price."

They continued to caress, to enjoy the feel of each other. Gentle hands ran through her long silky hair over and over arousing Beth. When his lips brushed across heavy lidded eyes down to her mouth once again, she felt a stiffness press against her hip. She sighed.

"If we'd met when we were young, we'd have had a house full of kids."

"Not a chance?" he said.

"Not a chance," she said.

Chapter 49

A week later, the phone rang early in the morning. A cup of coffee poised close to her lips, Beth thought, Lisa. Had to be Lisa at this ungodly hour.

"Have you read the morning paper or listened to the news yet?"

"Not yet. What's up?"

"Bruce Bradley is what's up. His name and photo are all over the news connected with some kind of pharmaceutical scam. From what I can make out, the man will not collect two hundred dollars. Instead he's headed straight for jail."

"Oh my God, I wonder if Frank knows. Talk to you later." *I wonder if Frank's involved.*

Beth hurried to the front door, read the paper on the way back to the cooling coffee. Details were enough to understand that a crime had been committed and Bruce was more than a person of interest. As far as Beth could make out. A new drug designed for relief from fibromyalgia had passed many tests but so far was not FDA approved. It was given to select patients. Somehow Bruce orchestrated a deal with an unnamed source within Vista Pharmaceutical to release pills to doctors who encouraged patients to try the new product. It was kept low key. These unnamed doctors kept track of the patient's reactions and reported back to Bruce. Evidently no harm came to the patients and many benefited and clamored for more. Vista Pharmaceutical and the principals were under investigation. Huge sums of money were transferred to Bruce Bradley's account somewhere on an island. There was no evidence of him splitting the bounty with anyone else and no other names had been revealed. The search for the doctors involved continues.

Disgusted, Beth sat back and recalled the overheard one-way conversation when Frank told Bruce, "Remember, everything's in your name." She was sure Frank was involved in some way.

The last line of the article chilled her. "The search for the doctors involved continues." If Frank was involved, it would hurt Susie. This has nothing to do with you, she thought.

The only sound in the house was the stupid clock with the googly eyes. "Tick—tock, tick—tock." She and Frank bought it to decorate their first little house. She ran across the kitchen, grabbed the clock off the wall, yanked the plug from its socket, and headed to the garage.

Lifting the lid of the trash barrel, she hurled the offensive clock in and slammed the lid.

Definitely time for a swim.

Over the next few weeks, the story petered out. Bruce was indicted, disbarred, and with the expensive aid of his celebrity lawyer, he received a slap-on-the-wrist sentence to a white collar minimum security facility. *Thank heavens no other names came to light.* The Bradley home was up for sale.

She had better things to think about. After Thanksgiving, a sold-out pre-Christmas Night of Possibilities needed planning.

Chapter 50

The long awaited Thanksgiving Day arrived and barring anything unforeseen, all would go well. Beth's daughter and son-in-law were driving her to St. Paul's and helping out. After that, they had a date with Frank for dinner at the country club. Lisa and her crew were volunteers and Sam would meet her at the church. He'd become a regular as often as his schedule allowed.

Dressed in faded blue jeans and a coral turtleneck sweater, Beth was ready for work. Sneakers were a must even if it snowed. The forecast was for a wintry mix, whatever that meant. She'd learned her lesson the first night wearing high-heeled boots and ending up with sore feet.

As an only child, Beth had observed her mother who was the hub of the wheel in a family of ten, the hostess of every holiday; Mom worked herself into a frenzy and the day after each family feast, she'd collapse in bed for several days. *I don't want to be like Mom. Not in that way. Competent, yes. Frenzied and overworked, no.*

Wednesday night, Beth stacked dinner plates on the dining table already covered with a holiday cloth. Now it was Thursday. Thanksgiving dinner was in the oven with the timer set just as the door chimes rang. It was a greeting Beth dreamed of come to life—radiant daughter, attractive son-in-law, arms outstretched for her. In the three-way embrace, Beth was certain she felt a kick from Susie's mound. A tentative touch and her hand was covered by Susie's pressed firmly. Kicks and rolls. They beamed.

Javier said, "Our baby." His dark eyes flashed with joy.

To Be Continued

Susie wore a body-hugging tee shirt with an unusual design. She stepped back so Beth could get a better look. A baby girl, blond curls spilling from a racing helmet, driving a pink sport car, one tiny fist waving a rattle. The caption read, "Watch Out World, Here I Come!!"

"Javier designed it after his new car." She reached up to kiss his cheek.

"Wonderful," Beth said.

"Mom, did you make the cranberry-orange sauce yet?? I like to see the skins pop."

"Sorry honey. I had to because we're pressed for time. We better go."

Susie headed toward the bathroom and Javier said in his soft Spanish flavored English, "Mother Malone, what may I do to help?"

Turning to this young man her daughter loved, soon to be father to her first grandchild, Beth saw in his sincere smile he meant well.

"Javier, call me Beth, please. It's not disrespectful." She squeezed his arm and noticing his face sadden, she said, "Unless you'd like to call me Mom. That would be my favorite. Think about it."

"Okay, Mom."

So far so good and it's only eleven fifteen Thanksgiving morning.

Javier drove their Hybrid with Susie in front and Beth in the back. Sitting in the back stirred unpleasant memories for Beth.

Over her shoulder, Susie said, "Mom, I bet it's been a long time, if ever, since you sat in the back seat of a car. Maybe when you were a teen ager, huh?"

Beth swallowed the lump in her throat. "You don't remember all the times when you were young and you sat in front with your father and I sat in back?"

254

Susie laughed. "No, Mom. Why in the world would you sit in the back seat? I'll never let our baby sit in front in my place. Would I, honey?"

Javier merely smiled.

Beth shook her head. *What a dunce I was. Somewhere in my daughter's mind she has a memory of her mother sitting in the back seat and it will surface when she has her own daughter. No more, kiddo. Be strong.*

Clouds billowed, darkened and snow seemed imminent.

"A quick prayer for the weather to hold 'til we're all safely back home," Beth said.

"Amen," echoed back.

Parking close to the great front doors, they hurried in heads bent against the wind. Near the entrance stood Sister Mary Margaret, tall as her petite stature could stretch, pride showing in the way she welcomed Beth and her family.

"Sister Mary Margaret, this is my family; daughter Susie and her husband Javier. They're here as volunteers today."

Sister clasped the extended hands and bestowed upon them her twinkling eyes and mischievous smile. "Thank you for coming and welcome to St. Paul's. Your Mum is a fine addition to our soup kitchen. She certainly knows how to take charge." Susie looked surprised at the compliment. "Get on with y' now, Beth. Tell your people what t'do and see what's goin' on."

Beth said, "Did the turkeys arrive?"

"Any time now, dinna fret."

Leading the way, Beth admired the huge banner saying Happy Thanksgiving strung across the dining section. Cardboard turkeys adorned dinner tables and the hall was festooned with colorful balloons tied with long streamers floating from the high ceiling.

Susie said, "What's your domain, Mom?"

Beth laughed. "The kitchen, of course. It's high tech and on Thursday's all mine. But not for too long. The regular chef is pregnant, due in a week. I'm filling in."

"Do you like doing it? It seems like a lot of work."

Beth picked up the pace, eager to see what lay ahead in the kitchen. "I came here to give something back to the community since I have so much. Yes, I like it. A lot." *A lot better than years trying to please your father. Did I really clean the dirt out of his golf clubs?*

When Beth opened the kitchen door, she was overwhelmed with the number of volunteers—old and young—aprons tied around their waists listening to clean-shaven Harold speak clearly about kitchen chores. Heads turned and she greeted the group. "I don't want to interrupt Harold. He seems to have everything under control." She introduced her family telling them Javier was an experienced chef and he was there as a volunteer.

Harold continued with his list. When Beth moved near him, he showed the written items to her. She asked if he'd mind her adding a few ideas to simplify and he nodded it was fine.

Quickly two kinds of stuffing were in preparation, three people worked on fresh vegetable platters and fruit cups. One large pot was reserved for turkey gravy and a mixture of flour and water was stirred carefully.

Cheers went up when the turkeys were delivered. Javier checked each one to make sure they were all fully cooked. Beth watched the big clock. Pies were due any minute. Sam volunteered for pie pick-up and delivery since the bakery was on his way to the church. A knock at the door. A volunteer opened and called out. "Sam's here with the pumpkin pies. He needs help bringing them in. Clear a table." The volunteers loved Sam's inside stories about the star jocks. They flocked around him whenever he showed up.

Four teens ran out and staggered back, carefully placing boxes on the table and running out for more. Every time the door opened, a cold blast of air swept through the warm kitchen. The table almost groaned with the boxes. At last they came back empty handed. Beth opened one box. The pie was gorgeous, crust fluted and so flaky she was tempted to taste it. So she did.

Heaven. Soon they had to be opened and placed on the dessert table.

She wore her chef's hat at a jaunty angle and the starched jacket half-buttoned. Beth hadn't cooked, stirred or peeled anything. Just watched and barked out orders. She liked being chef. Suddenly Sam came in the back door, walked directly to her, grabbed her by the hand and pulled her out the door. A few wolf whistles echoed from the kitchen. She steered him to the closest room; dark and quiet. Without a word, he wrapped her in his arms and kissed her long and sweet until they were breathless.

Coming up for air, Beth said, "What. . ." Her words were cut off with another kiss.

"I missed you last night," another kiss, "and this morning."

"Lisa, Maverick, and the twins are joining us for dinner." In the shadows she saw a look of pleasure on his face. "After they leave, I can thank you properly for the pies."

Holding hands, they strolled back to the kitchen.

Susie wandered into the lounge away from the kitchen. Cooking was never an interest unless it was sitting down to a meal someone else prepared. Spotting an obviously pregnant girl reclining on a comfortable chair, feet propped on an ottoman, she walked over and introduced herself. "You must be Karen. I'm Susie Delgado, Beth Malone's daughter."

Karen tried to rearrange her belly to a more accessible to no avail. She threw her hands up helplessly. "Pretty soon this will be over and I'll be holding them. Your Mother did a whole lot more for me than fill in as chef."

Pulling a chair next to Karen, Susie sat down. "What do you mean?"

257

"She saved my babies and probably my life just by shrewd observation by telling me to see a doctor immediately. I almost didn't but the way she took charge, the confidence in her words, and well, I followed her advice and I'm still here." She rubbed the shifting mound. "We're still here."

"My mother did that?"

A vigorous nod from Karen. "Sure did and she's been cooking for me every Thursday since. Everyone at St. Paul's loves her. If one of the babies is a girl, I'll name her Beth. I didn't want to know the sex. Old fashioned, I guess."

"Our baby is a girl. We're naming her Elizabeth Francesca. What about your husband, didn't he want to know?"

"Hmmm. I guess I'm not that old fashioned. There is no husband, sad to say. The father promised marriage after he graduates but so far. . ." Karen waggled third finger left hand, still ring-less. "nothing." Sister Mary Margaret is holding my job here with full health benefits and plenty of child care, so I'm okay." Karen gazed at Susie. "You're a lucky woman to have a mom like Beth. Be good to her."

The young women hugged. Susie rose and looked around. "I better make myself useful but first, where's the bathroom?"

"Follow the narrow hall. It's on the right and thanks for stopping by."

In the ladies locker room, Susie saw a woman with curly white hair at the mirror attempting to cover a bruise on her cheek with foundation cream. She was cursing like an angry sailor and finally sat on the bench next to the mirror.

Susie said, "Can I help? I'm good with make-up." Usually she didn't bother with strangers but there was something special about this church and her mom was involved. "I'm Susie Delgado. My mom's Beth Malone. Do you know her?"

The woman's face wrinkled with happiness at the mention of her mom. "Beth is the best. See this?" She leaned forward to show a thin scar near her eye. "Beth cleaned it and used a butterfly bandage so I wouldn't need stitches. What a sweet woman."

"Seems like my mom is an all around action hero at St. Paul's. Healing, protecting, feeding the masses." Using a makeup sponge, Susie applied cover-up to the woman's bruise. "How's that?"

"Looks great. Lucy's my name. Thanks for your help."

Leaving the locker room, Susie walked back toward the kitchen just in time to see her mother come out of a room holding hands with an attractive man. They had a sparkle about them as they dropped hands. Beth entered the kitchen, her companion continued walking.

Serving tables were already set up; Lucy's table almost overflowed with pumpkin pies and many more were in the kitchen. An assortment of holiday cookies and fruit cups were at the table as well. Lucy smiled with confidence and winked at Susie when she approached her station.

"Who's the man at the first table?" Susie said.

Lucy squinted. "Oh, that's Sam, your mom's uh, friend. Good friend. Now get along, young lady. Soup kitchen's starting."

Javier worked the vegetables, two kinds of stuffing and his special sweet potatoes. Quite at home, he ladled with a flourish and grinned often flashing pearly white teeth.

Beth was at her main course station dishing out turkey and gravy. The well she made in the mashed potatoes where the gravy was spooned always reminded her of the past.

She greeted the thin young man with a small son perched high on his shoulders. "Hi Pete's dad and hi Pete, up there. You're getting so big. Next time I think you'll have your daddy on your shoulders."

Pete dimpled and buried face in his dad's neck. "Nah. Too little." He led up three fingers, much cleaner than the first time she'd seen him. "I'm three." They moved on with a tray heaped full of food. Little Pete waved.

And Sam was next to her, not nearly close enough, she thought, doling out bread and crackers. All superfluous to Beth's mind but if you're hungry, you could always stuff some in your pockets to take home. Comfortable no matter what situation he was in, Sam smiled and chatted with everyone; not at all like uh, Beth searched her memory for the man's name. *Oh my. I had kind of a crush on him and Sister warned me not to get involved with Larry. That's his name. Larry with a secret agenda.* Not at all like Larry. She had a lot to thank Sister Mary Margaret for.

Susie went through the line to fill a tray for Karen. Smiling at everyone, especially the small children, she glowed with happiness. Stopping for a kiss from Javier, she had Beth fill the plate. "Mom, this is wonderful. For the first time, I'm speechless. Don't worry, I'll make up for it later." She turned to leave. Over her shoulder, she said, "I'd like to meet your friend, good friend Sam." And she was gone.

Beth stared at her back. It was bound to come out sooner or later and what's the big deal? But did she detect a sarcastic tone to Susie's remark? The mother/daughter relationship seemed to have mended and yet Beth always worried just a little about Susie's mood swings. Oh well, let it pass. This day turned out so beautifully. All the hard work and planning came together and made hundreds of people happy.

Sister Mary Margaret came up behind Beth and clasped her around the shoulders as Beth heaped yet another plate of turkey for a hungry family. "Your friends are an enormous boon to the festivities, Beth. Bless you for bringing such a spirited bunch."

Puzzled, Beth said, "My friends? Oh my. I've been so busy, I completely forgot Lisa, Maverick and the twins."

"Indeed. They set up all the tables with decorations. Such a tall healthy gang they are. The twins entertained the youngsters with songs. They brought guitars. Nice lads. Lisa and Maverick seem quite smitten with one another, don't you know."

"Hmmm. That I do know. Looks like we've had a successful Thanksgiving and the crowd is thinning out. Big clean-up ahead. Do you have enough volunteers?"

Another pat on the back from the little nun. "Not to worry. You and yours head back home when you've served the last. You must be hungry by now. Take a pie or two, if it serves your purpose. That Sam of yours brought more than enough." Sister moved around to face Beth. "I like him, Beth. He's a fine young laddie. I'll call you when our Karen gives birth. She and Susie had a fine chat and your girl helped Lucy with makeup earlier. Susie's a chip off the old block, she is. And her husband," Sister gave a little whistle, "what a courteous young man and so talented. I fancy his white teeth."

The two women embraced, caught up in the spirit of friendship and Thanksgiving.

A blanket of snow covered the church steps when Beth and Sam were ready to leave. The twins whooped with glee and ran to Maverick's truck for shovels and brushes, enthusiasm boundless. Just before Javier and Susie walked out, Beth brought them over to meet Sam who was laden with two pies and Beth's bag.

"This is my good friend, Sam Taylor. I've wanted you to meet him and this seems like a perfect opportunity." Beth's gloved fingers were crossed for good luck. "Sam, my daughter Susie and son-in-law, Javier Delgado."

Setting the packages on a nearby table, Sam smiled his warmest smile, the one that lit up even the serious brown eyes she loved. He extended a hand to Javier. They exchanged a firm shake. He turned his attention to Susie. "Your Mother's told me so much about you, your accomplishments as a teacher and," he included Javier, "your talent for designing cars. Tough industry. I'm so pleased to meet you both."

Susie, her voice snippy, said, " And what exactly do you do, Sam Martin, aside from volunteering here and being my mother's good friend?"

Beth felt a nervous tremor, wanted to smack her daughter for being so rude, wished she'd never introduced them.

Javier jumped in with, "Hormones. Sometimes Susie says the worst things I cannot understand. I wonder where my beautiful wife has gone and then she returns. All is forgiven."

Caressing her reddened cheek, he said, "Right, *mi querida*?"

"Si," Susie said. "Sorry. Blame it on my evil twin."

Sam retrieved the packages. "I'm not interested in the money your mother has, if that's why your pretty nose is out of joint. There's only one thing that interests me in this entire world and that is Beth Malone. For your information, I'm a sports agent." He beckoned for Beth to follow him.

"Be right there," she said.

The church had emptied out and only the clean-up crew could be heard finishing in the kitchen, while others clattered around folding chairs and tables for the following week. St. Paul's had a hollow sadness to it without the bustling crowd.

Beth moved in close to her daughter. "Susie, you're a grown woman. I've told you before, I hope your little girl will never talk like that to someone special to you. Hormones, my ass. What you said was the old bratty child speaking; the one who was so difficult to deal with. You're fortunate to have Javier who loves you so much." Beth turned to leave.

"Mom."

The sound of her daughter's voice made her wait to hear what came next. Beth didn't turn around.

"Mom, I'm so sorry. That was stupid and unforgivable and rude but please forgive me."

Oh fuffa. "We'll get together with Sam soon and you can say it to him. Happy Thanksgiving, kids."

She left them standing together in the empty cavernous entrance under the sign that read **ST PAUL'S WELCOMES YOU.**

Chapter 51

On the way to brunch at Susie and Javier's the Sunday after Thanksgiving, Beth felt both nervous and excited. Her daughter had invited them and that was a good thing.

Sam drove one handed, the other used to calm Beth. "My daughter, Allison, could be a moody little wretch sometimes and I found it better to speak my piece briefly and walk away. My ex would get into long non-productive discussions with Allison always ending with slammed doors and crying. It takes two to tango, dear. She always turned around looking for approval and acceptance from us. Remember this, Susie called us. Let's go in fresh, new page."

Glancing over at her lover, Beth sighed. "How'd you get so wise?"

"Practice."

"I haven't been here for a while," Beth said getting out of the car. "It was a non-descript little house before all this."

They stopped to admire the charming home with trees, a curved flagstone walkway and boulders scattered to fit the landscape. An impressive carved oak door opened; a smiling Javier beckoned. "Come in, it's cold out there."

Tempting aromas of coffee mingled with sautéed onions and peppers when Beth and Sam entered the house and climbed the few stairs to the main level. Beth stole a glance over the railing at the bottom level, the dreaded basement. *The level the kids joked about when they said I should sell my home and move in with them. In truth, if I hadn't gotten the settlement with money to live on and the house, where would I be now? And I never met Sam, of course. In the basement.*

"A tour of the house now or after brunch?" Susie said, arms open wide with an embrace for her mother and one for Sam.

Javier announced brunch was ready and that settled the question. After delicious Spanish omelets, fruit and coffee, Susie and Sam disappeared toward the back of the house with Susie mumbling something about showing him the nursery.

"Show you next, Mom."

Everywhere Beth looked, she envisioned disaster. Buffed wood floors instead of carpeting—Susie would slip and fall holding the baby; stairs without a gate—a tumble down each step. Sliders to the high porch—another danger. Left open, baby could wiggle through—*Oh my God, I'm letting my mother imagination go crazy. Give these young parents credit for some brains, please.* She took a deep breath and listened to her son-in-law, a sensible man.

"This is her way of getting to know your good friend. Let them be," Javier said.

"Sometimes you men know more than we give you credit for," Beth said.

When they finally returned, Sam said Susie was having Braxton Hicks contractions. Guiding Susie to the couch, he placed a pillow behind her lower back and elevated her legs.

"Javier, time the contractions and call the doctor if they get closer. Above all, be calm."

Clearing the dining room, Beth and Sam cleaned up the kitchen together, Beth marveling over Sam's behavior. "How do you know so much?"

"Pass the towel," he said and wiped the counter. "Allison, and also Gloria, my ex, had similar contractions. You don't forget . With Gloria, I wasn't as patient as I should have been. I guess it takes growing up and life's experience to mellow a person. I've become a big daddy to some of my clients and their wives. Everyone has a story you can learn from."

When they left, with Beth and Sam assuring the kids they'd be available anytime if needed, Beth knew splintered fences were mended.

Babies, babies. Sister Mary Margaret interrupted some heavy duty lovemaking by Beth and Sam when the phone rang. Beth dived for it.

Breathless, Beth said, "What?"

"Oh no. I dinna mean to, um disturb you, darlin' girl. Wanted you to know our Karen gave birth to twin boys just a few hours ago. Named one Seth after you. T'other is Ethan. Now go back to whatever 'twas that caused the breathlessness." Laughing, Sister Mary Margaret hung up.

"What?" Sam said. "Is it Susie?"

Snuggling next to him, Beth said, "No rush. Karen, the chef from St. Paul's, had twins and named one after me."

"Nice. Are you certain we'll never have a baby together?"

"As I told you before, not a chance," Beth said.

"Okay, then where were we before we were so rudely interrupted?"

She giggled. "I think page 47 in the Grandparents Do It Better manual."

"Yeah. I like that page. Now where's the whipped cream?"

A week later, Javier called at midnight, frantic. Susie's water broke, they were on the way to the hospital. Frank couldn't be reached, Susie was crying for her mother and if Sam was nearby, please ask him to come. Sam was dressed and ready in a few minutes while Beth wrung her hands and turned in circles. He steered Beth in the right direction as she jumped into clothes and ran to the car. She directed him to the hospital, the same one where Susie was born.

Sam stopped at every green light and drove through every red light. When Beth called it to his attention he muttered through clenched teeth, "Don't tell me how to drive."

So much for calm, she thought.

They hurried to the elevator after getting passes to Maternity. Beth buttoned and unbuttoned one button of her coat so many times that the thread wore out and it came off in her hand.

"It's taking too long to get there," she said. Everything's taking too long."

At the nurse's station, they were directed to the Delgado birthing room.

"Okay if I come in?" Sam said. Beth held his hand, knocked on the door and they entered.

"Mom," Susie cried. Another pain gripped her daughter and Beth almost fainted from the sight of the panting, sweating, and strain Susie was going through. She clutched Sam's hand then hurried to her daughter.

"What can I do to help?" Beth said, smoothing Susie's damp hair back. She asked Javier, who waited pale and anxious, for a cold wash cloth. "Wring it out, please."

"We're okay. You're here." Susie groaned as another pain gripped her. Javier hurried back to help with the breathing, panting, counting they'd practiced for months.

Beth saw the mound shift, tighten, felt a remembered contraction, almost cried out herself.

The nurse called for the doctor. A moment later he came in moving fast, stethoscope flying like a tie caught in a breeze.

Sam steered Beth out while the doctor checked Susie's progress. Beth didn't want to leave, not for a second, as if her presence might ease the pain and speed the delivery.

"All too familiar?" Sam said.

"Hurts too much when you see your own child go through the same thing. I guess it's a universal feeling, like it's okay for me to suffer but not my child." She squeezed her lover's hand. "Don't worry, I'll survive with you at my side."

"Always. This time is for you and your family. I'll be waiting right outside the door if you need me. "

Kissing Sam, Beth went in to wait and watch; to be there.

Susie and Javier did very well together from all the training classes they'd gone to. She had labored for many hours at home before the water broke and was ready to deliver a short time after their arrival.

"Push."

"I'm pushing, damn it."

"Crowning."

"Breathe and push."

"Come on, little one."

"Big one."

"Hold the head, ease the shoulders."

"Big girl!"

And she was out in the world, pink and beautiful. The first cry was almost a bellow from the new baby. Someone said, "I bet over nine pounds. I win." *When did babies get so big?*

Gazing at Elizabeth Francesca lying on Susie's tummy, Daddy Javier so proud after cutting the cord, Beth thought, it doesn't get any better than this. Susie was covered with a blanket looking triumphant; the doctor said Sam could come in and take pictures with his no-flash high tech camera while the little family bonded.

Sam snapped away with his super special camera, recording the event for posterity and Beth thought about the word bonding. In a few minutes of newness and joy, can a family bond? she wondered. No, at this momentous instant in time, they were caught up in the wonder of birth and what they created. Beth offered up a prayer for the three of them and knew she wanted to play an important part in the baby's future as her Granny.

When the nurse whisked the baby away to be cleaned up and swaddled, Susie said, "Mom, I'm cold. So cold." She was shivering.

"We need a blanket here, please. My daughter is cold."

"Hormones," said the nurse. "Blanket coming up."

And Beth did the only thing she could do. She wrapped her daughter in her arms, rubbed Susie's back, told her she was proud and whispered, "I love you."

"I want to be a strong warm mother like you, mom."

She thinks I'm strong and warm. Me, old back seat mom. How is that possible?

A warmed blanket dropped around them.

"Anything else, *mi querida*?" Javier said.

An impish grin from Susie. "I crave a corned beef sandwich and a pickle."

They laughed. "No more cravings." He opened a small cooler and presented her with a sandwich, gift wrapped pink ribbon tied around. "This was like diamonds to Susie during the last trimester."

Sam and Beth spent a few minutes visiting with the baby. All Beth could say was, "Oh, oh, oh" and touch the silky toes and miniature fingers waving like feathers. When huge blue eyes opened to meet Beth's, it seemed as though they were both startled.

"Well hello, Elizabeth Francesca. I'm your very own Granny and this is Papa Sam."

Baby eyes closed, the rosebud mouth puckered out and in. A baby kiss.

Frank bustled in after the fact, hair mussed. Beth could have sworn there was lipstick on his shirt collar and he reeked of perfume but so what. He was the new grandfather and proud of it. Susie had fallen asleep mid-sandwich so he shook hands with Javier, met Sam, hugged Beth and ran to the nursery to see Elizabeth Francesca. When he returned, eyes brimming with tears of joy, he kissed Susie's forehead gently and left. A part of the blessed occasion yet separate.

Chapter 52

It was late March, a year almost to the day when Frank walked out. Early morning peace was broken by the screech of tires braking to a stop followed by the slam of a car door. Beth had been admiring foundation flowers flourishing in the embrace of sunshine; purple grape hyacinths competed with yellow and purple crocus in a beauty contest. Spring was a little late due to the harsh winter and Beth had to smile at tulips pushing their way up in spite of some leftover snow. Yellow daffodils were up in bunches as were groups of large colorful hyacinth.

And the silence was disturbed. Who in the world was in her driveway so early in the morning she wondered and ran around to the front to see Lisa already ringing the doorbell. Lisa calling her name.

"Honey, what's wrong?"

Lisa turned at the sound of Beth's voice. Framed by the recessed doorway, Lisa looked as willowy as a model with hair askew, her face aglow with what? Close friends for almost a year, Beth thought she knew her friend's every mood but something was different. She looked as if she had a secret. A good one and couldn't wait to spill.

"Let me guess," Beth said and hurried close to her best friend.

Lisa grinned. "Three guesses."

"You and Maverick set the date for the wedding and want me to be the flower girl."

Lisa shook her head, curly hair blew with the breeze, and she held up two fingers.

"Was I close?"

No response except for a giggle.

"Hmmm." Hands behind her back like a caricature of a detective, Beth circled Lisa and sniffed the air like a bloodhound. "I've got it. You've lost all the weight that made you a Sequoia and now you're a Willow."

By now they were both laughing like kids and Lisa held up one finger.

"Oh no, one guess left." Beth sat on the top step and thought hard. She looked back at Lisa, still aglow and bursting to tell. "Oh. The rabbit died!"

Lisa sat down beside her and said, "Huh?"

"I'm almost afraid to ask, but are you pregnant?"

Lisa said, "The stick turned blue this morning."

And they both laughed and cried and laughed some more.

"What's with the rabbit?"

"Come in. We'll have some chamomile tea and I'll explain."

Over tea and toast by the fireplace in the family room, the two friends talked, excited with the news.

"What did Maverick say?"

Lisa's face turned rosy red. "Beth, he wants to carry me wherever I go in the house and this just happened this morning. When he saw the pregnancy test come out of the drug store bag, he almost fainted. Then he followed me into the bathroom and I had to throw him out until I finished the test. I let him in and we watched it turn blue together. Love at first pee. From then on, I was up in his arms like a delicate flower, all six feet of me."

"So what you're saying is that he's happy, you're both happy about this unexpected development."

"Well, yes. I believe we are." Lisa leaned forward, a wicked gleam in her big brown eyes. "But here's the rub, old chum."

Grinning, Beth propped her legs over some cushions on the couch. "Hit me with the rub."

"Now we'll have to get married sooner; like maybe tomorrow or in two or three weeks before I start blossoming into a Sequoia again." She inhaled a deep breath, exhaled and continued. "So what we want to ask is. . ."

"If I will have the wedding here and cater it etcetera and of course, I'll be honored, dear friend o'mine."

"And there's just one tiny thing more."

Beth sat up, pillows fell to the floor and she laughed. "Can't wait."

Lisa drained the cup of tea, finished the last bite of toast and smiled. "My Maverick has never been a religious man but he admires the way I go to services sometimes on Friday night and actually went with me a few times." At Beth's puzzled expression, Lisa said, "Yes, and for past few months, he's been taking instruction from the rabbi to convert to Judaism. We want our rabbi to conduct a service under the ceremonial canopy. Our temple is Reform, the service is mostly in English, very relaxed and our young rabbi sings and plays the guitar." She sat back and waited for an answer, then realized she hadn't asked the question. "It will be a small gathering, maybe forty people max. Is it too much to ask for?"

To Lisa's surprise, Beth ran over to the music system and punched in the disc with Fred Astaire and Gene Kelly singing, she used for the Night of Possibilities parties. Then she pulled fresh roses from a vase, wrapped them in a napkin and placed them across Lisa's lap. And last but not least, Beth danced around the room, a wide smile on her face. When the music ended, Beth fell across the couch, out of breath.

"What date, what time, oh what fun."

"You have an interesting way of saying yes," Lisa said. "May I keep the roses?"

Arm in arm, they walked to the front door. Lisa said, "I have to call Maverick and we'll get back to you with a date and time." She hugged Beth. "Before I go, tell me about the rabbit, George."

"Sounds like a line from "Of Mice and Men."

"So tell."

"Okay. When dinosaurs roamed the earth, the way you found out for sure that you were pregnant was by taking a blood test. A few days later, you'd get a phone call from the nurse saying you either killed or didn't kill the rabbit used in the test. A lot of rabbits bit the dust."

Lisa looked sick for a moment. "Barbaric."

"On that happy note, Lisa, we have work to do. This could be a whole new career for me, weddings in my home. Book me soon before my calendar fills."

Watching her best friend drive away carrying a precious cargo, the bright March sun warmed Beth's overflowing heart and she felt rejuvenated; a great way to begin Spring.

Wait 'til I tell Sam. He'll be so happy for them and a touch envious. I could cater small weddings, how about divorces? Mine will be final in a few months. Am I getting carried away?

Of course I am.

Three weeks later, the morning of the wedding, Beth's house was in a frenzy of activity. Lisa's twins were on the patio finishing the canopy, carpenter belts hung low over slim waistlines, some rock music on the loud speaker they kind of moved to as they hammered. A box of flowers arrived ready to adorn the wooden structure; pink carnations, yellow daffodils, purple asters, ferns and baby's breath. The florist's assistant, a pretty girl, long dark hair pulled back in a ponytail waited for that job. Beth noticed her sitting on an upside down crate very near the boys. She hoped the distraction wouldn't keep them from getting the job done. Almost twenty, they were too old to offer cookies as a reward. *Ah well.*

The cake was a tower topped by two tall figures made special order for the occasion. The groom was dressed like Maverick complete with cowboy boots. In his arms he carried his tall bride wearing a replica of Lisa's gown, curly hair blowing in an imagined breeze. Painted smiles captured the moment. Traditional bride and groom shapes were not special enough considering the real couple so Beth splurged and they became keepsakes and maybe their children would use them someday.

It was an April day without a cloud in the sky, warm enough to be outside in the sheltered area next to the big house. Chairs were aligned to form an aisle, the young rabbi showed up with guitar and briefcase in hand, longish hair clipped back. The guests, some friends from Lisa's bank, Maverick's associates and wives, Susie and Javier with Elizabeth Francesca, now four months old, in a carriage. Beth's arms ached to pick her up and kiss her—touch the blonde curls and rosy cheeks but restrained herself for the moment. Sam was a charming host, greeting everyone. The pretty florist girl, who somehow was now a part of the gang, had an equally cute girlfriend join her in rolling out a red carpet for the wedding party. Music filled the air.

"How the world can change, it can change like that, due to one little word, Married."

Maverick, proud and serious, blond hair slicked back, embroidered yarmulke perched at a jaunty angle, walked on the carpet; polished boots, pressed jeans, white shirt open at the neck. He moved next to the canopy.

The music changed to the traditional wedding march as Lisa, escorted by her sons, made her entrance. She floated toward Maverick, eyes seeing only him, a slight breeze caught the soft yellow and ivory flowered ankle length dress causing it to flutter. Her curly dark hair was pinned up in a coronet with small white daisies inter-twinned. The boys handed their mother to the man she loved and stepped to the side.

They moved under the canopy without having to duck their heads. The gathering sighed a collective sigh and the ceremony began.

Chapter 53

Six months later...

The invitation read:

You are invited to the 10th Night of Possibilities, December 15th. Join us in another evening of sumptuous dining and stimulating conversation where discriminating gentlemen and gentle women mingle in comfortable surroundings.

Donation to St. Paul's soup kitchen to be made in your name

RSVP *Beth Malone* 915.358.3939

Careful not to mar the polish on a fresh manicure, Beth slid the latest invitation into the scrapbook containing all the information about the singles gatherings she'd begun more than a year ago. The concept of bringing people together was a success and best of all, she'd met Sam at the first party. Their paths never would have crossed if he hadn't responded to the flyer.

After a lengthy discussion followed by many kisses, they agreed Sam shouldn't be a guest at subsequent parties. Instead he helped out in the library with Maverick, watching the CCTV monitor. Great investment. And the two men bonded as they watched the guests antics. Mating rituals, they called it. Over time, several guests helped themselves to trinkets not their own.

Without fuss, they were relieved of the treasures and taken off subsequent guest lists. Maverick made "Wanted" posters and Sam suggested fingerprinting them. Beth and Lisa laughed over their goofiness and Lisa slipped trays of food into the library to keep them out of mischief.

Beth applied finishing touches to her party makeup. The red hostess gown hung on the closet door ready to slip on. She missed Lisa more than usual at this moment; the camaraderie before the guests arrived; shared joy of all they'd accomplished. Beth grinned at herself in the mirror then laughed out loud remembering Lisa showing up at her door early one morning last March. Then came the lovely wedding and now she was expecting twin girls in a few weeks and on bed rest. Aunt Beth at long last. Visions of play dates with her granddaughter called "Tootsie" by everyone, and Lisa's twins flitted through her mind. And when did play become such a formal thing. Even babies needed appointment books.

Granny, Aunt, soon to be someone else's mate, all in the space of a year and a half. Beth Malone, you've come a long way.

The red dress went over Beth's head without disturbing the upswept hairdo she'd decided on for tonight. She twirled around and watched the dress flare out. *Sam will love it.* His plane would be landing soon; he should arrive at the party just as they gathered in the dining room. Beth had a surprise for him tonight. Beth glanced at her watch. Time out for a glass of Chardonnay.

A knock on the door brought Beth from her reverie. "Thanks for the five minute warning," she said. Beth opened a jewelry box and removed a slim diamond necklace. She fastened and admired it sparkling at her neckline; a gift from Sam in celebration of the divorce being final. One last thing to do. Beth opened another box and slipped on the ring Sam gave her as an engagement gift. Tonight would be the first time she'd wear it in public.

She called Lisa. "Hi best girlfriend. It's show time."

Just as the guests were seated and ready to dine, Sam arrived at the front door. Expecting to head to the library, he was ushered to the candle-lit elegance of the dining room. Beth, as always, occupied one head of the table. The other end of the table until now was always unoccupied. Sam was shown to the opposite head where a table setting was laid out. Beth clinked her knife against a crystal goblet. Talk ceased as all attention turned to her.

She said, "I'd like you to meet my fiancée, Sam Taylor. We met at the first Night of Possibilities."

Enthusiastic applause was followed by a champagne toast when Sam hurried across the room and planted a kiss on Beth's upturned mouth.

"To be continued?" he said.

"To be continued." she said.

More Great Books by Charmaine Gordon

The Catch

Tom Donnelly, once known as The Catch – every woman's dream guy, has fallen down every rung of the ladder he once worked so hard to climb. On New Year's Day, he realizes just how far he's fallen, and makes a list of resolutions to change his life. He vows to regain the trust lost from his family, his law firm, and his friends – and maybe even find the right woman this time.

Sin of Omission

A twist of fate intervenes when Shelley keeps a secret that threatens to break apart the Costigans and her future. A mysterious client, Deanna Rose, enters Haven, victim of a savage beating under strange circumstances. Shelley investigates and finds Ms. Rose has an unsavory past. With the reputation and safety of Haven at stake, Shelley is at risk to lose everything and everyone she cares about.

Reconstructing Charlie

Charlie Costigan has a secret. Home life gone from bad to the worst when she protects her mother from another vicious attack by her drunken father. Midnight. Clothes thrown into an old suitcase, she races for the bus with a letter to an unknown aunt and uncle. "This is my daughter. Embrace her as if she were your own." Determined, Charlie begins again. Alone with her secret.

Now What?

I held his cooling hand and asked the two words spoken many times during our years together. "Now what?" This time there was no response. I was on my own for the first time. When my fingers touched his wedding ring, I slipped it off and held it in my fist. The gold band was warm. I clung to him. "Come back to me, dearest." Sometimes what you wish for is more than you can live with.

Starting Over
Each morning, Emily Kendrick runs on the hard-packed sand of St. Augustine Beach to clear her mind and heal her heart. From the widow's walk of the house perched high on the dunes, a man trains his binoculars on Emily...

 **ALSO IN AUDIOBOOK!**

To Be Continued
Elizabeth Malone wakes up the morning after an amazing night of passion with her husband of forty years to find a note: Dear Lizzie, it's not you, it's me. Abandoned by her husband, disappointed in daughter Susie's casual attitude Dad's having a mid-life crisis, Beth decides to re-establish herself as the winner she once was. When Frank Malone returns, he's in for a big surprise!

Charmaine Gordon writes books about women who Survive and Thrive. Her motto is take one step and then another to leave your past behind and begin again. Six books and several short stories in three years, she's always at work on the next story. The books include *To Be Continued*, *Starting Over*, *Now What?*, *Reconstructing Charlie*, *Sin of Omission* and *The Catch*, just released.

"I didn't realize at the time while working as an actor in NYC, I'd become a sponge soaking up dialogue, setting, and stage directions. I learned many tools of writing during the years watching directors like Mike Nichols and actors including Harrison Ford, Anthony Hopkins, and Billy Crystal. And would you believe, I was Geraldine Ferraro's stand-in leg model, my first job giving me entrée into all the Unions needed to work. When the sweet time ended, I began another career and creative juices flowed."

You can reach Charmaine at
http://authorCharmaineGordon.wordpress.com

And on her FB page
http://www.facebook.com/charmaine.gordon

www.ingramcontent.com/pod-product-compliance
Lightning Source LLC
Chambersburg PA
CBHW061551170626
46811CB00001B/165

* 9 7 8 0 6 1 5 9 0 2 2 0 3 *